Praise for Rob

"Welbourn operates in the :
Easton]

"Welbourn has managed to encapsulate a generation."

"Few of us can so eloquently paint a picture."

"There's a confronting honesty in the way Welbourn
writes."

"Welbourn is a skilled writer."

"Bearing similarities to some of the best I've read."

"an exceptional piece of observational narrative"

"Genuinely gripping and heartbreaking"

"Welbourn portrays a realistic view of the world. It's raw,
fresh, and intoxicating."

"Fast paced and easy to read"

Great Romances of the 20th Century

Robert Welbourn

SRL PUBLISHING

SRL Publishing Ltd
London
www.srlpublishing.co.uk

First published worldwide by SRL Publishing in 2024

ISBN: 978-1915073-41-9

1 3 5 7 9 10 8 6 4 2

A CIP catalogue record for this book is available from the British Library

SRL Publishing is a Climate Positive publisher offsetting more carbon emissions than it emits.

Also by Robert Welbourn

Belonging, SRL Publishing
Ideal Angels, SRL Publishing

For Hannah

Still

Contents

Chapter One

Say Anything

God life is pointless.

I have two main issues in my life: 1) I am nobody, and 2) I am bored.

When I was a child, I used to wonder if I might be a robot. My theory was this: I have no proof I'm *not* a robot. Sure, I looked like a person, was made of skin and hair and flesh and stuff, at least on the surface. When I cut myself, I bled. When I injured myself, I hurt. When I felt happy I felt good, and when I felt sad I felt bad. I had all the traits of a human, but still, I was convinced on some days beyond belief that I was absolutely, definitely a robot.

Sure, when I cut myself I bled, but when Arnie cut himself in *Terminator 2* he bled as well. He had skin and flesh and blood and stuff; the robotic shit, wiring and circuits and that, was underneath. I never cut myself too deeply as a child, so I had no idea whether, under the shallow cut from which warm, red blood oozed, there were a bunch of green and blue and red wires, tiny little things that powered me instead of brains and nerves like other, actual, people.

I went to hospital a few times as a child; I was very clumsy, I fell down and knocked my head on the concrete playground on multiple occasions. As well as this, I fell out of trees, fell off walls and small buildings. I just generally did a lot of falling. So I'd fall, and go to hospital, and there I'd have an X-ray. The doctor would show my parents the X-ray, and of course I'd be in the room and be able to see it, too. So really, there *was* proof that under my skin and flesh and arteries and veins and stuff was bones. But: whose bones? Whenever a doctor showed me an X-ray, it could have been for literally anyone. When I fell out of a tree one sunny summer Friday morning and fractured, supposedly, my forearm, in the hospital the doctor showed my parents and myself an X-ray of a broken forearm. But there was no proof it was my arm. It could have been anyone's fractured forearm, absolutely anyone in the world. You might think this X-ray proved I was human, that underneath it all I was just guts and bowels and organs and stuff, but not me. No, I was deeply cynical.

I mean, I obviously still am deeply cynical, but at least now I'm an adult I know I'm not a robot. Or at least, I theorise that I'm not a robot. I still have no proof either way, but my train of thought now works in this way: if I am a robot, then someone royally fucked up. If I am a robot, what an absolute waste of time and money and resources. If this is the best that people can do when it comes to robotics, just fucking give it up. I ain't doing anything to prove the rise of robots will ever happen. If anything, I'm living (lol) proof that robotics is fucked, and, unlike in *Terminator 2*, we have nothing to worry about.

I mean, honestly, if the best that scientists can come up with is a robot with severe, borderline crippling, depression, who's so lonely that he'd kill himself if he wasn't such a coward, then fuck me. Give it up lads and lasses! If I, Oliver Jones, am your best effort, then it's time to find a new career, I'm afraid. I may pass the Turing Test, but at what cost? And I don't mean, like, philosophically or whatever, I'm not going all Phillip K Dick on you, I mean literally: what's the cost? If I am a robot, how much did it cost to make me, and was it (it definitely wasn't) worth it?

Anyway, what even is a robot? According to Wikipedia a robot is a "machine — especially one programmable by a computer — capable of carrying out a complex series of actions automatically". "Robots may be constructed to evoke human form" — okay so I definitely fit that criteria, I'd say I definitely "evoke human form". If only on the outside, at least. When I stand in front of a mirror, staring back at me is, ostensibly, a human being. The person, thing, whatever, that stares back at me has skin, has eyes and ears and teeth and a nose and hair and all that jazz. When I stand in front of a mirror and look at my reversed-facsimile, that facsimile absolutely "evokes human form".

But it's all just so surface, isn't it? What's underneath it all? Sometimes I find myself leaning in close, looking myself in the eye. I see nothing. The popular saying tells us that the windows are the eyes to the soul. Well, does that mean I don't have a soul, then? Because my eyes ain't windows to shit. My eyes are eyes, just two roundish objects, stuck in my head, that allow me to see, but that's about it. In literature, and in movies, narrators and characters talk about seeing the depth in someone's eyes, seeing beautiful azure pools of blue, of greens that are forest-like, browns that mix and swirl and come to life. Well, my eyes are fucking dead. That they're a light-ish kinda grey colour doesn't help: no one on TV or in films or books has grey eyes. You never read about someone having "beautiful granite-coloured eyes" or "his grey pools, like the concrete of a thousand schoolyards, made her fall in love with him in an instant."

My eyes, like the rest of me, are completely shallow. Sometimes I'm surprised I'm actually three-dimensional, because really, there's nothing to me. But I digress: what is a robot? A robot is "programmable by a computer". Well, what's a computer? A computer as we know it now is something electronic, a laptop, smartphone, calculator, whatever. But, like, computers used to be people. The term computer originated — I'm pretty sure — at NASA, when complex equations had to be done by hand. The people who carried out these complex equations were computers. So, like, computers can be human. So does that mean, similarly, that robots can be human? So does that mean I can be both a robot, and a human? I think, if so, that would solve a lot of my problems. Well, perhaps problem one anyway, that of me being nobody. I'd still be nobody, but at least if I knew it for certain, knew once and for all that I was a robot, then I'd be happy. As well as this, if other people knew me to be human, they'd be happy, too. If one day it does turn out that I'm a robot, and not a human, I expect to be scorned. People don't like what's different to them, and also people don't like the unfamiliar. If I had proof I was a human, whilst also knowing in my heart of hearts — my motherboard of motherboards — that I was a robot, I think everyone would be happy. Or at least, perhaps everyone would be slightly less *un*happy?

But then what the fuck is a cyborg? Heading back to our old friend, Wikipedia, we learn that the definition of a cyborg is "a portmanteau of cybernetic and organism — (is) a being with both organic and biomechatronic body parts." Well, that blows everything out of the water. Does that mean Arnie is a cyborg in T2? Now I think of it — I haven't watched the film for a little while — I believe he is, and even says this. I believe he calls himself, to John Connor, a cybernetic organism. But that doesn't help me. You know when you're trying to remember something, a line from a movie or a different movie that one actor has been in, and it's on the tip of your tongue, and then you remember and you get that incredibly intense feeling of satisfaction? I'm not getting that now whilst I think about cyborgs, and whether or not I might be a cyborg. The problem is, by its very definition a cyborg is partially human, has "organic body parts". Well, I don't feel like a cyborg. A cyborg feels very close to being a human, and I don't feel like a human at all. If I'm being honest, I don't feel like a robot at all either, but really I just don't at all feel alive in any way, so being a robot feels like the most natural descriptor to apply to myself. I wouldn't say I'm an animal or an alien, because these are both alive, and I'm not alive. So therefore I must be a robot. Or not. I don't even know. To be honest, despite how it may seem, I also don't even really care. Human, robot, animal, plant, alien, brick, horseshoe, whatever. I don't care what I am. All I care about is how alone I am.

Have you ever seen the film *Say Anything*? Released in 1989, written and directed by Cameron Crowe, it tells the story of Lloyd Dobler, played by a very young John Cusack, slowly but surely making Diane Court, played by an also very young Ione Skye, fall in love with him. And it's perfect.

Well, I mean, it's kinda perfect. It makes me feel, which is a change — sometimes for the better, sometimes for the worse. It makes me feel both wonderfully uplifted: I watch Lloyd and Diane, I watch them meet and get to know each other, make each other smile and laugh, they learn about each other's personalities, their likes and dislikes, their hopes and dreams. They learn and grow together, and though it isn't without its faults, their relationship blooms and blossoms and all the other floral metaphors, and they fall madly in love with each other. And watching all of this play out in the space of 100 minutes makes me feel wonderful. I love to watch their love, I love to watch them interact with each other. When they kiss for the first time, it's a perfect scene. Lloyd is teaching Diane to drive, and it isn't going well, but that's okay, he really likes her, he has the patience to take her through it. The car is jerking, Diane can't work the clutch very well, she bounces from first to second gear, Lloyd is thrown around the car. But he doesn't mind, and I don't mind either. Diane isn't perfect, and that's another reason we — Lloyd and I — love her. Because I do love her. Not Ione Skye, although in many ways I do think I may be in love with Ione Skye, at least as she was in 1989, but Diane Court. For the 100 minutes this film plays out on my screen, I am completely and utterly in love with Diane Court.

The film makes me feel equal parts wonderful and horrified. I feel wonderful because I'm watching these two people fall in love, I'm watching them take on the world hand in hand; they're going to face troubles, there'll be adversity in their lives, things won't always go to plan, but that's okay, they have each other. The film makes me feel horrified because I am so, so alone. I have no one. When I go through adversity, I go through it alone. When I wake up in the morning, and the sun is shining through my shitty cheap blinds, and I roll over and my arm graces the other side of the bed, it feels no warmth. It feels mattress, sheet, duvet, and nothing more. There is no other body beside me, there is no one to smile at me, bid me a good morning, ask me how I slept. There is no one to let me know that I exist, to remind me that in many ways I am actually a person.

There is no one.

There's a woman at my work who I'm in love with. So I want there to be a someone, even though there is no one. She's called Nicola, and she works in the PR team of the marketing department. She's fairly short, if I had to guess I'd say five feet and maybe two or three inches. Not tiny, not by a long shot, but I'm six feet and three inches, nearly four, so compared to me she is tiny. She has brown hair, parted in the middle, and it's always straight. It's so long, it flows over her shoulders and most of the way down her back, and I wonder how early she has to get up to straighten it. Our official start time in the office is 9am, but really if you're not there for 8, you're late. So how early does she get up to straighten that hair? And every day as well? Because even when she has it up in a ponytail or a bun, it's still straight. Even when her hair is 'messy', it's still straight. She's crazy. It's one of the things I love about her.

What else? She has brown eyes, I'm pretty sure, very similar in colour to her hair, which is a light chestnut shade of brown, not mousy but not far from it. I haven't ever really actually been that close to her, not close enough to really see her eyes clearly, so I'm educatedly-speculating at their colour. She dresses wonderfully: she's one of those women who work in offices who look amazing every day. One day she might wear a black skirt and a blouse with no sleeves and frills across the front. Another she might wear trousers with a checked pattern, all light and dark greys and whites and blacks, light colours and dark contrasting, with a plain shirt on top, or even a crop top or a vest or whatever. The office dress code, unless there's a client meeting, is pretty liberal, and I'm grateful for it. If we worked in finance or whatever and she had to wear a suit every day, I wouldn't have seen the glimpses of her breasts that I have seen working here, that I've stored up in my memory and that I masturbate to at night before I cry myself to sleep.

What else? That's about all I know about her. She's worked here longer than I have, so at least four years, because that's how long I've worked here. I work in the digital marketing part of the department, so our paths don't cross too often. In many ways, we're stuck in our gendered parts of the marketing department: she, in PR, has to meet people, to talk to them and woo them and generally be nice to them in order to get her way, and the company's way. She's one of the faces of the company, in media terms at least, and what a face. Whereas I deal mainly with data, which means I'm sequestered away in the corner like a goblin, hunched over my laptop, pulling out figures and sending them on to my boss. I don't even get to step out of my little cave corner to present the data in meetings or whatever, I simply format it into reports and my boss does the presenting.

It's probably for the best: I'm a terrible public speaker, I have no confidence whatsoever. Plus, I'm never more than about ten seconds away from bursting into tears, and that wouldn't be ideal in front of a room full of executives. I fucking hate this job, but it's also absolutely perfect for me and besides, I need it. I live alone, so have no roommates to fall back on: if I stop paying the rent, the rent stops being paid. So, as much as it physically hurts me to drag myself out of bed every day and schlep down to this office and create Excel reports about how many people visited our website and on what device and how they found it and what they did once they were on the site, I do it because I have no choice.

Well, I mean it's not all terrible, because I'll see Nicola in the office, and that makes things better. Not much; maybe one or two percent better, so rather than the day being 100% a living nightmare, it's only 98 or 99%. But then, she's only human, which means she goes on leave, or is ill, or works from home, or is out visiting clients or media partners. And on those days I truly, truly want to just scream until I bleed and am fired. On these days, as I walk into the office, my pace becoming exponentially slower the closer I get, like a number being continually halved, except unfortunately I will eventually reach zero, I cannot avoid it, on the days I get there, waiting to see her face, expecting it, and not: those are the really bad days. On those days, the little data goblin that I am is so pronounced I imagine people can feel it, because they tend to leave me alone more than they normally do. I'm not well liked in the department, but I don't mind. I'm not there to make friends, although I wish I could. I'm not there to fall in love, although I have. I'm just there to work and get paid and pay my way until I die, which hopefully will be any day now.

On the days I know Nicola won't be in the office, for example it's a Tuesday and the previous day I found out she was going to be away for the whole week, I silently pray to a god I don't believe in that I'll be hit by a bus or something. That as I step off a curb a four-tonne metal box will sweep me off my feet and we will, DENNIS system-style, separate entirely. On the days I know I'm not going to see Nicola, death is the preferable option.

And I've never even had a proper conversation with her.

We all want to be Diane Court. I don't mean that I'm secretly trans and this is my coming out. No, it's much more basic than that: we all want to be wanted. I think, really, that's the most basic desire every single person on this planet has, is to be wanted. To be desired, to be

11

needed, to be actively sought after, I think that's all we really need.

Although, even as I say it, I think it might go a bit deeper than this. To be wanted is to have someone want you somewhere. And to be wanted somewhere is to have somewhere to belong. And I think, really, we all just want to feel like we belong somewhere. With someone who belongs there with us.

It's not like I'm not trying to be happy. I've recently started manifesting, and as I walk to work this morning I'm chanting under my breath, "today will be a good day, today will be a good day, today will be a good day."

I'd never heard of manifesting until a few weeks ago when Emma, my sister, sent me a link to a *Teen Vogue* article about it. She WhatsApped me the link accompanied solely by a few laughing emojis as commentary, so I assumed she was mocking it. I was prepared to mock it, too, to scorn at it, but as I read the article I found myself less scornful and more hopeful. Manifesting, the article said, is the idea that you will your dreams into reality. Can you blame my sister for her emojis? When you say it like that, it does sound laughable. But as I read the article, wanting to laugh but instead wondering if this was a potential game-changer, it occurred to me that it's just another way of saying, 'fake it 'til you make it'.

Because that's essentially all it is, manifesting is incredibly similar to faking it until you make it. The idea of *fake it 'til you make it* is that if you pretend to be confident, you'll become confident. If you pretend to be happy, eventually you'll actually be happy. If you pretend to be successful, at some point you'll be successful.

And isn't that basically what manifesting is? If you pretend to be happy, you're willing yourself to be happy.

You're manifesting happiness. So whilst people like Emma scorn at the idea of manifesting, think it's something teenage girls do in order that Harry Styles will completely out of the blue message them on Instagram and declare his love for them, it's something millions, tens of millions probably, of people do all over the world every day. It's all just marketing really, isn't it? *Fake it 'til you make it* is tried and tested, it's old school, it's been around forever. Business people say it, professional coaches say it, serious people doing serious jobs use the phrase, so it's an acceptable phrase. Manifesting? No thanks, that's something teenage girls do, something that comes from social media, something a serious person would never even consider. Manifesting is decidedly unserious behaviour.

But whatever. I'm manifesting today to be a good day, because really, what's the worst that can happen? If today does end up being a good day, amazing, great success, the manifesting has worked. If today turns out to be a shit day, or really just a completely and utterly nondescript day like almost every other is, then I haven't lost anything. Manifesting is completely free, it carries absolutely no risk attached to it whatsoever. Worst case scenario; I've chanted under my breath for no reason. Low risk, potentially high reward. Isn't that the capitalist dream?

"Today will be a good day, today will be a good day, today will be a good day…"

At one point I realise I must be saying it louder than I realise because as I'm waiting to cross Broadway, lined up alongside millions of other commuters waiting to cross, facing down a million other commuters waiting to cross in the opposite direction, I can see a couple of people giving me the side eye. There's a person next to me, female presenting but I don't want to assume: she's wearing a power suit, navy blue with the faintest of white stripes, and she's looking at me like I'm truly, madly, deeply insane. Of course she's right, but not because I'm muttering under my breath, or should I say over my breath, apparently. I'm truly, madly, deeply insane because I'm 28 years old and have no idea if I'm a robot or not; amongst many, *many* other things. I want to grab her by the shoulders, I want to turn both our bodies so we're facing each other, and I want to tell her that yes, I am insane, but to me she's also insane. The suit has working in a bank or law firm or something similarly bullshit written all over it, and I want to scream at her that she's insane, she may not be muttering under her breath at 7:46am on a Tuesday morning on the streets of New York City, but she's still insane. I want to spin her by the shoulders and point out other people and tell her that they're all insane too, each and every single person at this crossing is insane, both on our side and the other side. We all, every single day, bend over for the capitalist machine, every day we sell our labour-value, we allow ourselves to be exploited for surplus-value, and though we may whine, complain, be unhappy about it, ultimately we do nothing. And isn't that completely and utterly insane?

Obviously, I don't do this. Obviously, I look at her out of the side of my eye, and reduce the volume of my manifesting. The light soon grants us permission to traverse the road and we do, and as the two opposing groups of people intertwine and move through each other like corporeal presences, I lose sight of the woman, and she's gone from my life forever.

My company has its offices in a building on West 45ᵗʰ Street, next to the Museum of Broadway, just down from Times Square. I have to cross at Times Square each morning, and as I stand waiting for the light to change, for an inanimate object to give me permission to move, I can't help but think about how ridiculous it all is. Even before 8am, Times Square is packed with tourists, all with their cameras taking pictures, smiling and happy and stuff, visiting a place they've seen on TV, have known about for years, finally seeing it in the flesh: the myth becoming reality. And I'm there, making my way to a marketing office to do marketing. They're living their best lives, I'm living my worst.

Times Square is a weird-as-fuck place anyway; all the lights, adverts, it's a pure capitalist dream. And when it rains, the lights are all reflected on the ground and it's like there's two of it, one capitalist nightmare isn't enough and another must be forced on you. It's oddly beautiful in a way, in the way that only New York can make steel look pretty. In no other city on the planet, at least as far as I know, do you pay so much money to come and look at offices and apartments from the outside, to stand and stare at girders. The contrast of their lives vs mine is so weird: the Instagram life vs real life. I'm not sure which I hate more.

My office is the closest I ever get to the Upper West Side, except when I meet up with a bunch of people to get day-drunk in the park on a weekend, an event that's happening with decreasing regularity as we (they) all grow up and begin to get married, have kids, live what is supposedly a proper life. I live in Soho, way, way down from where I work. I don't always walk to work, it takes like 50 minutes, an hour, it sucks, but this close to pay day — on the wrong side of it — I don't really have a choice. When I lived in London it was great, as a student I somehow wangled my way to a pre-paid travel card which meant I could get the Underground every day, I didn't have to deal with the changeable temperatures and climates like I do here. If there's one thing New York does amazingly, it's having ridiculous weather that can change on a dime. I'm not one for carrying an umbrella, so I've been caught out on more than one occasion.

I'm still manifesting as I reach my building and, checking my phone to see it's 7:55, I make a mad dash for the elevators, slipping into one just before the doors close. Even though it's early the elevator is crammed, had I known how full it already was I definitely would have waited for the next one but it's too late now, I'm here. People around me look annoyed and I hate myself for it, but the doors have now closed and the metal box is ascending, so there's nothing any of us can do.

I surreptitiously glance around at my fellow passengers; there are a couple of people I recognise from my company, but I don't know them so don't acknowledge them in any way, as well as various people from presumably the various other companies that have offices in the building. Satisfied there's no one I need to interact with I pull my phone from my pocket and scroll through all the usual feeds on all the usual apps — only in New York would an elevator have cell service, because God forbid we go 30 seconds without looking at social media. Despite the fact it's not even 8 on a Tuesday morning it's incredible the things people are up to. Someone I went to university with who also somehow ended up here has just finished yoga in the park and has posted a sweaty selfie on Insta; a guy I met once and then followed on Twitter for reasons since lost to the annals of time is evidently training for an Ironman race and is living his best life telling his 417 followers all about his now-daily exercise routine; I'm shocked to see my parents drinking wine, before remembering they live in the UK so it's 1pm there, and though still perhaps a bit too early for a drink, a lot better than 8am. Yes, my parents have social media, and yes, it's a whole thing I don't want to go into. Easier just to chuck them a like then keep scrolling.

The elevator finally grinds to a halt on the 27th floor and I step out, immediately entering my company's reception area. Matthew, the impossibly handsome 20-something receptionist glances up as the elevator doors open but looks right through me, saying hello to one of the people behind. I use my swipe card to open the glass door into the actual office and navigate my way through to my desk, dropping my bag onto the floor and my arse onto my chair.

Before I've even taken my laptop out my boss, Neil, swoops down on me, and I inwardly sigh. It's going to be one of those days; fuck manifesting.

"Morning, Oli, how you doing? Listen, did you manage to pull the usage reports for the new logistics campaign? Brielle's on my ass and I have better things to do than deal with her, so if I could get her the report it'd be great."

"I'm nearly done, just gotta finish it off and I'll get it over to you."

"Okay great, do you think you could get it over by 9.30? We have the weekly all hands at 10 and I just know she'll be on my case about it, so it'll be good to have some time to digest it beforehand."

"Yeah no worries, boss."

"Thanks, pal."

He walks away, allowing me to finally take off my coat and actually get settled in. I'm such a liar: I haven't even begun the usage report. But it's okay, because Neil is an even bigger liar: he never asked me for one. Luckily this kinda report takes about five minutes, so really I could have it over to him by 8.05, but what's the use? I'm the only data person in the entire marketing department, and as such half of my job is making sure no one else knows how to do my job. If they knew just how little I actually do, how little time all my tasks actually take, there'd be a landslide of new work falling on my head, and that's something in which I have absolutely no interest.

I envy Neil in many ways, he's such a normal person. Glancing to my right at his desk now, which is about 10 feet away from mine, I can see he has various pictures of his wife and kids. He has a "world's best dad" mug, as well as some truly awful artwork I sincerely hope was done by his kids, otherwise I'd be concerned. He seems to genuinely love his wife, and his kids, and genuinely love his job. He goes on about Brielle riding him all the time, but I know secretly he actually likes it, and only bitches about her to me and everyone else so he seems like one of the guys. I did used to think he and Brielle might be having an affair. I only stopped thinking that because I stopped caring.

Tom sits down next to me, also to my right — he's my buffer to Neil — five minutes late as usual, but no one notices, or if they do, no one says anything. Now Tom I truly am jealous of; he's one of those people who is just effortless, and as such everyone loves him and he can get away with anything. This morning he reeks of alcohol, and I can see a hangover written all over his face. I wonder what he got up to last night.

"Quiet in here this morning," he mumbles quietly, his words slurred a little.

"Yeah man," I reply.

"Where is everyone?"

"I'm not sure, only just got here myself."

He turns away from me to Neil.

"Neil!" He shouts, far too loud for the distance between them, which is about two feet, but as I say, no one says anything, he gets away with it.

"Morning, Tom. What's up, bro?"

Yes, Neil actually calls people *bro*, in all seriousness. Not me, he's never once referred to me as 'bro', but he does so to everyone else. Males at least.

"Where is everyone, boss?"

"Let me see," Neil raises his hand and begins to tick people off his fingers. "Brielle is in her office, Jacinda is coming in late, some appointment or something, Amrit and Sheena are pitching to this furniture company upstate…"

I zone out, letting the noise wash over me, allowing it to become so much background buzz. As I wait for my laptop to finish loading up I glance around and realise Tom's right, the office is very quiet. I feel the panic begin to rise within me, building like how I imagine the pressure must in a volcano before it erupts, as my eyes move across the room, towards the desk, towards my Mecca: *her* desk. It's empty. But maybe she's running late, or is making a coffee, or already in a meeting. I force myself to zone back in just as Neil delivers the news which breaks my heart, and confirms how shit the day is going to be.

"…and Nicola is unwell, probably going to be out most of the week Lin says. Food poisoning or something."

For fucks' sake. Manifesting really is a crock of shit isn't it? I mean, today might still be a good day, but I'm struggling to see how. Neil is already on my arse, Nicola isn't here, Tom smells like he bathed in Maker's Mark; I'm struggling to see what positives will come from today, at least until 6pm when I'm finally allowed to leave this hell hole.

With a sigh I pull Neil's report and, attaching it to an email, I auto schedule it to go to him at 9:18, ahead of the deadline enough to look good, not so far ahead as to be too keen, or look like I've done it too quickly, and get up to go make myself a coffee. I have no Nicola to get me through the day, so caffeine it'll have to be. What a world.

When I was a kid I wanted to be, in turn: a writer, a policeman, a politician, Prime Minister (when I still lived in the UK), a rockstar, and then happy. I have achieved none of these things. I am a data analyst in the marketing department of a midrange marketing agency that, even having been here for four years, I'm still not entirely sure what we do. Luckily, I don't really need to know. I live in Excel and Google Analytics and various other programmes that deliver me cold, hard facts. I don't need to know any of that marketing shit thankfully, although working in the marketing department it probably wouldn't hurt.

I did used to have hopes and dreams, even over and above the ones listed above. I used to dream of travel, of seeing the world, seeing all 190-odd countries, experiencing every bit of culture on the planet. And once I did I was then going to change the world, to change the planet. I was going to take the best bits of these cultures and share them, make English people more Polynesian and make the French more Australian. I was going to go to Japan and make them more Greek, then go to China and learn how to make Colombia more Chinese. I was going to be some sort of saviour, some sort of modern-day Jesus. People were going to worship me. Now I'm just glad if I can make it through the day without crying. I fail almost every day.

In *Say Anything*, when Diane brings Lloyd home for dinner for the first time, her father asks Lloyd what he wants to do with his life. At this point he's just graduated High School and teaches kickboxing to kids. He says to

James Court, played by John Mahoney RIP, that he doesn't want to sell anything, he doesn't want to buy anything, nor does he want to process anything as a career.

Around the table are a few of James' friends, business associates and whatnot, and following Lloyd's little speech there's silence, before the adults all scorn Lloyd. He then talks about potentially becoming a professional kickboxer, it being a burgeoning sport in 1989 America. The adults are confused and disappointed, Diane is concerned about their reaction, and Lloyd is, well, Lloyd. Whilst this scene ostensibly plays out in a comedic manor, it's actually a very telling scene in the film.

All media has to have conflict, and the conflict in *Say Anything* is that James doesn't think Lloyd is good enough for Diane. James is a businessman, a capitalist: he owns a very successful nursing home and reaps very large profits from it. Diane is incredibly smart, applying to go to the best colleges all over the world. Lloyd is an army brat, living on a pull-out couch in his sister's living room, far from being the most academically gifted student. He wants to fight for a living, whereas the Courts are intellectuals. James sees Lloyd as being from the wrong class: he never actually says it, he uses lots of other issues to describe to Diane why he doesn't like Lloyd, but it's all there in the subtext. Diane is wealthy, intelligent, beautiful, Lloyd is stupid, poor, and ugly. In many ways it's a classic case of class warfare, the kind that happens a billion times a day, every day, in every country in the world. Thankfully, as in all good romcoms, love wins. It turns out James is so successful because he's been stealing from the residents of his care home and their families, and the movie ends with James in jail and Lloyd accompanying Diane to England, where she's won a scholarship. Lloyd 1, James, 0.

I've considered various different careers since I joined the full-time work force. I seriously considered being a social worker, even went so far as to send off for some information from a couple of local colleges, but then I had a realisation one day: much as the basis for conflict in *Say Anything* is class warfare, so it is in social work. I ran through a bunch of scenarios in my head, the potential kinds of issues I might be faced with and came to one conclusion: they could all be solved by money. In fact, basically every problem on this planet is caused by money, namely most people not having enough of it. Poverty is the cause of so much suffering on the planet, every day, and it's a political choice. The upper class drain money from the middle and working-class, and hoard it all for themselves. If their money was invested into education, healthcare, youth clubs and all that kinda shit, then kids would probably be less likely to turn to drugs, prostitution, and crime. If parents weren't paid poverty wages they'd be able to work one job with decent hours and spend time parenting their kids, reading to them and playing with them and bonding with them. If schools had proper funding they'd be able to properly educate kids. If private healthcare was abolished people wouldn't risk bankruptcy every time they fell over. If ifs and but were candy and nuts...

I don't want to be a social worker any more. I don't want to be anything. Well, in the workforce that is. I do want to be one thing, and one thing only: I want to be in with Nicola.

Friday. Finally Friday. TGIF. TFIF. TFIFFF. I've wished away another week and here we are, it's finally fucking Friday. Neil was right, Nicola hasn't been in the office at all since she fell ill. It's been a literal nightmare. Considering I've basically only ever exchanged about 18 words with her in the four years we've worked together, I miss her terribly. There are work drinks tonight which I agreed to attend on the basis that she would. I now have absolutely no desire to go, but it's too late to back out. Maybe I could have changed my yes to a no on Wednesday or Thursday, but I was hit with an extreme bout of optimism that Nicola would recover, and would be at whatever bar we're headed to at 5pm, in approximately 45 minutes. Yes, you read that right, 5pm. Not 6pm, oh no: the reason we're going out is that it's the end of Q2, and Q2 it turns out was very successful for the company. We made a shitload of money apparently, and so we're off to celebrate, a whole hour earlier than we'd normally be allowed to leave. Praise the lord for the bosses!

But alas, Nicola is still unwell, so I have to go to drinks and suffer through them. I figure I can possibly slip away after two, three maximum, I probably only need to spend an hour or two socialising before I can disappear into the night. Not like a sexy vampire or anything, not at all, but more like a weasel or something, I suppose less disappear into the night and more skulk back to my apartment and hide until Monday morning.

The office is buzzing, there's a palpable excitement in the air. Neil is the ringleader: he's been talking loudly all week about how he's gotten a pass from his wife to stay out as late as he wants and get as drunk as he wants. Hopefully he'll be more reserved than he was at the Christmas party when he did some bad coke and after trying to fight a waitress puked all over himself and our table before bursting into tears and being taken home by Brielle. I mean, it was pretty funny, I'm not going to pretend it wasn't, but it was awful to see as well. The man has a wife and kids, why's he doing coke in a restaurant bathroom at a work party?

Beers are being passed around the office and Tom hands me one. Despite the fact I'm 28 and am, in all the technical ways, an adult, it's still a queer thrill to be drinking in the office, at my desk, during work time. I feel like a naughty child doing something I shouldn't, despite the fact that the beers were literally brought into the office by my boss. I guess it's the old id vs ego scenario: the rational part of me knows full well what's happening is fine, but the emotional part of me, the irrational part, still wins. Who needs facts when you have feelings? Fuck you, Freud.

Even though it's only 4.15PM, people are gathering their things, laptops being turned off and placed into bags, jackets put on because, even though it's early July, the weather is oddly cold today. People have finished their drinks and trying to remember if our office recycling bins can take glass, and no one seems to know so they all get put in there anyway, if it isn't recycling it's wish-cycling which is basically as good. Soon there's a mass exodus and we all wait in the lobby, the elevators slowly ferrying groups of people down. The entire company is coming to these drinks, obviously illness and leave aside, which means it's a relay to get us all down to the ground floor and out of the building. I'm one of the last, absolutely refusing to push into an already full elevator, happy to wait my turn. Soon it's only me and one other person left in the lobby, a woman I don't recognise. She's looking at me, and when I look at her we make incredibly awkward eye contact and both look away, me looking at my shoes, the floor, the abyss, her looking wherever she looks.

A soft ding announces the arrival of the elevator and as its doors silently glide open I see it's empty. Neither of us move until I gesture with my arm and she smiles slightly and enters, and I follow. She's already pressed the button for the ground floor, and we stand side by side in silence as the elevator descends. Does she work for the same company I do? I could swear I've never seen her before. The one beer in me threatens to make me social; she is very attractive, and I'm about to turn to her and ask her, politely of course, who she is, but before I can the elevator dings again and we're on the ground floor, the doors open and the final two of us rejoin the crowd. She moves out of the elevator and approaches a group of people who I think are lawyers, or maybe they work in the finance department. Either way, they're not marketing, and I guess that's why I don't know her. I stand for a moment watching her, until the elevator doors begin to close and I realise if I don't move I'll end up going back up into the building, and so waving a hand to make the sensors open the doors I dash out and find Tom and Neil and the rest of marketing.

"Finally, what took you so long?" Neil asks me, but then continues before I can answer. "Right, that's everyone, let's head out.

"Where are we going?" someone asks.

"The Perfect Pint," Neil replies to the unknown voice. A chorus of groans meet his answer.

"But that's a total tourist place," a voice remonstrates.

"It'll be full of people taking pictures and being all in the way and annoying and that," another says, equally annoyed.

"For fuck's sake Neil," a third voice announces, to general laughter.

Regardless of all the complaints about location, everyone follows Neil out of the building, turning left and entering the next building, a small Irish pub.

Out on the street I hesitate for a moment. There's a feeling in the air, the anticipation that was covering the office like a fog has come with us. Or perhaps it's our proximity to Times Square that makes the air feel palpable, gives it a certain tension. Times Square is one of those places that doesn't feel real, it doesn't seem like it should actually exist. Even though I grew up in England I was raised by American TV and films, and so Times Square is one of many places I felt like I already knew when I got to New York. But nothing could have prepared me for it actually being real, which was a huge shock to me when I first visited.

I moved here when I was 22: I did my undergrad in Media Studies in London and then was offered a place to do my MA at NYU and was never going to turn that opportunity down. I landed in New York a week before my course started and spent that week exploring, visiting all the places I'd seen and heard and read about, seeing them all come to life. Some, like the Statue of Liberty, were disappointing: it turns out it really is just a massive statue, one that's not even actually that big compared to the skyscrapers that have been built since the French shipped it over. Others, like the Empire State Building and the view from its roof, were even more amazing than I'd imagined. And then there was a third category, in which Times Square fell: places that just, for one reason or another, didn't seem real. Six years I've been in New York, four years walking through Times Square nearly every day, and yet, and yet. Seeing it for the first time was how I imagine it'd feel to see a Minotaur or Medusa in the flesh: very confusing. Something I felt like I was already so aware of, and yet being there, seeing it, it was so alien to me. New York is less a city and more a collection of mythologies, and Times Square is one I still haven't been able to reconcile.

Dragging myself away from my asinine thoughts I follow the group into the pub, gratefully accepting the beer someone, Tom I think, hands me. A cheers is called in praise of the Q2 profits, and then all pretence is cast aside and the real drinking begins.

I stand a little in the back and off to one side, observing. I used to see myself as somewhat of a David Attenborough character, simply observing the animals in their natural habitat. This was back when I used to try and find reasons for why I was so aloof, so out of the picture, so uncomfortable. "It's on purpose," I'd tell myself, "I'm better than these people, I'm Jane Goodall watching the apes." Thankfully now that I'm a little older, a little wiser, and very aware that I'm just a bit socially inept, I don't try and excuse myself. I simply stand far enough away to be left alone, whilst remaining close enough to not look weird or aloof, two things I hate being accused of, despite how true they may be.

Anyway, in a place like The Perfect Pint, when a group as large as ours comes in, there's nowhere to go. It's not a huge place, and we are a relatively huge group, so we take up 99% of the space. I couldn't escape even if I wanted to, which now I think of it makes me shudder a little. I really hope there isn't a fire.

I finish my beer and am about to go to the bar and order another when one finds its way to me. I take it gratefully and looking up from the beer in my hands to say thank you to the giver I see it's the attractive woman from earlier, my elevator companion. I'm not sure what to say, so I go with a trusty acknowledgement of her kindness.

"Thank you, that's very kind."

"You're not from around here are you?" she says, a slightly drunken lilt in her voice. No "you're welcome", no pleasantries of any kind, she's straight into it.

"I'm not," I reply. She looks at me as if waiting for me to say more, and when I make no move to she continues.

"So where are you from, then?"

"Oh, I'm from England."

"England, wow!" she says, and whether it's because she's drunk or just American, she genuinely sounds like I've blown her mind. "What's England like?"

"Erm," I falter. What *is* England like? "England is England, I suppose," I say, lamely.

I'm nervous, but not the usual kind of nervous I am when I talk to people; no, this is the special kind of nervousness that I only feel around absolutely stunning women. Because that's what this woman is, absolutely incredibly beautiful. I was wrong before, attractive doesn't even start to cover it. Now we're talking, and not just awkwardly avoiding eye contact in an elevator, I can see her properly. She has platinum blonde hair, so light as to almost be silver, and her eyes are yellow, like a cat's, and I wonder if she wears coloured contacts or something? She's shorter than me but not by much, she must be much taller than most women, and I momentarily wonder if that's why she's talking to me, because I'm one of the few men in here, in the world, taller than her. It may be 2023 but some things still hold, and I think most straight women want the man they're with to be taller than them.

"England is England," she says, mocking me in an exaggerated Cockney accent — the same accent all Americans do in impersonation of an English person no matter where they're from or whatever accent they may actually have — and she starts to laugh. I try to as well but I fail, instead just watch her. Even though she's somehow already pretty wasted, it's barely 6pm, she's still incredible, her laugh is still musical. Incredible? What does that even mean? She's so pretty I just can't describe her, I can't do her justice. We humans are but ugly rocks on the beach of life, and she's a mermaid.

"What's your name, England?"

"Oliver."

"Aren't you going to ask what mine is?" she says, starting to look a little peeved now.

"What's your name?"

"Sophie."

As she says it she reaches her hand out, but as I go to shake it she grabs my forearm and pulls me into a hug. I stand frozen, not sure how to react: I'm not a hugger, not at all, particularly not with people I don't even know, and so my response is to freeze. You know people talk about fight or flight? Well that binary is bullshit, because most people do the third option, which is to freeze. I'm a total freezer, and I'm frozen right now.

Eventually I unfreeze enough to move to hug her back, despite my every muscle and sinew screaming against it, but I once again freeze when she whispers in my ear:

"Well, Oliver from England, do you wanna fuck?"

Chapter Two:

Sliding Doors

Is this my *Sliding Doors* moment? Is this the dime upon which my life will turn: if I say yes, my life will play out in a certain way following that yes, Sophie and I will go to either her place or my place or a hotel or maybe even just the bathroom of this bar depending on how drunk and really horny she actually is, and we'll have sex, and then my life will continue for 50 or 60 or 70 years, and then I'll die. However if I say no, will my life take a completely different path, will the events that happened to me, and that I made happen, after I said yes, be completely different if I say no?

Really, the answer is: it's literally impossible to know. I have two thoughts on the matter: 1) there are no *Sliding Doors* moments in life, and 2) every single moment in life is a *Sliding Doors* moment.

The thing about life is, despite how much it can feel like it, it's not a movie. Fuck, I'm not even the main character in my own life, I'm just a tertiary character in the lives of others. I'm a character actor, I don't have the spotlight, I don't steal the show, I'm just kinda there. Rather than being the main star of my own movie, I'm a background character in the movies of everyone whose life I come across. In some movies, for example my parents', I play a pretty big role; in other peoples, like, say, Nicola's for example, I barely play a role at all. But I do play a role. It may be "non-speaking extra" or "idiot who keeps walking into the shot", but whatever, both of those are still roles, no matter how minor.

Dear Shakespeare, if the world truly is a stage, and we are all truly merely players, then tell me this: where's the fucking exit?

Because life isn't a movie, there are no *Sliding Doors* moments, because how would we ever know? The whole thing about the movie is the fact that those literal *Sliding Doors* on the train fracture her onto two separate timelines, and we as the viewer sitting at home or in the cinema watch both play out. We see how Helen's life veers off in two different directions, how getting on the train makes her life play out in one way, and not getting on the train makes it play out in another. And even though in the movie there are slips, where the two timelines sort of kind of bleed into each other, really Helen has no idea what's happened; in each timeline she's just a woman living her life, doing what she does, taking it as it comes. And that's all we can do: I am living the life that I'm living, in the year 2023, in New York City, and that's all I can do. There may be other mes out there in the infinite alternative universes, if you're into that kind of thing, but really, I'm just me. So no, there can be no *Sliding Doors* moment in life because, like, how would we even know?

Or: every single moment in life is a *Sliding Doors* moment. This is a bit of a stretch, but one could argue that, because our lives play out from moment to moment, because we only really exist in the present, then every moment is a *Sliding Doors* moment because every single thing that happens to us, every single thing we do, shapes how the rest of our life will play out. If I have sex with Sophie, then the rest of my life will follow on from that. If I don't have sex with Sophie, the rest of my life will follow on from *that*. But really, the same applies to everything. Say Sophie hadn't approached me, and I'd gone to the bar like I'd originally planned. If I'd ordered a beer, the rest of my life would have played out from that decision. However, if I'd ordered a cocktail, the rest of my life would have played out from *that* decision. If I'd have ordered a Coke and some food, my life would have played out following *that* decision.

Maisie Peters sings that all she does is think about the past, but the past doesn't exist, not really. We may remember it, but the human memory is remarkably infallible, and incredibly prone to misremembering things, or even inventing memories. That the justice system relies so heavily on eye witness testimony is an issue for people much smarter than me to figure out. But really what I'm saying is, every moment is a *Sliding Doors* moment, or none is. But even if you subscribe to the every moment theory, then that still negates each *Sliding Doors* moment as a *Sliding Doors* moment, because if everything is something, then that something becomes redundant. As Sean Bateman argued in *The Rules of Attraction*, not everyone can be beautiful, because if everyone is beautiful then no one is beautiful, because it's a universal standard, not an achievement. But then again, as Rupert so eloquently put it, Sean Bateman is a rich mother fucking mother fucker, so you can only take what he says with a pinch of salt.

Sophie is looking at me. I should probably answer her.

I want to say yes. I'm desperate to say yes, but for the moment I say nothing. Sophie releases me from the hug, and we're once again standing facing each other, the appropriate amount of space apart for two people who are supposedly having a normal conversation. She's looking at me expectantly, sipping her drink through a straw, apparently this bar still serves plastic ones, I thought that was illegal, or is that just in England? My parents insist on keeping me up to date with all the latest news from back home, and it often gets jumbled up in my head with what I've read about my new home, and I find at times I'm not sure what's English and what's American. And also what I've invented or dreamed or wished or am half remembering from another life.

I know my focus on the straw is my mind delaying, distracting itself from the real question. My brain does this a lot: I think its logic is that, if it can distract and delay, then in that intervening period someone may swoop in and answer for me. And not just now, here, with Sophie, but always, in every scenario. I don't have ADHD, I got tested a few times as a kid, so I can't blame being easily distracted and often lacking focus on that. I suppose I could probably blame it on the crippling depression and crushing loneliness, but that already shoulders the burden of about 80% of my life and my problems, so I should probably cut it some slack.

I'm staring at Sophie, forcing my eyes away from her straw and to look her in the eye. She's looking at me, still with that expectant look on her face. Oh fuck, I better answer. What am I gonna say? Fuck it, I'm gonna say yes. If this is my *Sliding Doors* moment, then I can do a lot worse than the rest of my life playing out after I've seen this woman naked.

"Yes."

"Yes?"

"Yes."

"Yes, what?"

"Yes, I do want to fuck you."

Sophie blanches as I say this, and I'm mortified. Did I

mishear her?

"That's nice?" she says, her voice rising at the end to make it a question, like she's speaking to a toddler who's showing her a nice rock or something.

"Do you want to come back to my place, or should we go to yours?"

"Why?"

"To have sex?"

Her face changes in the second it takes me to say this: her expectant look had been replaced by a confused one, and now that look slowly slips off her face, and she begins to smile, small at first, just a ghost of one creeping into the corners of her mouth. It grows, spreading towards the centre where the two halves of it meet and become one whole, a smile that takes over her face, creasing her cheeks, making lines appear beside her eyes and on her forehead, her eyes themselves light up with it. Then the smile becomes a laugh, again small at first, just a chuckle I can barely hear over the noise in the pub, the music and TVs and many people having many discussions, some more animated than others. Slowly her laugh becomes more pronounced, not just louder but bigger on her, her mouth opens and closes with the sound of it, and she — and I can't believe this, she literally does it — she tips her head back like some sort of fucking cartoon or something, like a parody of a human, and then her head is bucking back and forth like a chicken, she's in hysterics, people are turning to look at us, at the woman laughing maniacally, at the man standing watching her, not laughing for some reason, just looking very uncomfortable.

Because that's basically what I've become; I'm no longer a man so much as I am the feeling of being uncomfortable come to life. I am the personification of discomfort, and ironically for the first time in my life I feel comfortable in my skin. I feel like this is the natural end point for me as a person, to stop being a person and become a feeling, and a bad one at that. At least now I know my role.

Sophie's laugh has overtaken the bar, I look around and there isn't a single conversation still taking place, literally everyone has stopped and is looking at us. I can see Tom and Neil looking at me, both inclining their heads slightly, silently asking what's going on. I shrug back, trying to convey my honest answer: I have absolutely no idea. They look from me to Sophie, then back to me. She's still laughing, and even though it's probably only been 30 seconds, a minute max, it feels like we've been here forever. I feel like I've lived in this moment always, I was born here and the 28 years since that tragedy have been spent here. Hey, I finally found where I belong!

"Oh no, oh my," Sophie coughs, her laughter slowing down now, she looks like she's getting herself under control. "Oh, I'm sorry, Oli."

I didn't ask her to call me that. She didn't ask me. I fucking hate being called Oli.

"Are you okay?" I ask her.

She wipes her eyes with her sleeve, taking care to remove any mascara that's clumped in the corners by her tear ducts. She's stopped laughing entirely, and most people have stopped watching us, have rejoined their conversations. A few people are still looking at us warily, particularly those proximate to us, but I ignore them as best I can, focus on Sophie, try and figure out what on earth is actually going on. Try and figure out if I'm going to have sex or if I should turn and run.

"I'm fine, I promise I'm fine. I just didn't think…" she's stopped wiping her eyes and is looking at me now, and her face has fallen.

"Didn't think what?" I ask her, my heart beginning to pound. I have half an idea what she's about to say and I'm petrified.

"I didn't think," she hesitates, before letting the next words spill from her mouth in a rush. The semi-drunken slurring is long gone from her voice, she's now speaking very clearly. "I didn't think you'd take me seriously."

Yeah, that was what I feared she was going to say. And, as expected, it crushes me. I am destroyed. I don't know what to say. What do you say in this situation? No one has prepared me for this. I mean, girls used to make fun of me at school, tease me and stuff, but never like this. They'd call me names and throw stuff at me, laugh when I asked them out, but they never played with my heart like this. I'll give those teenage girls credit, they were mean, and they were cruel, but they stopped short of ever destroying me. Sophie has not given me that courtesy.

Her face has completely changed now; in her defence, at least she looks mortified. Her mouth is moving, it looks like she's trying to say something, but no words are escaping her lips. I feel like I should say something but I have no words either, I have no thoughts I want to convey. My mind is blank, I am no longer here, no longer in this pub in anything but body. The ceilings are no longer above me, but simply my fleshy form. The ground underneath me has swallowed me, I am in literal hell, I wish to burn, please, because my skin and flesh searing would hurt less than this. I think Sophie has finally found her words but I hear nothing except a rushing noise, like gale force winds blowing directly by my ears. In fact, everything is rushing, the world has started to spin in front of me, I feel dizzy, I feel weak. I have to leave. My two options are leave or collapse, and I really don't think this moment needs me collapsing to complete it. Sophie is still talking but I turn away from her and leave the pub, I glide across the floor weaving between tables and groups of people. I think I hear someone, maybe Tom, shout my name, but I ignore it. I do not know where I'm going to, but I know where I'm going from, and that is this moment. The only way to make it end is to flee it.

I eventually make it to the single door that denotes entrance and exit and burst through it, like a whale bursting through the surface of the ocean. I gulp the air into my lungs, feeling slightly better just for having escaped the oppressive atmosphere of the pub. I stand hunched over with my hands on my thighs, gasping and drawing in huge breaths, willing the oxygen to fill my system, getting a bit light headed as it does. I hear a noise and turning slightly I see the pub door open and Sophie comes out, still with that mortified look on her face. I see her quickly scan the street before her eyes land on me and she moves in my direction, but I'm not able or willing to deal with her so with a gargantuan effort I stand upright and begin to walk, moving in the direction of Times Square. Sophie follows me.

I move as fast as I'm able, weaving through crowds of locals, tourists, and everything in between. People leaving work, going to work, moving from their first job to the second. People taking pictures, pictures of the buildings that fence Times Square, pictures of the crowds that fill the ground level, pictures of themselves and each other. I move as quickly as I can but each time I risk a glance over my shoulder I can see Sophie still behind me, she's reaching out for me but can't quite get me, but I know if I slow down she will. I think she's shouting apologies but I ignore her, I keep dodging people, turning to the side and now and then going up on my tiptoes, making myself as tall and thin as possible. I curse my height, because even as I put both people and distance between myself and Sophie I know she'll be able to see me, my head sticks out above the crowd. I had planned to lose her in the mash of people gathered in Times Square like fucking Jack Ryan or something, but my height stops me.

Sophie is still behind me so I inwardly tell myself a big 'fuck it' and I start jogging, still trying to avoid people but not as much, bumping into some, hearing shouts of "hey" and "watch out" and "fuck you" but I ignore them, my only focus now is getting away. I move north across Times Square and head up Broadway, no longer looking back, simply making my own way, fuck Sophie. I jog the 15 blocks up Broadway to Columbus Circle and duck into the station, running down the stairs before swiping myself through the barriers and onto the platform. The first bit of luck of the day strikes me: a train is waiting, doors just starting their beeping as I head down the stairs. Unlike Gwyneth Paltrow there are no kids blocking me and I get on the train, the doors closing behind me as I do. I sit with my back to the platform: I no longer care if Sophie is behind me, I figure there's zero chance she got on the train with how little time I had to spare, so I assume I'm free. The train moves away and I relax for the first time in what feels like forever. Well, I relax as much as I'm able. I feel a bit better from the light jog, my brain has very kindly bestowed me with a handful of endorphins, but even as I sit on the train the image of Sophie laughing fills my head. I close my eyes but that only makes it more visible; I push my hands into my eyes, rubbing them until it hurts, but no matter how hard I try I can't erase the image.

I ride the D train to Lafayette and walk the five minutes to my apartment building on Greene Street; the journey calms me somewhat, and as I enter my block, a five-storey building painted jet black that you wouldn't believe was real unless you saw it, I check my mail: spam, spam, marketing garbage, spam, bill I can't afford to pay. I shove the bill into my pocket and chuck the rest in the trash, moving past the eternally broken elevator to the stairs. Thankfully I'm only on the 3rd floor so it isn't too bad, and actually the climb gives me a few more endorphins, so by the time I get to my apartment door I think I might be able to make it through the night. I'm quickly removed from this idea, however, when I feel something hit my hand as I put the key in the lock, and looking down I see it's a tear. I feel another, then another, and only then do I realise I'm crying.

My eyes blur with the moisture and it takes me an age to open the door, the couple of beers I had at the pub combined with the one in the office have stayed in my system and as well as crying I'm a bit tipsy. I eventually make it into my tiny, shitty little rent-controlled apartment and, throwing my bag and jacket onto the couch, I head straight for the bathroom and try to masturbate the sadness away. Unfortunately I'm so sad I can't get a proper erection, and after maybe an hour I give up and go to bed, lying staring at the ceiling. What a fucking catch-22 eh? The only way to rid myself of the sadness overwhelming me is to masturbate, and yet I'm just too fucking sad to be even able to. No one tells you that shit when you're growing up. You don't see that in the movies.

One of the biggest differences, for me at least, between *Say Anything* and *Sliding Doors* is the amount of love I'm left with when the credits roll. Because a good romcom, I don't care what anyone says, makes you fall in love. I'm mostly straight, which means I invariably fall in love with the female lead, the love interest usually, more than the man doing the chasing. Romcoms are still incredibly hetero-normative; I know *Bros* came out recently, but I haven't seen it yet. Besides, the best romcoms were made in the 80s and 90s anyway, I'm always wary of newer ones. Although there are some exceptions: see *(500) Days of Summer*.

Whenever I watch *Say Anything*, which is pretty regularly, by the time the credits roll I am deeply, deeply infatuated with Diane Court. The problem is, once the credits end, I'm kinda, not. I'm in love with Diane Court, but I never really fall in love with Ione Skye, not truly. I lust her for the 100 minutes the film plays, but once it's over, so am I. I do fall in love quite a lot with Lloyd Dobler, but that's the opposite of Diane/Ione; I'm a lot more in love with John Cusack than I am with Lloyd. That's perhaps because some people theorise that Lloyd actually becomes, ignoring the name change, Rob Fleming in *High Fidelity*, which is not only one of my all-time favourite books, but also one of my all-time favourite movies. It's a rarely good adaptation. It's not ever included in my list of top romcoms, however, for one simple reason: it's about breaking up and getting back together. Unlike Diane Court and her commencement speech, I do not believe people should go back. I'm of the opinion that when people break up, they break up for a reason. And unless they're living in a sitcom, and the break up is over a misunderstanding that's simple to resolve, I don't believe there are issues that can be solved by breaking up. I think once you're apart, you're done, that's it. None of my exes have ever wanted me back so I've never tested this theory.

Now take *Sliding Doors* for example: by the time the credits roll 99 minutes later I am completely and utterly in love with Helen Quilley. And not only this, but I'm completely and utterly in love with Gwyneth Paltrow.

There's this one scene in the film, when the Helen on the good timeline — the one where she has short hair, thanks director for doing that and making our lives easier — and is doing the grand opening for Clive's restaurant. In this scene she's wearing a very simple black dress, and her very short hair is propped up somehow, and in it she's weaved some small red flowers. Fucking hell. There are no words to describe my feelings for Helen/Gwyneth in that scene. She looks just so incredibly beautiful, so incredibly stunning. I think part of the power of the scene comes from the fact that not only has she arranged this kick ass party, but it's going really well, and so she's feeling good, feeling confident. For the first time, or one of the first times, in the film, she's back to her old self, ready to take on the world and fucking win. And this confidence is so incredibly sexy. It's obvious I'm in my late 20s when I say something like that, that confidence is sexy. But whatever, it is. Although that scene only plays out for a few minutes, and is ruined by dickhead Gerry appearing, kissing her in front of James and causing a huge misunderstanding that threatens to ruin their burgeoning relationship; although it's only short, a small fraction of the whole dream, that scene is everything.

There's a moment in it: Gerry has taken Helen outside to talk, and James is inside, watching them through a window. At first he's trying not to stare, just stealing a glance now and then, trying to be tactful and give them space (James is great like that you see, he's an absolute prince, and not in the sarcastic *Catcher in the Rye* way but in the genuine fairytale way, kinda). What makes this scene so perfect is if we step out of Helen and into James, and we watch Helen through his eyes. They're in that perfect early stage of the relationship, when all they have and all they want is each other. James is desperately crushing on Helen, and all he wants to do is see her, speak to her, smell and hear her, learn about her. All he wants to do is touch her, not necessarily sexily, a hug, hold hands, even something so little as brushing arms together will create an energy in him that nothing else on this planet could even come close to matching.

That early stage of the relationship is everything. Even though you're seeing someone your crippling fear of dying alone is bigger than ever, because before you met the person you'd resigned yourself to dying alone, and despite crying yourself to sleep every night you pretend you're okay with it, pretend you've made peace with it. But then someone comes along, someone who changes things. They do many things, but one of the biggest things they do is they banish that fear of dying alone, they push it to one side. For the first time you're optimistic, you think that actually you're not going to die alone, you're going to spend the rest of your life with this person, maybe everything will be okay, maybe you're just a normal person after all and you do fit in, you will actually be happy.

The problem is, the fear of dying alone is never banished fully, and is only pushed to one side. And because of this, because you've taken the spotlight off it, it's shadow looms larger than ever. The fear, because it no longer has you, is fighting for you. It draws more and more power, it threatens to take over you. Dying alone is one thing: going from being with someone to being alone is about the worst thing imaginable. I don't want to die alone. I don't want to lose my Helen, if I ever meet her. I don't want to lose the feeling of touching the skin of the woman in the black dress with flowers in her hair. I don't want to lose the sound of her voice first thing in the morning, and the sight of her after a long day at work. I just want someone to love me, is that too much to ask? Is that even possible?

What am I talking about? I've found my Helen: it's Nicola of course. How fucking idiotic of me. Depression causes memory loss, have I mentioned that? Apparently to the extent you can even forget The One. Madness.

July bleeds into August and the heat is relentless; the capitalists have buggered off to the Hamptons or wherever, places with sand and beaches and more importantly, functioning aircon. New York is such a weird city: as the city constantly pumps out hot air, for someone like me who's normally a summer lover, I've slowly grown to hate New York summers. Sure it's nice to go sit in the park, take a few tins or a bottle of something, bask in the sun and pass the time of day, but those days are few and far between. Really, the reality of New York in August is hot heat, hot humidity, and stickiness. I see people running as I walk to work, wearing only a t-shirt and sweating through it before I've gone two blocks, and I wonder how they're not just spontaneously bursting into flames. I feel like I'm going to just watching them.

August in New York is arriving at the office a sweaty mess, fearing the elevators more than usual because oh god the smells; we're all in this together, we all suffer through the same heat, but that's where the camaraderie ends. We might exchange a nod, maybe even a little chuckle about "the state of things", but we don't want to smell each other, we don't want to have to deal with each other's rank odours. In the elevators we're forced to. At least it's only a few seconds, a minute or two max, and then the doors slide open and release us, and we live to fight another day. Or at least, we live to fight until our next elevator ride.

It's been over a month since the incident in The Perfect Pint and I haven't seen Sophie once. Whilst I generally tend to fall in love with all beautiful women who speak to me, tend to view every single one of them as The One, spend my days picturing our lives together, there's one sure fire way to avoid this: absolutely fucking destroy me. Because that's what Sophie did, she ruined me. The rest of July was a blur. Sitting here at my desk, a Monday morning in August, I couldn't say what I've been doing for the last few weeks. I could make an educated guess that I've been going to work, struggling through the day, returning home, crying and watching films, and then trying and failing to sleep. That's the set menu, so it's what I assume has been happening.

I mean to be fair it could still be July for all I know, because nothing has happened. Things have quietened down in the office: because everyone with any money fucks off from the city until the heat dies down, marketing grinds to a halt. Well, it slows down at least. The decision makers aren't in their offices, aren't receiving our emails or flyers or seeing our billboards. We mainly sell to other companies: companies that sell to the public, this is their time to shine, particularly with the massive influx of tourists who seem to want to know what it's like to be cooked whilst you're still living. But the business money holders, the people who buy stuff from our company, who pay our salaries, they're nowhere to be found.

Obviously we still have to come in all day every day, god forbid we get any time off. That's the one thing that makes me consider going back to England, actually getting some vacation time. And then being able to afford to use it. I love New York, I think you have to be dead inside not to, but fuck me New York doesn't love me back. Even if I moved back to London I think I could cut my rent in half and use the leftover to exploit the city's proximity to Europe. And get a bunch of trips in before the EU really takes its gloves off and starts charging us Non-EU residents for visas and shit. Yay, Brexit!

I'm sitting at my desk, headphones in, some spreadsheet or other in front of me. I'm occasionally wiggling my mouse, making sure my computer doesn't go to sleep, making sure I don't go to sleep, when a shadow falls over me. I ignore it at first, willing it to go away: today is not a good day, no amount of manifesting on my obscenely sweaty walk this morning has changed that, and I just don't have it in me to speak to anyone. I pray for the shadow to go away, but when it doesn't I sigh and force myself to lift my head up, force my chin to rise and my eyes to see who's bothering me. My heart stops: it's Nicola.

I look at her for a moment, paralysed, and it's only when she starts gesturing at me to remove my headphones that I realise I'm still wearing them and pull them off my ears, let them rest on my neck, their weight a momentarily comforting distraction. I'm so excited. I'm so scared.

"Hi, Oli, how're you?"

Fucking *Oli*. Although it doesn't sound so bad when it comes from her mouth. She gives it a totally American lilt, her voice fairly high-pitched and slightly clichéd but basically I am enraptured.

"I'm, erm, okay, erm, yeah, good thanks." I'm stuttering and stumbling like the idiot I am.

"That's good."

She looks at me for a moment and I realise I didn't ask her how she is. Fuck.

"How're you—"

"Listen what are—"

We speak at the same time, each's words drowning the other's out. We exchange an awkward laugh before she speaks again. I purposefully stay quiet to avoid making this whole ordeal more awkward than it is. Why can't I just go back to quietly loving her from a distance? It's much easier, much less potential for disaster.

"I'm good, thanks," she smiles softly, like someone might when they're talking to a child or someone with intellectual disabilities. I don't mind, her smile is so beautiful she can use it on me any way she pleases. "Listen, this is a bit random but what are you doing a week on Saturday?"

I pretend to think for a second, knowing full well already that I have no plans.

"I think I'm free," I say, trying to keep the fact my hands are shaking from reaching my voice. I sit on them, trying to do it in a way that she can't see, and therefore making it really fucking obvious what I'm trying to do. She doesn't say anything, just continues to talk in her beautiful voice through her beautiful smile formed by her beautiful mouth.

"Do you want to come to a wedding with me?"

Why is she asking me? But also: yes, yes, more than anything in the world, yes.

"Erm, I guess, okay, sure?"

"Great. It's at the library, you know the Schwarzman building on 5th? The ceremony is at 1.30 so meet outside at, like, 1, maybe?"

At the library? Fuck, does that mean it's going to be stupidly posh? Because that can't be cheap, getting married in New York Public Library, that place is an institution. Oh god, I'm going to be so out of place, I've literally only just been invited and I'm already dreading it.

"Yeah, no worries, sure, sounds great."

"Okay great, see you then."

"Yeah, brilliant."

She turns and walks away from my desk and I let my

entire body go when she does. It's taken everything in me to restrict the shaking to my hands, but now she's left me I can let it take over me. I awkwardly stand up, my legs not quite wanting to but I force them, and I shamble to the toilets, locking myself in a cubicle and finally breathing out. What the fuck just happened? Did Nicola actually just invite me to a wedding? Did that actually just happen? It must have done because otherwise why would I be shaking so much? I have absolutely no idea *why* she invited me to a wedding, completely and utterly out of the blue, but that's something to think about and dissect in an unnecessarily minute level of detail another time. That's something to massively overthink later. But it must have happened; only something of that magnitude could cause a panic attack this large to come this quickly. I close the toilet lid and sit down, put my head between my knees and draw deep breaths in through my nose, let them out through my mouth. I do this until I think I'll just about be able to survive the day; I glance at my phone and see it's nearly lunchtime, just half an hour to get through then I can go out, ostensibly to get some food but really to calm down, I might actually go and get a drink. In the movies when someone is shaken up they go to a dive bar and down a shot of whiskey: I've never done that in my life, but first time for everything and all that. Nicola has just invited me to a wedding, so stranger things have very much happened, and very recently. Is this my life now? Beautiful women and whiskey? 'Cos I'm not exactly not okay with that.

Another difference between *Sliding Doors* and *Say Anything* is that *Sliding Doors* doesn't address class in the same way that *Say Anything* does. Where in *Say Anything* Lloyd is looked down on by Diane's father and his peers as being too low class, there are no such issues in *Sliding Doors*;

Helen and James are very much of the same class, at least we can assume. It's never made clear what exactly it is James does, how he comes across his money. At the beginning we see him in Helen's building, indeed he even retrieves for her the earring which she drops in the elevator. But then after Helen is fired, in the timeline she makes it onto the train she bumps into James, and this is where their acquaintance — in this timeline at least — truly begins. But then again, such is the non-standard make up of the working world that a man can't be judged by being on a train in the middle of the day. Perhaps that's my subconscious classicism coming into play: the very outdated idea that good, respectable people are in work between the hours of 9am and 5pm, Monday to Friday. If you're not in a shop or an office or on a building site or whatever during those hours, you're some sort of layabout, some sort of lazy, shiftless scumbag. James could be a freelance journalist, travelling from one report to another; he could be a travelling salesman, conducting large amounts of his business thanks to London's extensive underground network. James might be on leave when the whole shebang of the film kicks off, and is just out and about, doing whatever. He says on the tube to Helen, before she shows any real interest, that he's just had some good news, but again it's never made clear what this is. Now that I think of it, there are a few missing details in the story in *Sliding Doors*.

But they don't matter, because love. As The Beatles say, all you need is love. Everyone knows that. Because as James says in *Sliding Doors*, everyone knows all the Beatles lyrics, they're born doing so. The mother knows them and passes them on to the baby, and voila! You come out of the womb singing *Yellow Submarine*. I mean, in reality not quite, but still, perhaps in the UK in the 90s, not too far from the truth. Before the internet really kicked globalisation into 6th gear and the world went a bit mad, the Beatles were perhaps as much as a mascot for England as Queenie was. Before she died anyway, no one gives a fuck about Charles.

I wonder if there's no discussion of class in *Sliding Doors* because they're all at least middle class, if not pushing upper middle: in the timeline with the short hair, Helen opens her own PR agency and does Clive's aforementioned restaurant opening, and does a bang up job of it. Clive is a chef, a hot young chef in central London. James is… whatever James is, but you'd assume something middle/upper middle class, like attracts like and all that. I mean the man *rows* for fucks' sake, and then after he rows he and his fellow rowers go to a pub and sing the kind of weird song you only get from private sports club, which are upper middle class at least. Maybe the reason class isn't discussed in *Sliding Doors* is because the film centres around the kind of people who don't discuss class, because it's never been an issue for them. But equally likely, maybe there is huge class discussion in *Sliding Doors* but I haven't picked up on it yet as I haven't seen the film enough times. I've only watched it a handful of times, unlike *Say Anything*, which I've seen at least 30. How do I know this? I once watched it every day for a month. It was not a good month emotionally, even if it was spectacular from a cinematic point of view.

It's the day before the wedding and I've figured it out. What have I figured out? Why Nicola has invited me. She hasn't spoken to me since inviting me, not even in the course of work; we've kept our usual lines of demarcation, unbeknownst to her but everything to me. I've stayed my distance: like Homer when he asks Marge to prom in *The Simpsons*, he doesn't approach her again for fear of her not going with him. I don't approach

Nicola because a) I just don't, it's not what I do, I love her from afar; b) I can't just talk to her, why and how would that work; and c), most importantly, right now I'm invited to the wedding, but if I talk to her I may find she's changed her mind, found someone else or decided to go alone. That may be the case as I sit here right now, but if I don't know I don't know. Schrödinger's Wedding Invite. Fair play to *The Big Bang Theory*; you can argue all day about whether it's actually any good or not — early seasons pretty decent, later stuff not only not funny but quite offensive, actually — but it did bring a lot of scientific terms into the mainstream, such as Schrödinger and his cat malarky. Much like how even though the *Harry Potter* books are far from the best written books in the world, they got kids reading, and that's much, much more important.

I was initially quite happy at all that lay before me: I figured the wedding was Nicola's friend, or family member, cousin or whatever, who knows. I didn't care really. But the more time passed the more I wanted to know details, and without her speaking to me, and me not speaking to her, I couldn't ask for any. And so I did what any self-respecting person would do in 2023: I went on the internet. The library's website has public listings of what's going on, even for the private events. I guess the people who have events there are fine with it; I think you only hold an event at the library to show off, and having your event listed on the library's website certainly speaks to that. It took me all of five seconds to find the listing; there's only one wedding this weekend, so what else could it be? Mr Elijah Parker and Miss Jennifer Nguyen.

Finding the listing I sat for a moment, a distant part of my memory trying to make a connection. Elijah Parker, why did that seem familiar? It's a pretty generic name, could be anyone; I'd surely seen that name somewhere online, or read it in a book or heard it in a film or something. Elijah Parker. I mean it's not exactly fucking Zsa Zsa Gabor now, is it? So I wracked my brain, trying to find the significance, when it slowly dawned on me: London. 2014. King's College. Bisexuality. Elijah and I had a very brief affair in our second year of uni.

Well then. That's something I'd completely forgotten about. As I say, the past doesn't exist, aside from some memories that may or may not be real. And these had not been memories to me, at least not consciously, until I saw the listing and the synapses that form the connections in my brain formed this one. Elijah Parker. We had some fun together.

It wasn't a great love affair, not by a long shot. Really, I can't even call it an affair. We drunkenly hooked up a few times when I was drinking too much and contemplating my sexuality. I wasn't contemplating it in any big way: it wasn't so much that I was attracted to men as it was that I couldn't attract any women, and sometimes when I got drunk enough I'd adopt a mantra of any port in a storm. Elijah happened to be a port I visited on a few occasions, /eing as it was just down the hallway from my room, my home port.

Was it just coincidence that Nicola had invited me? Elijah and I haven't spoken in, what, seven years? It must be, the last time I remember seeing him was graduation. I left for New York a few months later and haven't heard a thing about him since then, I have absolutely no idea where he even lives, in what country, on what continent. Is it possible he's been living in New York the entire time I have, but we've been completely unaware of each other? Or maybe he's been aware of me but has had no interest in getting in touch? I wouldn't blame him if this was the case, I mean why would he want to get in touch? We were decent friends, and aside from a few weeks of drunken blowjobs in the twilight hours when the rules don't apply, when some people are still up and others just getting up, the nether zone between night and day, we weren't anything. It's not like we were boyfriend and boyfriend, he wasn't my great love, and as far as I know I wasn't his. Even if I was, sorry Elijah, that was the beginning and the end of my adventures with bisexuality, I'm fully straight now. Although, is straight the right term? Is there a term for when you're a man who likes women, but those women are all fictional characters in romcoms? Actually, yes I think there is a term: fucking loser. That certainly fits me.

I'm just thinking about logging off, sneaking out a bit early, when my phone buzzes. I pick it up from the desk in front of me and see it's a message from a number I don't have saved. All it says is, "just in case". I figure it must be Nicola, and am proven right when I look up from my phone in the direction of her desk and see her smiling at me. I give her a thumbs up and immediately regret it, and pressing 'reply' on my phone I simply type 'I'm so sorry I just gave you a thumbs up'. She replies with a laughing emoji, to which I reply that I'm looking forward to next Saturday. The two ticks appear, letting me know she's read it, but no reply is forthcoming. I wait a few moments before putting my phone back down and packing my shit away. Time to end this day, end this working week, time to get ready for next week. Yes, it will take me that long to get ready. Mostly it's to mentally prepare myself, but also much more practically. Because I had a realisation this morning: I don't own a fucking suit.

I bet James owns a suit. James also gets to kiss Helen. And even though they're obviously only acting, James get to sleep with Helen, to see her naked and touch her. Fuck my life, why am I not James? Why do I have to be me?

Chapter Three:

(500) Days of Summer

I found out recently that not everyone thinks about death all the time. In fact, lots of people don't think about death some of the time, or even at all. I think about death constantly.

Weddings in real life are nothing like weddings in movies. For starters, how often do you see someone get really drunk at a movie wedding and try and fight someone, or try and seduce a clearly not interested or even already spoken for bridesmaid? Or even just give a really inappropriate speech, or try and get involved when the bride and groom cut the cake or have their first dance? I'm sure there are examples in films and on TV, but I'm also sure they're the tiny minority. Most movie weddings I've seen are clean, well-ordered, well-behaved affairs. The bride is beautiful, resplendent in her clean white dress; the groom is beautiful, too, in his clean and pressed suit. Sure he might have some worries, there may even be misdirection enough to make the viewer think the wedding might not go ahead, but he always turns up in the end. I mean, with the exception of *The Graduate*, and Ross and Emily in *Friends*, has anyone on TV or in a movie ever actually not gotten married?

Elijah and Jennifer both turned up on time, said all

the right things and were, in fact, married. They are married, the whole ceremony went off without a hitch. So actually, their wedding was very well reflected in movies; no one at Elijah and Jennifer's wedding got too drunk, no one threw anything or tried to fight anyone, no one tried to sleep with anyone who was already otherwise engaged — at least not in an obvious way, if it did happen I missed it — really, everyone, at least as far as I know, was very well behaved. Even Nicola and I were, although if I'm being completely honest it wasn't the most fun day.

I knew it was off to a bad start when I couldn't even bring myself to manifest that it would be good; I didn't want to go, no matter the fact that I was going with Nicola, I was going with *her*. I used to think, watching her across the office, that if she invited me to go to hell and get tortured for all eternity I'd be like, "sign me up, we going now, yeah?" Even this week that feeling remained: up until the wedding actually happened, I couldn't wait to go. I spent Friday night and Saturday morning thinking about Nicola; I wondered what she'd be wearing, if it'd be conservative, or if she'd been wearing something a bit more sexy, a bit more suggestive. I wondered if she'd have a bag, or if she'd want me to carry things for her in my pockets. I wondered if she'd have a jacket, or if the day would be warm enough she wouldn't need one, and then in the evening when the sun went down and it was a bit cooler, I could give her mine, gently drape it around her shoulders like Cary Grant or something, do what it is supposedly gentlemen used to do.

(Don't you find it odd that people pine for the days of men like Cary Grant or John Wayne, as if they wouldn't beat the shit out of you and rape you at the first opportunity? Men are not nice; men have never been nice.)

As it is, Nicola is wearing a red dress, fairly figure-hugging but not entirely, enough give that it doesn't ride up or bunch up or anything when she sits, and she doesn't look too uncomfortable that she's eaten, and had a few drinks besides. The dress is gorgeous: it's light red, thin straps hold it on her shoulders, and the dress itself starts about three quarters of the way up her breasts, so it shows enough of them that you can't help but stare, no matter how hard you try, you can't help but find excuses to glance at her, to glance down at her, but it covers enough that it's modest, if you asked me under oath to describe it I'd say it was fairly modest, not at all too sexy or inappropriate. It runs past her knees, about midway down her shins; it's fairly conservative in this way. She's wearing heels, similarly coloured red shoes with similarly thin straps, the heels perhaps an inch or two, nothing major, at no point today has she stumbled around. If anything, she's handled herself incredibly well. I don't know why I sound surprised, I don't know what I'd been expecting. Any judgements I'd made on this woman were my own; apart from the little I know of her at work, I know nothing about her really, so any judgements made exist only because of my own assumptions and prejudices, because of my own experiences, and have nothing to do with the fact or reality of her existence.

The Parkers, as they're now known, have also made it through the cutting of the cake and their first dance unscathed. I'm watching them now from where I stand on the edge of the dancefloor, and they look beautiful; her dress is stunning, it's a full dress that covers her shoulders, sleeveless, flows down her waist before blooming just below it, it looks like a Victorian dress or something, one of the ones that was so thick and heavy it had wooden framing inside it. But Jennifer's looks incredibly light, she moves with such grace, it's like watching a Disney Princess or something. Elijah just looks besotted; all day I've been watching him and he's barely taken his eyes off his bride. And I can't blame him either, it isn't just the dress that's beautiful, but she is too. Black hair, straight and coming down to her shoulders, framing a perfectly symmetrical face, her nose and eyes and cheekbones all sitting perfectly on her small but not too small face. She's beautiful, I don't know how else to describe it, and from his face Elijah clearly knows this, even if he's clearly unable to believe it. He's found his one, and as happy as I am for him, which I am, I swear — I think — I also hate him quite a lot. I want to find The One, and more and more I'm beginning to think that I won't, that maybe even there is no one for me, that I'll die alone. Unless there's an equal split of straight men, straight women, gay men, gay women, and queer non binary people, basically unless you can split the world exactly in two — perhaps removing the polyamorous people, they're too confusing a variable in this grossly oversimplified metaphorical equation — then there isn't one person for everyone. It's just maths, really. If there are three billion men, but only two and a half billion women, then half a billion men won't have a one. I think I'm in that group, I don't think there's a one for me. Now *that's* something you don't see in movies.

The couple haven't left the dancefloor since their first dance; they did a slow dance to *At Last* by Etta James, a beautiful song, dancing for only perhaps a minute before others joined them. Nicola and I did at first, dancing slowly and awkwardly. I've never danced with someone at a wedding before today, so I only have TV and movie weddings to go on; so I took her hand and pulled her onto the dancefloor, and once we found room we faced each other. I put my arm around her waist, and held out my other for hers; she put her arm around my shoulders and put her hand in mine. We danced like this for a couple of songs, but it was not incredible; we were awkward, we did the awkward dancing of two people who not only have never danced before, but don't even really know each other. We were clunky, we kept bumping into each other, both moving in the same direction when we should have been moving in opposite ones, or vice versa. At one point our foreheads collided, I'm not even sure how, and I can't speak for Nicola but it really hurt me. After a couple more slow songs the music sped up a bit and we tried to dance faster but this just made things worse, and so after three or four songs when Nicola told me she was going to the bathroom I was relieved, didn't even watch her go before going to the bar. I grabbed my third drink of the day; I'm pacing myself, the last thing I want to do is get really drunk. I might not have a one, but then again I might, and it might be Nicola and this might be my shot. I'm not going to get stupidly drunk and blow it, I've been there too many times, there's no coming back from that place.

So now I'm holding my third beer, half drunk, watching Elijah and Jennifer as they continue to sway in each other's arms, as they continue to be completely and incredibly in love. Part of me is melting with joy for them, part of me wants to kill them, wants the roof to cave in and all the happy couples to die. Probably a bit extreme, but it certainly would make me feel a lot better, and honestly, I don't think enough people at this wedding have taken my feelings into account.

I'm debating whether to try and bum a cigarette off one of the few people I've seen smoking; I decided not to bring mine in some completely misguided attempt at not smoking all day, and all I've achieved is being desperate for a cigarette, and being pissed off that I don't have any. I'm just looking for one of the potential culprits when I feel a touch on my arm and turning to my right I see Nicola at my elbow. We make eye contact for a brief moment, before she nods towards the doors, I think intimating that she wants me to go outside with her. As I move she does too, moving ahead of me, and she puts her arm behind her, holding her hand out, and I grab it, feeling the warmth and softness of her hand in mine, the smoothness of her palm, even as it's folded and creased with lines. Her hand is small, really small, it feels so fragile in mine, and I want to really grab it, really squeeze it, but I don't want to risk breaking it. She leads me through the crowd, people watching the couple as I'd been, dancing in their own little groups off the dance floor, sitting and standing and talking and laughing and generally celebrating life and love and all of us here.

Nicola wends her way slowly but surely through the crowds with a practised expertise and passes through an open door into a small courtyard within the building; the sun is low enough that it shines right in my eyes as we reach the outside and I'm temporarily blinded, the shine so bright I can't see a thing, and I'm glad to be holding Nicola's hand because otherwise I fear I'd fall over, I'd collide with something and hurt myself, I'd become Vonnegut's Billy Pilgrim and become completely unstuck. But Nicola still has me, and she must see that I'm struggling because her other hand finds my other hand and I bump into her, so she must have stopped. I take a moment, two, and then my vision clears, the world slowly falls back into place in front of my eyes, and when it does she's facing me, looking at me with a look on her face I can't quite place; it might be that she likes me, it might be that she's horny, she might be drunk, she might simply be hungry, she might be trying to reconcile the plot of *Lost*. Then she leans in to whisper in my ear, and I'm shocked by her words.

"Well, Oliver from England, do you wanna fuck?"

Nicola's words shock me, but what shocks me more is that they don't feel like the most intimate thing that's happened between us today. We've spent all day together; well, since 1pm anyway, and it's now nearly 9pm, so only actually eight hours, but still, under the circumstances, that counts as the entire day. I feel like we've seen more of each other than most people do in several lifetimes, it's almost been like our own little marriage in fast forward. We've seen each other looking our best, her in the aforementioned red dress, me in my brand-new suit; we've seen each other eat, a thing that I think is happening less and less with potential couples these days seeing as taking someone out on a dinner date is just a bit old fashioned now, a bit of a faux pas; not that there's anything wrong with it, but it's just a bit…binding. If you take someone out for a meal, then really, they're stuck there until the end of the meal. If you take someone out for drinks, or to a museum or something, then they have plenty of chance to escape if the person inviting them turns out to be a weirdo. Which I feel like is happening more and more at the moment, I feel like I read many more stories about weirdo men doing weirdo things on dates with perfectly normal women than I used to. It's probably the movies that are to blame; we men all grew up being told to date women a certain way, and not only this, but to not take no for an answer. Women weren't told this, they were given a completely different rulebook from us. And theirs gets updated all the time too, they get patches and new software, whereas we're still stuck trying to date women the way our fathers did. That is to say, unsuccessfully. And sexist-ly. It doesn't work.

The most intimate moment between Nicola and I wasn't our dancing, wasn't our sharing a meal —

alongside 248 other people — it wasn't sitting side by side and watching two people get married; the most intimate moment between us today was just now, when she took my hand.

I feel like holding hands is about the most intimate thing two people can do. I know that it isn't, at least not technically; surely having sex is the most intimate thing people can do, that's literally what being intimate means. But having sex with someone is easy — or at least I used to find it easy, when I was younger, now it's basically impossible — but finding a woman to hold hands with is nigh on impossible. I've 100%, absolutely definitely had sex with more women than I've held hands with. I don't know the numbers for either event, but I know for a fact I've had my penis in more vaginas than I've had my hand in other hands.

That's definitely the most intimate part of *(500) Days of Summer*. When Tom and Summer are in Ikea, the first time, when it's all going right. They're having a grand old time doing what couples do in that early part of the relationship: they're having fun. They're shopping for something for Summer, and pretending to be tired at the end of a long day they drop into a show living room. When the TV doesn't work they go into a show kitchen, and when the sink in this kitchen doesn't work they go into another show kitchen. They then end up in a show bedroom in which they kiss. Cut to them walking around Ikea, and Summer reaches out and takes Tom's hand; there are no words, no look exchanged, no nothing, she simply takes his hand and they walk away from the camera. Hell, the very next scene is them having sex for the first time, and yet them holding hands in Ikea is the most intimate part of their day, and if I'm being honest of the entire film.

No matter what happens between Nicola and I for

the rest of this day, for the rest of our lives, no moment between us will ever be as intimate as just now. When she took my other hand, so we were both holding both of each other's hands, if I hadn't still been blinded from the sun and therefore able to concentrate, I might have broken down there and then. Because it's not the sex I'm even after; yes I'd like to have sex with Nicola, I want to take off her red dress, slide the straps down her shoulders, kiss and bite them, unzip the dress and let it fall from her, exposing the other three quarters of her breasts. I'd like to see what underwear she's wearing, if she is wearing any; are they big, is she wearing granny pants to tuck it all in because the dress is form fitting, or are her pants also form fitting, a small thong or something. Are they green like her dress, or black because she's hoping someone will see them or red because they're the first pair she pulled from whatever drawer she keeps them in. Or is she wearing no underwear at all? Is her entire outfit the red dress and red shoes, and nothing else? I want to know all these things and more, I want to learn these facts; I want to place my lips on her body and kiss every part of it. But more than this, more than anything, I want to hold her hand again.

Because holding hands with someone is different. Sex can be an act between two people who care about each other, it can be a tender loving act which each uses to truly confess their love for the other. Sex can be a thoughtless, feeling-less act, two bodies mashing together in a way that's mutually pleasurable. Sex can be everything in between, it can be 100% feeling, 0% feeling, or any percentage in this window. Holding hands is different; holding hands is 100% about feeling. I've never held hands with anyone I didn't care about deeply; I've never gone out with friends, gotten super drunk, and then taken a girl home and held hands with her. A girl has never held hands with me to make her boyfriend jealous, or to upset her ex, or to ward away other potential suitors. The only people I've held hands with, and the only people whose hands I've held, I've well and truly cared about. They've meant something to me, and holding hands with them has been a way to solidify this bond, to give it a physical form. Sex is ostensibly about making babies and having fun. Holding hands is about so, so much more.

I can't be imagining things, did Nicola just say that to me? My memory isn't amazing, but I'm 99.9% certain she used the same words as Sophie, verbatim. She can't have, surely? Or if she did it's just coincidence, surely?

I'm speechless, flummoxed, not a clue what to say, but thankfully I'm saved, the effort by Nicola smiling at me and apologising.

"I'm sorry," she says, "that was mean of me."

I still have no idea what to say; why is it mean of her? What did she mean, did I mishear her? What's even going on?

"I shouldn't have said that, but I heard what happened a few weeks ago with that woman from HR and I couldn't help myself." I'm still unsure, unmoved, not laughing or smiling, and this fact seems to penetrate into Nicola's brain. "I really am sorry, what she did was a terrible thing, embarrassing you like that in front of everyone."

Oh fuck, did she embarrass me? I mean she fucking mortified me, but I thought it was a contained moment, that there had been no breach, that it happened when it happened but was immediately forgotten about, people moved on with their lives. But clearly not, clearly people have been talking about it; Nicola wasn't even there so someone must have told her. I wonder if they laughed when they did. I want to cry.

I haven't said anything for what must be at least two or three full lifetimes now, and so I force my tongue to move and my lips to form word shapes.

"What?"

"Y'know, a few weeks ago in The Perfect Pint, that woman from HR who—"

"—I know what you're referring to."

"Oh good, I'm sorry, it's just that I—"

"—why are you referring to it?" I try and keep my voice steady, to keep the anger and the hurt out of it. I don't think I'm doing a very good job.

"Well, it's just—"

"—just what, Nicola? What is it *just?*"

"Oliver, I'm sorry, I—"

"—you what? You should be sorry."

She looks abashed, which makes me feel a little better, but I'm still dying inside, probably outside too, and I want to stay with her, she's probably The One, I want to spend all my time with her, but I can't. I am not Schmidt from *New Girl*, this isn't going to be a goosebumps walk away. This is just going to be a regular, old-fashioned storm off.

"I need a drink," I mumble, more to myself than Nicola, and then turning away from her I walk in no particular direction. I do actually need a drink, and something stronger than a beer, but now the tears are coming and I don't want Nicola to see them so I just walk away from her, walk in a straight line, putting distance between what was once my great love and is now my great shame. "I think the bar is that way," I hear quietly behind me. It's Nicola's voice but I have no interest in her words, I just need to be away from her, away from everyone.

I stumble back into the library and navigate my way

through it somehow, managing to avoid bumping into anyone, getting drawn into any conversations, quickly moving through various rooms and up and down staircases until, finally, I burst through the front doors and am back on 5th Ave, the relative quiet of the library is replaced by the noise of midtown Manhattan in full swing; car engines rev, horns are pressed in anger, in warning, in fear, people talk to each other, shout at each other. In the distance there are sirens, whether up in The Bronx or across the river in Brooklyn who knows, wherever they are they're not here, and though what has just happened to me feels like it should be a crime even if there were police here there's nothing they could do, nothing they would do. Even if it was a crime, based on simply he-said-she-said who are the police going to believe, a lurching, semi-drunk crying monster like myself, or Nicola, sweet Nicola, with her soft olive skin and perfect brown hair and her hands, oh her hands, they must be made out of some precious material because I've never felt something so beautiful, something so right, never has my hand fitted somewhere so well. OJ's glove didn't fit, but mine certainly has. The glove has fit, so I guess don't acquit? Who knows, I'm rambling, my thoughts are not rational and I'm going to go home. That is, at least, until I spot Elijah standing at the bottom of the steps, on the street proper. I'm about to try and sneak back inside, hoping he hasn't noticed me, but then he waves at me and there's nothing I can do but wave back and watch as he starts to walk up the steps towards me. This is a conversation I cannot handle right now, but short of running away what other options do I have? And I'm 28 years old and this is simply an awkward social situation, I can't run away. Although saying that, I've just run away from one, so why not another? Unfortunately, in the time it takes these thoughts to run through my mind Elijah is with me, and it's too late to do anything other than take and shake his outstretched hand.

"I suppose I should say congratulations," I say, unsure why these words from *(500) Days of Summer* are the first that come out of my mouth. Why am I the way I am?

Elijah looks at me funny before he replies, his brows furrow and his head tilts slightly, not like a dog per se, but not *not* like a dog.

"Thank you?" he replies back, unsure.

"What a wonderful day," I say, cycling through all the things I've ever heard people say about weddings in films. "Congratulations, really." This time my voice manages to at least sound a little like a normal person's and I see Elijah visibly relax, his shoulders fall slightly, some awkward tension leaves his body.

"Thanks man, really, I appreciate it." He takes a drag on a cigarette I didn't even notice he was holding, and when he sees me look at it longingly pulls the pack out of his pocket and offers me one. I gladly accept and place the cigarette between my lips. I'm searching for my lighter when, with a click and a flash of hot air, Elijah lights it for me. The gesture is oddly intimate.

"Really, Elijah, it's been a beautiful day. The venue is stunning," I sweep my arm behind my back to the library. "Jennifer is stunning, you look great, the weather has held off," this time I gesture generally to the sky, "really man, it doesn't feel like it could have gone any better."

Elijah takes another drag off his cigarette before he speaks, and when he does his voice is grave, more serious than I'd anticipated.

"Absolutely, it's been a great day. Jennifer is really happy, and that's all that counts, isn't it?"

I think it's a rhetorical question, but when I see Elijah looking at me, a look of near pleading on his face, I realise he's waiting for an answer. What the fuck am I supposed to say to that?

"I dunno man," I stumble over my words, "I think you're both supposed to be happy?"

"Are we?"

I shrug.

"I know weddings are about the couple getting married," he continues after I don't verbalise an answer, "but let's not kid ourselves: weddings are for women. Hetero weddings anyway," he looks at me out of the corner of his eye as he says this, but I ignore it, take a drag on my cigarette, watch a woman on the other side of the street trying and failing to hail a cab. For some reason they keep ignoring her, and I feel bad as I watch them glide past, lights on, not bothering to stop.

Elijah keeps looking at me, and I think I know why, but I'm desperate to be wrong. It's because it's his wedding day, I tell myself, he's just taking stock. I'm technically one of his exes, so it makes sense that he'd ruminate over me on what's the most romantic day of his life, the beginning of the rest of his life. Jennifer is the future, whereas I'm firmly in the past. I guess he's just separating the two, partitioning off his life before today, moving on from it to his new one.

We both smoke in silence for a minute or two. He finishes his cigarette and I think I'm going to get a reprieve until he lights another. I force myself to talk; if he's going to force us to have this awkward moment, I'm going to power through it. He can ruminate on me all he wants, I'm just trying to get home without being absolutely destroyed any more than I already am.

"Shouldn't you, y'know," I gesture to the library again. "Shouldn't you be inside?"

"It'll be fine."

What does he mean?

"What do you mean?"

"Oh, no one will miss me for five minutes."

"Are you sure?"

Now it's his turn to not answer verbally and simply give me a look. I absolutely cannot read it, his face is a blank.

"Don't you wanna, you know, go see your wife?"

"I do, I very much do. However I'm not sure she wants to see me."

As much as I want to pursue this line of conversation, as much as my curiosity wants to get the better of me, I can't help but blurt out my next words.

"Elijah, why am I here?"

He looks taken aback and it takes him a few seconds to compose himself.

"She's hot, isn't she?"

"Jennifer? Yeah, she's incredibly beautiful. You've done well there, mate." Mate. My dread at hearing Elijah's answer has reverted my vernacular back to full English. I can't remember the last time I called anyone mate, people over here don't like it.

"No, not Jennifer," he smiles, I guess what would be called a rueful smile, though I'm not entirely sure if that's correct. "The woman you're with, Nicola is it?"

"Oh, Nicola." Her. "Yeah, she's okay I guess."

He looks at me now with a mixture of confusion and disbelief on his face, cocking his head again; I know this look, it's the look people give me when I've said something stupid. This look I do recognise because I see it a lot.

"'She's okay, you guess'?" Elijah drops his cigarette and once again immediately lights another. I hope he'll have the stamina to last the wedding night; where the fuck did that come from? "She's not okay, Oliver, she's incredibly beautiful. That dress, fuck man! I just want to kiss those shoulders you know?"

"Elijah, are you—"

"—yeah, yeah, I know it's my wedding, I shouldn't be saying this about another woman, particularly one of my wife's best friends, but man, come on, just look at her. Do I need to take you back inside right now to look at her?"

He's smiling now, and I can't help but smile too, some of the tension dissipates between us and I feel slightly better.

"Fine yeah, she's obviously incredibly beautiful, honestly man in terms of looks I think I'm completely in love with her."

"Of course you are," he says quietly.

"But the thing is, she's also a fucking cunt."

"Woah man, what?"

I've forgotten that the c-word is about the worst possible word you can say in the US, Americans fucking hate it. Give an insane person an AR-15 and watch them blow away 50 school kids in 10 seconds, no bother. But say cunt? Oh my, we won't stand for that. "Horrific deplorable violence is okay, as long as no one says any naughty words." The *South Park* movie will never not be relevant.

"Sorry, forgot you Yanks hate that word. She's beautiful, yes, but she's a piece of shit."

"What do you mean? Tell me."

And so I tell him about Sophie and The Perfect Pint, and I tell him about Nicola just now. When I finish telling the story, which doesn't take anywhere near as long as I'd thought it would, Elijah is looking at me with an expression I can't quite read.

"What?" I ask him.

"Are you kidding?"

"What do you mean?"

He sighs, rubs his eyes, looks at me again.

"Oliver, I say this with all of the love in my heart: are you fucking kidding me?"

"Elijah, I'm really not. What are you on about?"

"So this beautiful woman you're having a lovely day with, presumably" — I nod confirmation — "makes one joke, admittedly perhaps not a great joke, or a well-timed one, but a joke nonetheless, and you, what, you have a fucking tantrum and run away? Literally?"

"But Elijah, it's not—" I begin, but he interrupts me.

"—don't 'it's not' me, Oliver. I know you, remember? I know what you're like. I know we haven't seen each other in years but some people change, some people grow and become better versions of themselves. You were never one of those people. Tell me, what do you know about her?"

I list off what little knowledge I have; I start to tick facts off on my fingers, but stop when I struggle to get past three.

"So to sum up, you know virtually nothing about her?"

"I suppose," I reluctantly admit.

"And yet in the course of this conversation you've mentioned the word 'love' at least once, and called her The One."

"Yeah, and?" I say, now very defensively.

"Oh, Oliver," Elijah sighs, runs a hand over his face, leaving it cupping his chin as he looks at me again. "You haven't changed at all."

"I—" I begin to protest, but Elijah talks over me again.

"No, Oliver, you haven't. How many women did you fall in love with at college? And how many of them had you spoken to, had any sort of meaningful conversation with? How many of them had you simply seen once and decided they were your perfect woman?"

Thankfully he continues speaking and doesn't want answers, but I am terrified of what those answers might prove to be when I inevitably think about them later.

"You used to do this all the time, Oliver. You'd see a girl walking across campus, see her in one seminar, or at the pub, or on the bus or whatever, and that would be it. You'd be walking down a corridor and you and a girl would do that awkward little move-dance-shimmy where you keep getting in each other's way, and she'd smile at you, and that would be it, you'd be completely and utterly in love with that person."

I wish he'd stop talking. I can't take this, having my personality laid bare in front of me. Isn't this supposed to be a wedding, a happy time? I didn't come here prepared to be psychoanalysed. I don't like it.

"You even did it to me!"

He says this loudly enough that a couple of people on the street look up at us. He lowers his voice before he continues.

"Do you remember why we stopped seeing each other?"

"I—"

"Oliver, shut up, let me finish. We stopped seeing each other because your Film Studies TA emailed you to tell you she really liked your paper on *Hitchcock*. Do you remember that?"

It sounds familiar but I can't say that I remember it specifically. Even if what Elijah is saying is true, and I have no reason whatsoever to doubt him, no doubt that memory is either repressed, as many of mine are, or has simply fallen out of my head, one of the wonderful side effects of depression they never tell you about. Depression causes memory loss, have I mentioned that?

"She sent you this one email telling you she really

liked your paper, and that was it, you broke it off with me and we were done. Fucking hell, Oliver," he laughs in a forlorn way, "she did it from her uni email to yours! She didn't even use her personal email address, or yours. She was clearly just a young TA trying to do right by her students, trying to encourage them, and you fucking went off the deep end. It was ridiculous. When I finally got over the hurt do you know what I felt?"

"No," I manage to squeak out a reply, so quietly I doubt Elijah hears. But it doesn't matter.

"I was embarrassed!" He shouts this and not a few people down on 5th Ave look up at us, a couple of people stop walking to watch our, by now, quite animated discussion. "We had a good thing going on, and you ended it because you fell in love with your TA because she sent you a nice email. Fucking hell, Oliver! I never told you this, but did you know she sent me one, too? And Linda? And Oli S? And Leena?"

This can't be happening, surely it can't he must be lying.

"I know what you're thinking, and I'm not lying, I'm not saying this just to hurt you. When it comes to women, Oliver, and men come to that, and love, you've spent too much time watching movies, and not enough time living in the real world, talking to actual humans."

I don't know what to say. All of this is becoming a blur to me, because my mind doesn't want to handle the fact that everything he's saying is almost definitely completely and utterly correct. My mind wants to dissociate in order to stop me from hearing this, but I'm unable. I'm forced to remain present and hear my flaws laid bare. Do I deserve this? Does anyone?

"I loved you, Oliver. Like actual, real love. I didn't love the idea of you, I didn't love the thought of you: I loved the actual you. I loved the physical you, the mental you, the *present* you. And you broke my fucking heart."

I still don't know what to say. I know I should apologise, I should tell him he's right, I should tell him I'm sorry. I'm not, I don't feel a thing, but I should at least pretend. I'm looking at my shoes, past them at the ground, studying Elijah's discarded cigarette butts, avoiding eye contact, but when I look up I'm relieved to see Elijah isn't looking at me but beyond me, behind me back to the library. His face lightens and he lifts a hand in a small wave, and forcing myself to turn around I see the only other person here I don't want to see: Nicola.

She's standing by the doors, the way her face looks she's clearly been looking for someone, and I can only assume that someone is me. As if she's the person I need to see right now; between my last conversation with her, and this one with Elijah, I don't want to see any people, I want to die.

"Oliver, look at me." Elijah hisses an angry whisper that I can't help but listen to. "There is a beautiful woman coming down those steps, coming to see you. Yes, she made a bad joke, but that's all it was, a joke. Fuck knows why, but this woman seems interested in you, even if only a tiny bit. Don't throw it away because she teased you."

He's right, I know he's right, but god I wish he wasn't.

"Oliver, I promise once I've said this last I'll leave you alone."

I look him in the eye, and I see such sincerity I can't help but hang on his every word.

"Also don't do the other thing you do, which is be too much. You're clearly in love with her, or at least you've convinced yourself you are; don't blow it. Don't go full on, full Oliver like you always do. Take your time, go slowly, talk to her and get to know her. For some reason she's looking for you, for some reason she wants to speak to you. Use that."

He puts his hand out and I shake it, and then before I know what I'm doing I pull him into a hug. We stand there for a moment, perfectly still, holding each other, I can feel his skin against mine, smell his aftershave, and it's comforting, accepting, it feels like home. I want to tell him I love him, that I really am happy for him, but no words will suffice for this moment. Instead we hold each other until we don't, and then he moves past me. I hear him exchange a few words with Nicola, the sound of her voice resurrecting me somewhat, and I stand and wait for her to reach me, which she does a moment later.

There's so much to relate to in *(500) Days of Summer* that sometimes it feels less like a movie, and more like just watching my own life. I mean hell, there's a bit in the movie where we watch Tom watching a movie of his life, whilst we sit and watch a movie of his life. It's all very meta in ways that *Say Anything* and *Sliding Doors* aren't; those two films were released long before meta became the be all and end all, back when we could enjoy things for what they were, what they are, instead of needing constant references to things we know and love, references to ourselves and each other. Back before we needed films to be aware of themselves.

In many ways I am Tom Hansen. The narrator explains that he grew up thinking he'd never be happy he met The One. It's funny, because the movie says it in a disparaging way, as if looking for The One is something stupid, as if pinning all your hopes of happiness on finding that one person is something only a crazy, irredeemable person would do. And maybe it is; but more importantly, what if it isn't? I am desperately searching for The One, because I know she's out there. It may not be Nicola, as much as I currently feel like it is, but it's definitely someone. I both want, and will have, my happy ending.

I will have my happy ending. I will have my happy ending. I will have my happy ending. Not like that, you fucking pervert.

I am Tom Hansen in that he has his *Sliding Doors* moment: when things are going well between Summer and he, and Summer begins to open up to him, the narrator tells us that this is the night everything changed for Tom. I mean come on, if that's not a *Sliding Doors* moment almost literally spelled out there, then what is? If Tom isn't living his *Sliding Doors* life, then are any of us? Seriously, are any of us?

I could go on and on about Tom, but actually it's Summer who says the thing in the movie I find most relatable, and I think is most applicable to modern life. In the beginning scenes of the movie, in the early days of the 500, Summer has just moved to LA from Michigan. When Tom asks her why, she tells him: boredom.

A-fucking-men sister, I feel that.

Summer, aged however old she is in the film, it feels mid-20s, maybe 25 or 26, 27 at the oldest, has cottoned onto something most people never figure out, and that I was unfortunate enough to figure out by the time I was about 22; life is fucking boring. It's impossible to say what Summer finds so boring about life: maybe it's not life but Michigan she finds boring. Maybe it's working and socialising she finds boring. Maybe it was growing up she found boring. Who knows. What matters is that Summer is bored, and oh brother can I relate to that. I am so. Fucking. Bored.

The thing is, it's difficult to be happy at relating to Summer, because she's also a fucking idiot. In the karaoke bar when she, Tom, and McKenzie are talking about relationships and stuff, Summer says she doesn't believe in love, and doesn't like relationships because they're messy and people get hurt. Firstly, you don't believe in love, Summer? Well then I think you might be insane; as McKenzie says, it's not like Santa. Love exists, love is all around us, love is all we need. It isn't an opinion, it's just a fact. And yes, relationships are messy, and yes, people's feelings do get hurt, but so what? That's a risk you take, that's the gauntlet you run. You might get hurt, yes, but you also might be happy. Like, you might find actual, genuine happiness. And isn't that worth taking a risk for? Sure, you might be fucking broken and never recover, but it's worth a shot. High risk, yes, but for the highest possible reward. To me, it's a no brainer.

Nicola approaches me sheepishly, looking at her feet, at her hands, anywhere but me. I see this out of the corner of my eye as I too look anywhere else. I want to look at her, she's so incredibly beautiful, but it hurts. I'm just another joke to her. I thought her inviting me here meant something, but as usual I'm just the punchline.

"I'm really sorry."

She says it so apropos of nothing that I jump a little. I'm already on edge so it doesn't take much to startle me, but still.

"I'm sorry, Oliver," she repeats, and hearing my name coming from her mouth is everything. I again don't respond, but this time look at her so she at least knows I've heard. She clearly takes this as a sign to continue speaking, and when she does her voice is quiet, soft, she sounds sorry, she sounds abashed, and I nearly forgive her just for her tone.

"I'm sorry for what I said, for that joke, it wasn't funny. I don't even know why I said it; when Torrey told me I couldn't believe it, I mean what an awful thing to do."

"Yeah," is all I can muster by way of reply.

"I mean, what was Sophie thinking? In what universe was that funny? If it makes you feel any better, Torrey told me her boss tore into her the Monday morning when we were back at work. From what I've been told she got a big lecture, being in HR and all, about her responsibilities and shit. If it was me I would have fired her ass, chucked her out on the street without so much as a goodbye."

I'm looking at Nicola as she says this and she seems so genuine that I can't not believe her. It's dark outside the library, the building itself is lit from below by spotlights so it almost appears to loom over us, but the top of the steps where we stand is in near total darkness; I can't see Nicola's eyes, can't try and read how she actually feels, so I have to take her at her words, at face value.

"I just… I just…" is all I manage to say before I start crying, before the tears start falling. My shoulders buck up and down, my arms hang languidly at my sides; I feel five years old, a lost little boy with no one to comfort him when a girl is being mean to him. I miss my parents. I miss London.

"Come here," Nicola says, and she pulls me into a hug. It's warm, her skin is so soft and she smells so nice, her perfume invades my nostrils and seduces me, I give in to her and bury my head in her neck, weeping in earnest, truly letting myself go now she has me, letting it all out.

After a few minutes I pull away, release myself from the hug, and wipe my eyes on my jacket sleeve. Probably not a gesture with a great deal of decorum but fuck it, dignity went out the window a long time ago. About 15 years ago by my counting, the day I discovered girls.

"It's okay, I know." I know Nicola is just trying to reassure me but it's a bit patronising, but also I don't care. Just to be here with her, now she's apologised and I've believed her, is enough for me. "Do you want anything?" I shake my head. "A drink?"

"No thanks," I mumble a reply.

"Do you want to go inside and dance?"

I do want to dance but not inside, not in the library, not at this wedding. I want to dance in my apartment, in Nicola's, I want to dance in the park or on the moon or anywhere else we'll be able to be alone, just the two of us, the music our little secret. I want to hold her in my arms and feel the weight of her, the warmth of her, I want to smell the hair on top of her head and feel the truth of her existence in my hands. I want everything. But I don't want it here, and so I shake my head again.

"Do you want to go home?"

This time I nod, again wiping my nose with my sleeve, again forgetting what I'm wearing, again forgetting who I'm with. If Nicola sees, and there's no way she doesn't, she doesn't say anything. Instead she says, "come on then," and she takes my arm and leads me down the steps.

Once at the bottom and on the street she has no problem hailing a cab; who wouldn't stop for that face? As one pulls up she opens the door and I get in, and for one brief moment I think she's going to follow me, but she simply stays standing on the curb. She leans down and looks at me in the blackness of the back of the cab.

"Take care, Oliver, text me when you get home."

"I will," I manage to mumble, before she stands up and closes the door. I give my address to the driver and then he pulls away from the curb with a definitely illegal U-turn, other cars honking as he does, for a brief moment I think we're going to be in a crash and I wonder would it be so bad? I glance out of the window and see Nicola waving. I wave back, and then the cab shoots off down 5ᵗʰ and Nicola gets smaller and smaller until she's no longer visible, and I'm alone once again.

Chapter Four:

Empire Records

A snapshot of a Saturday in Central Park: in attendance are myself, Elijah but no Jennifer, Tom from work, Lottie, Alfie, Munir, Deandra, Luna, and Amir. There aren't often this many of us, but on this sunny September Saturday the stars aligned and we're all free, and all not only able, but willing, to come and sit in the park and do nothing for many, many hours.

Even though we've ticked over into September the sun is still shining, it's still incredibly warm, the temperature pushing 30 degrees. I'm wearing a pair of blue denim shorts, showcasing my brilliant white legs for the world to see, and a plain black t-shirt. There's so much skin on show, not just in our group but in the park as a whole; Tom, Alfie, and Amir have taken their shirts off and are laying topless, sunning their abs. Because they all have abs, and that's probably why they're shirtless. If I had abs I'd probably be shirtless. Elijah demurred, saying he's still carrying a little honeymoon weight, and I'm glad he did because it means I'm not the only man here still wearing a top. The women are in various stages of undress; Lottie has taken off her t-shirt and so has on just a teal bikini top above the waist, but she's kept her shorts on; Deandra has gone full bikini; Luna is wearing black jeans and a black long sleeve t-shirt, and whilst she's made no move to shed any layers, she doesn't look at all uncomfortable. Although this doesn't surprise me; we met at uni, post-grad that is, and she was a fully fledged goth, wearing only black, no matter the weather. She had this floor length leather trench coat she'd wear every day, and I mean *every* day, I'm not exaggerating. Whether it was minus 10 and bucketing it down with hail, or 35 degrees and absolutely sweltering, Luna would turn up to class in her long trench coat, and she never once looked unhappy or in any sort of discomfort. She's not pale like goths usually are, I think I heard someone say one of her parents is from Spain, so that would explain not only her skin complexion but also her not dying in the sun like I am, a pale man from the UK, where the sun did shine once, but I'm pretty sure it was just the one time.

Luna is older now, obviously, that's how time works, and though her dress sense has aged with her, i.e. she doesn't wear the trench coat any more, she wears blouses and three-quarter jeans and other supposedly adult items of clothing, I think she's still a goth at heart. I think even though she's a grown up, a proper person with a job and bills and a cat, she'll always be a goth at heart, hence all the black, as well as long sleeves, in the brilliant sunshine.

Deandra didn't hesitate, on the other hand, to take her clothes off as soon as we found a spot in the south part of the park and had our blankets spread out. I don't know her that well, she's a friend of Luna's who I've met a few times and have her number, but I don't think we've ever messaged; the first time I met her, after we exchanged our hellos and told each other it was nice to meet each other blah blah blah, she immediately took her top off. She was wearing a bikini then as well, but it shocked me a little bit. I'm not used to women undressing in front of me; even the ones I've slept with, it's always been a pleasant surprise when it's turned out

I'm not dreaming, and the woman I'm with is interested in me enough to show me her body. Deandra isn't showing me her body, at least not per se; she's showing off her body in general. And like the guys, I don't blame her. If I had her slim, toned body I'd probably show it off too.

The scene: we're sitting in a vague circle, a pile of alcohol in the middle, all of us sitting or laying down, a rabble of people, we have cares in this world but none of them presently on show. We look like a Diet Coke advert or something, a group of people in our mid to late 20s having it all. It's nearly midday and people are discussing getting lunch, getting some sort of food anyway, we've all had a few drinks and are planning to go out for drinks tonight — I'm not, I'm going to bail, I haven't told anyone this yet although I'm sure no one will be surprised — so people don't want to peak too soon and not be in any fit state to go out. Food is the proposed solution.

"What about the deli on 57th?" Luna says. "They do amazing sandwiches."

"If I'm thinking of the same one, I know someone who had raw chicken from there and had to go to the emergency room." Elijah said.

"Oh, shit, really? I can't afford to go to the hospital," replies Amir to general laughter, myself included.

"Obviously," says Alfie, grinning, and Amir grins back and playfully punches him on the arm. Alfie rubs the spot when Amir turns away, I think their versions of playful are slightly different.

"There's a deli on 79th that's really great," Tom says, the first words he's uttered for quite a while. A few people startle; they must have forgotten he was there.

"That sounds great and all," Lottie says, adjusting her top, "but some of us work two jobs and can't afford to eat on the Upper West Side." She says it playfully, although she definitely means it as well. I'm glad she says it, because I can't afford to eat there either, but if people said they wanted to, I definitely wouldn't have said anything. No one wants to be *that* guy.

"Well what do you suggest then, Lottie?"

"We could eat each other?" she says, raising an eyebrow.

"You mean like..." Tom says, leaving the suggestion hanging in the air. Is this flirting new, or have I just not noticed it before? Tom and Lottie are old friends; that they are is how Tom and I are spending time together outside of work, Lottie is our common denominator.

Lottie flutters her eyelids in an exaggerated fashion.

"Well, Tom," she purrs, "what I mean to say is, if you can afford to eat on the Upper West Side, then I think you fall into a certain category."

"Oh?"

"Oh, indeed." The whole group has stopped and is watching this interaction, we're all waiting to see where it's going. Lottie and Tom know we're all here and can see and hear them, right?

Tom looks very excited, I don't think he knows anyone in the world exists except for he and Lottie. I can see a look in Lottie's eyes though, even if Tom can't; she's taking the piss.

"You know what it's time for Tom?"

"No?"

"EAT THE RICH!" she shouts and jumps on him, laughing, and then she's laying on top of him and he's laughing too, and suddenly Deandra jumps on them and before I can even tell what's happening there's a pile of bodies in front of me, all skin and limbs and laughter. There's just Luna and I who haven't joined in; we haven't moved from our respective positions, we're both just passive observers, wanting to be involved but not wanting to move, I can't speak for her but from my point of view I don't want to touch anyone, make any physical contact. I could pretend it's because it's so warm that all the bodies will be sweaty, as I lay here now and watch them writhe and squirm I can see skin glistening, whites and browns and olives and slight oranges shining in the afternoon sun. I could pretend that, but really: I don't want to touch this pile of people, I only want to touch Nicola.

Eventually they disentangle themselves and once everyone is back in position Lottie says, "but seriously, what are we gonna do? I'm hungry AF." She actually says 'AF'.

"Oliver, you're very quiet, what do you think?"

I zone back in and realise everyone is looking at me; eight pairs of eyes, sixteen eyes all staring at me, putting me on the spot. I'm the focus of everyone's attention and I don't like it, it's too much. I open my mouth to try and say something but nothing comes out, I have no words prepared, and my subconscious is apparently unable or unwilling to take over, to come to my aid. I sit there flapping my mouth like a fish before Elijah saves me.

"I say we do the deli on 57th."

"But what about the raw chicken?"

"Fuck the raw chicken!" Elijah shouts, a few nearby people turn to look at us, but after a moment or two of awkward silence everyone bursts out laughing, myself included. I'm not sure what's funny, not sure what we're laughing at, but it feels good to laugh, it feels good to join in. I've basically spent the last few weeks either at work trying not to cry or in my apartment crying, so it's nice to have a change of scenery and a change of emotion.

Elijah is on his feet, and Amir, Alfie, and Tom drag themselves to theirs.

"The men will go," Amir announces. "We'll go hunt whilst you women — and Oliver — stay here and look after our home."

"Men bring food," Alfie says, imitating a Neanderthal. "Men save day. Women happy. Women thank men."

"Alfie," Lottie says, fluttering her eyelids at him.

"Yes, dear?"

"Go fuck yourself."

Everyone laughs again and the four guys walk off, head towards the deli, leaving the rest of us laying there in anticipation. I hadn't realised until someone mentioned food but now I think of it I'm absolutely starving; I spent the morning laying in bed staring at the wall, and by the time I realised how hungry I was it was too late for breakfast, so the three tins of gin and tonic are all I've had today. It's fun, yes, but probably not overly practical or healthy. But then again, whatever.

"So you and Elijah are hanging out again, then?"

I'm startled from my reverie when I realise this sentence, spoken by Luna, is addressed to me.

"I guess so," is all I can mutter back.

"What happened there, then?"

"I'm not sure," I say, though this clearly isn't a satisfying enough answer as no one says anything; the women are all looking at me now, I feel like they've been waiting for an opportunity to grill me like this.

I sigh before I continue; they're not going to let up until I tell them, so I may as well just get it over with.

"I'm not sure," I say again. "Like, before I went to his wedding I hadn't seen him since graduation. We'd messaged a bit afterwards, when I was still in London before I came out here and he came back here and moved back in with his parents, but that didn't last long."

"What happened?" someone says.

"Nothing happened," I say. "We just drifted I guess, the way people do. I missed him, but that feeling soon passed. To be honest, I'd forgotten he existed until Nicola invited me to his wedding."

"Why did she invite you?"

"I'm not sure of that either."

"Haven't you asked her?" Lottie asks, incredulous.

"Nope."

"But, like, why haven't you? I'd be dying to know."

"I dunno. I was going to on the day, but I never got round to it, and then we've barely spoken since."

"What?" "Why?" "What the fuck?" General murmurs from the group.

"Have you heard what happened?" I ask.

"No." "Nope." "Elijah said something about her making a bad joke but that's all."

"I'm not going to go into it," I say, my voice catching as I do; just remembering it makes me want to cry all over again. "But, yeah, basically she made this joke that she thought was hilarious but I very much didn't. And I know it's only a joke or whatever, but still."

"No that's fair," Luna says.

"Do you think so?" Lottie asks her.

"Sure, do you not?"

"Well I mean, it's just a joke isn't it?"

"Maybe to her, but clearly not to Oliver."

"Yeah, but."

"But what?"

Lottie and Luna's discussion takes over the conversation and I'm happy to let it, happy to fade back into the background. I let them talk, removing myself from the conversation, and I gaze around the park as I do. It's a strange place, emblematic of New York as a whole I suppose, and how weird of a city it is.

From where we're variously sitting and laying, from

where we're positioned, if I look around at ground level we could be anywhere that isn't urban; we could be in upstate New York, we could be in the Midwest, we could be in Yorkshire or Northumbria or anywhere. All you can see from this level is green; the green of grass, of trees, the greenery of flowerbeds and planet life. However, the moment you look up the illusion is immediately shattered; over the tops of the trees you can see the buildings, you can see man's metallic touch on the world, and it destroys the calm and quietness that envelops the park. Because as well as seeing the buildings you begin to hear the traffic as well, all of urban life's noises come to haunt your ears. The buildings look ominous in a way; they're all so huge, so absolutely vast, they reach into the sky and sometimes, on a cloudy day, they pierce it. There are no clouds today, the beautiful blue of the sky is unbroken, but still, the tops of the buildings are hundreds of feet in the air and it's a little unnerving. It's almost as if they're waiting, waiting for you to drop your guard, so they can advance. Like that kids game, Ice Cream I think it was called, or maybe What Time is it Mr Wolf? The game where one person stands against a wall and with their eyes closed counts, and the other players advance on them when their eyes are closed, but have to stay perfectly still when they turn and open them, and if you get caught moving you're out. Or even more so, it's like the topiary animals in the book of The Shining, slowly advancing when you're not paying attention, but in a much more sinister way. I don't feel safe in the park, not when I look up. I feel watched, I feel observed. I feel hunted.

Central Park is emblematic of New York in another way: it's almost more of a vibe than a real place. Obviously it is a real place, but it just doesn't feel like it half the time. It feels like a giant movie set, or just one big Instagram background. That people, me for example, live their perfectly mundane lives here, feels a bit ridiculous. It feels so underwhelming, getting up every day and walking to an office. You're in New York, the greatest city in the world, land of opportunity, according to that song by Alicia Keys and Jay Z there's *nothing* you can't do. So why the fuck are you on Microsoft Excel?

Silence has descended on the group like a fog. I pull my gaze back from the skyline and see everyone is looking at me: shit, someone must have asked me something. Luckily I'm saved from not knowing how to respond by the return of the guys, who come bearing multiple paper bags which they put down on the blanket between us all and begin unloading, placing all manner of foodstuffs in front of us all. Once the food is unpacked there's still a bag left, and from this Elijah produces a couple of bottles of Grey Goose and some lemonade, as well as some solo cups for us to drink from. Evidently the boys decided that this little group hang needed to be ramped up a bit. Fine by me; the conversation with the women has got me thinking about Nicola again, and thinking about Nicola makes me sad.

The conversation has moved on to other things, I've thankfully been left behind. Lottie asks me if I want a drink and I'm about to answer when my phone vibrates; looking at it my attention is drawn away from Lottie, from the group, from the park, and is focused into one thing and one thing only; Nicola has literally just messaged me.

Snapshots are a funny thing, because essentially that's all life is, is a collection of snapshots. Because often a snapshot is all you need; even though they're only small by definition, they can still hold so much. So many memories, so many events, so many actions. Lives can change in a snapshot, they can begin and end and move onto another path and never be the same again. I'm trying to avoid talking about *Sliding Doors* moments yet again, but I'm destined to fail.

Look at *Empire Records*: it takes place over the course of a day, perhaps a little over 24 hours, from one night to the next. And look what happens in that time: Lucas turns $9,000 into $18,000 in Atlantic City, then loses it all. Empire Records — the store the movie takes its name from — is at once sold and then saved from Music Town, a big conglomerate threatening to take over. Deb shaves her head following her failed suicide attempt, Corey tries and fails to seduce Rex Manning, Gina tries and succeeds to seduce Rex Manning, Corey and Gina go from best friends to worst enemies back to best friends. Corey moves from trying to lose her virginity with Rex Manning to declaring to AJ that, yes, she does love him the way he loves her, and she does want to be together. You watch the film over the course of around 110 minutes and whilst it feels like a lifetime, it's only one day, one fictional day, and everything changes.

It's not a romcom in the traditional sense; whilst ultimately AJ and Corey do end up together, they're not the focus, and their love isn't the story. If anything, *Empire Records* is a romcom about a group of people's love for a music store, the last of the small independents holding out against the faceless corporations trying to take over and uniform the world. Joe, the manager of the store, is the guide for this collection of oddballs and misfits, he watches over them, rescues them, saves their lives. And in return they save his; whilst it may not seem like it when you watch, everyone in this film needs each other. Everyone plays their part, and without them they could not succeed.

Whilst it may not be a romcom in the traditional

sense, it satisfies my one major need: it makes me fall in love. In *Empire Records* I spend the entire film completely and utterly in love with both Liv Tyler and Renee Zellweger, both of whom are impossibly young and impossibly beautiful. Nicola actually looks a lot like young Renee Zellweger, only with slightly darker hair. I wonder if the film means more to me since I've noticed that, since I first laid eyes on Nicola and made the connection. I'd seen the film myriad times before meeting Nicola, and loved it so much, but do I love it more now? Did I just like it before, and do I love it now? Am I completely and utterly insane, and do I need to be stopped? I've no idea how old Renee Zellweger was when the film came out, but I have no idea how old Nicola is now, so it's all swings and roundabouts, I suppose.

In the movie, Lucas, he of the aforementioned missing $9,000, says, "I'm guided by a force much greater than luck." And whilst it's not clear what he means, he's a typical young pseudo-zen pretentious dickhead, I happen to agree with him. I'm guided by a force much greater than luck; I'm guided by Nicola.

Sitting at my desk, yet another day passing me by, a meeting invite pops up in my Google calendar: it's for a 1:1 catch up with Neil. This can't be good. I accept without looking at when it's for, and am surprised when a reminder immediately appears in my Gmail telling me the meeting is overdue. I begin to think Neil must have got the time wrong, and I'm about to ignore it when Neil wanders over to my desk and, placing a hand on the back of my chair, asks me if I'm ready to go. Go where? To the firing squad?

I stand up and follow him to one of the impossibly white meeting rooms, a small one which has two chairs and a table that's unnecessarily low to the ground, forcing you to really lean forward in your chair to reach it. Who are these tables designed for? I get shorter people need lower tables, but then why have such high chairs? It doesn't make sense. I'm rambling. I'm nervous. Although for what reason I don't know; am I about to be fired? Maybe, but that wouldn't explain my nervousness. I literally couldn't care less if I get fired. A job's a job, I'll get another.

I sit in the chair closer to the exit, force of habit for if I want to make a quick escape. Not that anything will happen, this isn't like a fucking movie, in which I'm sitting across from a retired spy who still carries a gun. No, it's for my anxiety. It's standard practice I carry over from bars and restaurants, placing myself as close to the exit as possible so I can leave with as little fuss as possible. It usually doesn't work, but it's almost always worth a shot.

"Thanks for joining me, Oli."

I grunt non-committally.

"How're things?"

"Fine."

"Just fine?"

Oh god, he wants me to open up or something. No, thank you.

"Yeah, just fine. I think it's going well isn't it?" I push the focus back onto him.

"I think it is, yes, at least from what I can see. Your work is always excellent and you never miss deadlines, so I have no complaints."

"I'm glad to hear it." I don't care at all.

"With this in mind, do you remember the all-hands meeting last week?"

"Yes." No.

"Good. I know it was only spoken of hypothetically

then, but the need now arises: are you still okay to help Nicola with the copy?"

What the fuck? Nicola? Copy? Nicola? Volunteering? Nicola? Fuck, this must have been what people were talking about in the meeting. I'd zoned out completely, and when I zoned back in people were looking at me, asking whether it was a yes or no, and not wanting to draw too much focus, or admit that I wasn't paying attention, rather than asking them to repeat the question I simply took a gamble and said yes. Everyone looked pleased when I did, a collective sigh went around the room, and so I assumed I'd given the right answer. No one has said anything since, until now at least, so I'd also assumed I got away with whatever it was. Apparently not.

"Erm, yeah, sure. Why not, what's the worst that could happen?"

Neil laughs, he seems to think I'm joking. I'm not joking, I'm genuinely asking.

"Good man, I'm glad to hear it."

Sensing the meeting is over, or perhaps wishing or willing it to be, I start to rise, but Neil isn't finished, and so from a half-raised position I lower myself back into my seat.

"How are things going with Nicola?"

Things? Going? Nicola? They're not, at least not to my knowledge.

"How do you mean?" I ask, present in the conversation for the first time. What does he mean?

"I'm not normally one for office gossip" — I mean, come on man, exhibit A, literally right now — "but I hear it's going well. You went to that wedding didn't you, one of your old college friends?"

How the fuck does he know all this? Have people been talking about me? A sense of dread is creeping up my spine, it's like water falling in reverse, I'm suddenly very uncomfortable.

"Yeah we went to the wedding but…"

"But?"

What does he want from me?

"Well, yeah, we went to the wedding, but that's about it. We haven't really spoken since, I mean we've exchanged a few texts but that's about it."

I'm not lying, we have exchanged a few texts — when she messaged me when I was at the park asking if I wanted to meet up, but I was busy and told her so. It fucking killed me to turn her down, but I was actually having a good time with the group and wanted to see how long it would last; I so rarely enjoy anything that I wanted to hold onto the moment, even in the face of the one asking to spend time with me. A few days before that I'd messaged her asking how she was, but no reply. We've only had these fragments, fractures of half-dreamed conversations. We haven't exchanged any full sentences, not face to face, since she put me in a cab after the wedding; I'd done as she asked and text her when I got home, but other than replying with a smiley face that was the extent of that conversation. I'm desperate to talk to her, but I'm terrified. What if I blew it? What if my reaction to her joke ruined any chance we ever had of getting together? What if, what if.

"That's not what I hear."

"And what do you hear?" I'm pissed off now, the thought that my private life is being banded around the office is not kismet. And besides, how can he have heard differently? Unless someone is making stuff up, or there's a second version of me that's dating Nicola in ways I can only dream about. That would actually be very helpful, supposing I could slip in every now and then and hold her or kiss her or have sex with her; like that show *Severance*, but with love instead of work. Otherwise it's just someone else in a relationship with her, and that's my worst nightmare.

"I've heard she really likes you."

I haven't heard this.

"Okay."

"I've heard that's why you were the person asked to help her with the new copy. Obviously you have experience, and did a degree in Creative Writing, so that helps, but still…"

He lets the sentence hang there. Copy experience? A degree in Creative Writing? These two things are not true, I have neither of them. Shit, they've mistaken me for someone else. Fuck, I need to keep it under wraps so no one finds out. This might be my only chance with Nicola, I need to make it count. I need to spend time with her in a structured environment with other people around, where I'm not allowed to drink. As much as I want to take her on a real date, just the two of us, get dressed up real nice and try and seduce her, I know all I'll do is get drunk and tell her I love her, and women do not like it when you do that. Believe me, I have extensive experience. No, I need to spend time with her here at the office, where I can use my work personality and make her think I'm a real person. Sure, if it goes well we'll have to be alone at some point, but hopefully by then she'll like me so much that when she sees my real personality it won't put her off too much.

Anyway, if we do get together she can work on me. Women always work on men, they love it. Look at Corey, making sure AJ doesn't waste his drawing skills; Summer convincing Tom to pursue his architectural dreams; Laura getting Rob to start DJing again in the aforementioned and not totally okay *High Fidelity*. Men want to find The One; women find someone they like, and make them The One. I don't know which is crazier.

Well, I obviously do, it's women: The One exists, all you have to do is find them. And even if it's impossible, surely it's easier than making The One from someone who isn't The One? Starting from scratch is easier than coming in halfway through, surely?

I must have been quiet for a while because Neil is looking at me. What was the last thing either of us said? Oh shit, I need to talk. Time to put on my work personality. Fake it until you make it baby, or at least until 6pm when you can go home and cry into your pillow.

"Oh, yeah, it'll be great to use those skills again. And great to spend time with Nicola, of course…"

Neil smiles at me, a bit lasciviously but not entirely. Like, he's a creep, but not a total creep.

"Good man. Right," he slaps his thighs with his hands. "Thanks again for doing this, I really appreciate it. Not just because it makes me look really good to Sarah, so thanks."

"No problem. What happens now?"

"I'll speak to Nicola's boss and confirm we're all good, and then you'll hear from someone. It may be Nicola, may be her boss, it may be me. Someone will get the ball rolling."

"Great, looking forward to it."

We get back to our desks; I barely make it, I'm shaking all over, although whether through anticipation or fear or anxiety or a mixture of all three who knows. It's a little after midday so I decide to take an early lunch, stretch my legs, try and walk off some of this adrenaline currently making me its home. I stagger to my feet, to the elevators, and once in the lobby stagger out of the building. Fresh air is good, I gulp it down. Oh shit, is everything about to be different now? Am I completely and utterly fucked, but, like, in a good way? Is that even possible? Is Nicola going to fall in love with me? Is everything finally going to be okay?

I'm on my way to meet Elijah for dinner. It's a Thursday evening and we're meeting at The Angry Immigrant, a new place just opened on Church in Tribeca. I'd never heard of it until he invited me but according to Elijah it's a great little place, it's creating a lot of buzz in the society pages and we're lucky to get a table, thankfully he knows the chef and so was able to get us a reservation for tonight at 8pm. These are all Elijah's words, none of them really mean anything to me, except to think that it sounds like it's going to be my nightmare: incredibly busy, incredibly loud, the kind of place that's just a little bit offensive to all of the senses, but just when your discomfort will be about to reach fever pitch the food will come, and at first you'll scorn because the portions are tiny, little scallops or radishes or whatever looking ludicrous in a tiny pile in the middle of a vast white plate, the empty space causing your anxiety to reach levels previously unheard of, but then you'll take a bite and the food will be so incredible, so delicious that every previous bad thought you've had about the place will disappear and you'll make your peace with it, you accept you'd go again at the drop of a hat. I fucking hate places like that. I'm dreading tonight.

It isn't just tonight that I'm dreading; a sense of dread has been following me for a few weeks now. Admittedly it's always there, hanging just above me like a bell jar, but in the recent few months it's been so far above me as to be nearly invisible, I've nearly been able to live my life free of the shadow it casts. I think it's Nicola. I was perfectly fine watching her from a distance, being distantly in love with her; now we've spoken, spent time together, now there's a very real chance something may happen between us, especially as we're going to be working closely together on this new project at work. When I watched her from a distance it was fine, that's all it was, quiet regarding, I could never lose her because I didn't have her. But now? Now that there's a chance I can have her, there's also a chance I can lose her. And if I do finally get her, but then I do lose her, then what? Then what will I do? Then who will I be? She's the centre of my universe, she's my sun; so how will I cope if she isn't?

Elijah's invitation came completely out of the blue. I don't know how he even got my number, he must have got it from Nicola or something. Because they must know each other, for her to be invited to his wedding. And not just invited, but to have a plus one as well, she must be someone to him, some relationship to him, some part of his life. I wonder if I'll find out tonight. I don't know if I really want to know or not.

He text me earlier today, I was just sitting at my desk, wiggling the mouse, pretending to work. I've created this report that I can run when I'm really bored; it doesn't actually do anything, doesn't pull any meaningful stats or anything, but to the uninitiated it looks like I'm doing actual work, pulling numbers and data that will actually help the company achieve its quarterly forecasts or whatever. I run it on days like today, when all other options fail me. When there's nothing to read online, when all my socials are quiet, when my head won't let me escape into it. Sometimes I watch the report, stare at the numbers feeling like Neo when he first sees the Matrix. Mostly I just zone out, sit there and let it tick over, being just present enough to answer any questions about the fake report that may be aimed at me. I'm a very bad employee. I very don't care.

I didn't expect to hear from Elijah again to be honest,

at least not one-on-one. Since we're part of the same friendship group now, though, I have no idea how that's happened, we do see each other occasionally, like that time at the park. But I didn't think we were of the 'hang out without the rest of the group' kind of persuasion, I didn't think he cared about me that much; if anything, I thought he still kinda hated me for what I did to him all those years ago. Hell, he probably doesn't care about me, because really who can care that much about someone they're not in love with? I assume he cares about Jennifer dearly, at least enough to marry her anyway, but other than her, people are just people. I care dearly about Nicola, I worship at her altar, but other than her? Sure, people exist, but to me that's all they do. I'm sure to them I'm simply an existence, too. It's not worth getting particularly het up about.

He messaged asking if I was free tonight, knowing that I would be, knowing that I always am. I told him yes, and he said about dinner. I couldn't think of any excuse not to so here I am, walking slowly to the restaurant. Google Maps said it'd take me about 15 minutes, but if I really try I can do it in 30. My feet drag, my legs have to be forced into every step. I spent the brief time back at my apartment crying, lying in bed trying and failing to bury the sound of my sobs with the pillow. It was soaking wet from my tears when I left the apartment, hopefully it'll be dry by the time I get home. Not so I can sleep on it, but so I'll be able to tell in the morning whether or not I've cried in my sleep.

I turn onto Church and see the place. You can't not really, it's massive. It looks like it was probably a warehouse at some point, like 90% of Tribeca. The sign on the front is huge, letters must be about 10 feet high, bright red, shining into the dusk. At night you must be able to see this place from space. As it is, I can see it from where I stand, on the corner of Church and Reade, and there's no backing out now. Particularly as I can see Elijah in front of it, his head is down and he's looking at his phone, and suddenly mine rings and I take it out of my pocket and see it's Elijah, and he must see me do this because the call ends before I can answer it and then Elijah is waving at me. With a sigh, I force myself to cross the road and approach him. No backing out now.

"Hi, Oliver," he says, his accent a strange mix of English and American, of New York and London. Most of his words sound pretty firmly New York, but then sometimes he sounds just like me; or how I used to anyway, I guess by now I must have a weird hybrid accent too.

"Hello," I say, taking his outstretched hand and briefly shaking it. His hand is warm, slightly damp, it feels alive and the feeling makes me shudder, but thankfully so little that Elijah doesn't notice, or if he does he doesn't say anything.

"Shall we?" he says, opening the door and gesturing for me to enter. I do, and as I step through the open door I'm immediately hit with a wall of noise, my worst fears confirmed. The place is chaos.

I can't hear myself think; between the buzz of conversation, the shouting of various wait staff and all the chefs, and the music blasting over the top of this, my ears feel like they're going to explode. The room is dimly lit; I can just about make out a bar to my left, an open kitchen to my right, and with Elijah behind me ushering me ahead I feel like I'm in the pass at Thermopylae and am about to be absolutely fucking obliterated by 300 Spartans. The lighting is low, to the point where I wonder how it's possible to eat, and then realise eating is beside the point. This may be a restaurant for all intents and purposes, but it doesn't exist to serve food. The

Angry Immigrant exists as a place to be, a place to be seen at and heard at, to post online. People don't come here to eat, they come here to come here; they come here to tell people they've been here, to strut into the office tomorrow and sit with a shit-eating grin on their face until someone says, "what did you get up to last night?" and then they'll tell them, oh how they'll tell them.

The walls are a dark red, a deep blood colour, and this fact doesn't help my anxiety. After walking for what feels like five billion miles, but is probably only more like five feet, I reach the hostess stand. A beautiful, harried looking young woman in all black looks at me questioningly, but I have nothing to say to her. I stand there for a moment, the pair of us regarding each other, before Elijah steps up and gives his surname and tells her of our reservation. She turns without a word and leads us to a small table by the floor to ceiling windows; the walk is treacherous, the tables are so close together and there are around a thousand waiters and waitresses moving about the place carrying giant trays of plates and glasses. It's organised chaos, and my anxiety levels are peaking with every passing second. Eventually we're seated and I pick up a drinks menu, pretending to read it but mostly just holding it in front of my face until my tears stop. Thankfully they soon do and I lower it, regard Elijah regarding me.

We make some small talk, Elijah asks how I am and how my day was, how life is, all that jazz, but my dread is driving me and I cut him off mid-sentence.

"Why are we here?"

He's taken aback but only for a second, he quickly resumes his calm demeanour.

"What do you mean?" he says with a laugh.

"Elijah, cut the shit. Why did you invite me here?"

"Well I have this reservation, and Jennifer couldn't

make it and I know you live nearby so…"

I stand up to leave; my dread and anxiety, which I had hoped to keep at normal levels, won't allow me to sit through this dinner if Elijah won't be honest. Luckily, my standing seems to spur him towards the truth, and I slowly lower myself back into my seat as he speaks.

"Okay, fine. Jeez man, what's up with you? I invited you here because I'm worried about you man."

What the fuck?

"What the fuck?"

"What?"

"Why are you worried about me?"

"Well, you know…"

"No, I don't know, please tell me."

"Well… it's… I mean—"

I cut him off.

"—Elijah, just fucking tell me. Why are you worried about me? Why do you even care? We haven't seen each other for nearly ten years, and then all of a sudden someone I work with, someone I'm crazy about but didn't think knew I even existed, is inviting me to your wedding. Then I'm at your wedding having a shit time and you're there trying to psychoanalyse me or whatever. Then we're at the park and everything seems totally normal. And now you're inviting me out to dinner, just the two of us. What the fuck is going on? Where have you been this last decade? What do you want from me?"

I stop, catch my breath, drink my entire glass of water. I have no idea where our waitress is so I flag down one passing the table and order a beer and a shot of vodka. I don't think about price or if Elijah wants anything. He invited me so he can pay, and he's a big boy, if he's thirsty he can order himself a drink. When my drinks are delivered I down the vodka and sip the beer, appreciating how it cleanses my mouth of the taste of paint thinner branded as a luxury refreshing drink. Elijah watches me, looking thoroughly shocked. I had no intention of upsetting him but now I have, I'm glad. I'm pissed off at him, although even I'm not entirely sure why.

"I…"

"You what?" I snap at him.

"I'm sorry."

Fuck. Of all the things he could have said, I wish he hadn't said this. I immediately feel terrible, because he truly does look sorry, and I feel bad for having a go at him. Maybe he is just trying to reconnect, to revive our friendship, and I've been treating him like a piece of shit. My anxiety has gotten the better of me and I've lashed out at an innocent party. I'm such a prick. Can't wait to get home, tonight's cry is gonna be a biggie.

I can't think what to say so I sip my beer, wait for him to continue. Eventually he does.

"The reason I've been in touch so much… is Jennifer." Jennifer? I don't know the woman, never even met her until her wedding, barely spoke two words to her at it. "She wanted me to reach out to you. Her and Nicola are old friends, they went to college together, have known each other since they were 18." How old are they? How long has that been? "Nicola was always invited to the wedding obviously, but seeing as she's single, and the guest list was long, she didn't originally have a plus one. It was only when Nicola mentioned you, and Jennifer mentioned you — and someone else dropped out — that I realised we had to give her a plus one, so you could be that one."

I don't know if it's the beer or the vodka or the atmosphere of the place or the revelations, but my head is spinning. I order another beer, knowing it's probably a bad idea but doing it anyway. My entire life is a bad idea, so fuck it.

"What are you talking about, Elijah?" I'm struggling to follow him. "I'm, like, struggling to follow you."

"Nicola is in love with you."

"What?"

"I said—"

"—I heard what you said. What do you mean?"

"Well, I meant what I said. Nicola is in love with you."

"But, like, what?"

"Nicola and Jennifer hang out all the time, and Nicola comes over quite a lot. She's a great girl, actually—"

"—woman."

"What?"

"She's a great *woman*."

Elijah sighs, rolls his eyes.

"She's a great *woman*, and she talks about you all the time. Although obviously for ages I had no idea it was you. I mean how many people are there called Oliver in New York? I never made the connection. It was only when Nicola showed Jenn a picture of you and I happened to see that I realised that her Oliver was also my Oliver."

"I'm not your Oliver."

"What?"

"I'm not *your* Oliver, I haven't been for a decade." I say this angrily, my dread has become white hot and I'm furious.

"Fine, you're not my Oliver. Fucking hell man, it's semantics, lighten up. Anyway, when I saw the picture I mentioned I know you, that I knew you, and both Nicola and Jenn jumped on me. At first they wanted me to invite you to the wedding but I told them you'd say no if I did. Just out of interest—"

"—Definitely would have said no."

He leans back in his chair, a smug grin on his face, satisfied that I've said this.

"I knew it. Anyway, I told them this and that's when Jenn told Nicola she should invite me. We moved a few tables around and gave her the plus one, and the rest is history."

He finishes talking, takes a long pull on a beer I didn't see him order or receive, and sits back, waiting for me to respond. How the fuck do I respond to that? I want to go home and cry and scream and lock myself away and never see the world again, but sadly that's not really an option. At least not until dinner's over.

I don't know what to say.

"I don't know what to say."

"That's okay, man," he says, "I do. Are you okay?"

"What? Stop asking me that."

"But I want to—"

"—But I don't care what you want," I shout, standing up without realising it. "Why do you care if I'm okay? Why are you suddenly so invested in my life? You didn't care ten years ago, why should you care now?"

People have stopped what they're doing and are staring at me. I'm staring at Elijah with a fury I didn't think possible. Who does he think he is, coming to me after all these years and inserting himself into my life? I'm doing just fine, thank you. I can handle this mess perfectly well. I'm still alive aren't I?

"Oliver, can you—"

"Can I what?" I'm still standing, still shouting. "Do you want me to stop shouting? To sit down? To have a *normal* conversation?"

"Actually—"

"—Well tough shit." Although even as I say this I realise I have no plan, and so will have to sit down eventually. The moment to storm out has passed, and I'm stuck here. Slowly, reluctantly, theatrically, I retake my seat. I drink the last dregs of my beer and order two more. I say nothing else.

"Oliver," Elijah begins, pleading in his voice. "I'm worried about you. I saw you at the wedding, I watched you dance with Nicola, you're clearly crazy about her."

I stay silent, I don't want to give him the satisfaction of confirming that he's right.

"You like her, and she likes you. If this were anyone else I'd be quite happy to sit back and let nature run its course, but I know you. I know what you're like."

I continue to say nothing. To open my mouth would be to prove him right, and I don't want to do that. We both know he's right, it doesn't need saying out loud.

"Nicola wants to be with you. Jenn wants you to be with Nicola. I want you to be with Nicola. I want to help make it happen."

"Oh, and how are you planning to do that?" I'm angry, but also genuinely interested. I want to be with Nicola, too, but I don't know how. Perhaps this will actually be good for me.

"I have no idea," he says with a sigh.

"Are you fu—" I start to say before cutting myself off. I'm not going to start another argument, I can't be bothered. "Don't you think you should have thought of that before inviting me here?" I ask him, unable to keep the amusement from my voice, unable not to have a little laugh at Elijah's expense. Because I am amused now; Elijah's grand scheme has fallen at the first hurdle, he's done little to no preparation, and I find that fact very funny. He laughs, too, at me, at himself, presumably at the whole damn scenario.

"Probably," he says, amusement in his voice as well. He laughs some more and I join in, and the tension breaks. Now we're just two friends having dinner. "I don't know, let me think of something."

"The something you should have thought of and brought to this dinner?"

"Yeah, that something."

"The something that means Nicola and I get our happily ever after?"

"Yeah, that something."

"Are you going to save my life, Elijah?"

"I'm going to try."

Like how I'm Summer and her boredom in *(500) Days of Summer*, I'm also Lucas in *Empire Records*: "My life is a package tour and I'm simply the passenger." A-fucking-men brother, I feel that.

I'm also Corey: "I didn't realise that it really was love because it was more than love and it wasn't just some stupid feeling in my stomach like everything else and I'll never love anybody as much as you and I hate you! I hate you!"

Love and hate are so close as to be nearly indistinguishable. I think there's a small part of me that hates Nicola. The rest of me worships her.

Chapter Five:

10 Things I Hate About You

Elijah calls me (ew) to tell me he's thought of the something, and when, after some cajoling, he reveals what it is, I can't admit to being anything other than slightly underwhelmed.

"Seriously?"

"Seriously."

"That's your plan?"

"That's my plan."

"For fu—, okay, Elijah, if you think that's a good idea."

"I do my friend, I really do. Comfortable, controlled setting, friends around in case of need, private so no strangers to potentially complicate things. I've assessed all the options, factored in all the variables, and this seems like the best way to get this whole thing in motion."

"A dinner party?"

"Yes, my friend, a dinner party. Keep saying it, it'll keep being true."

I sigh, audibly, on purpose, trying to make obvious my frustration. If Elijah hears me, which surely he must, I do it right in his ear with exaggerated volume, he ignores it.

"Fine, fine, whatever."

"That's the spirit."

"Fuck you."

But I say this last with a smile in my voice, and soon we're both laughing.

"Do I need to bring anything?"

"Just yourself. And maybe a bottle of wine. Nothing too cheap."

As if that needs saying. But nothing too expensive either, wine is too much of a gamble to spend too much money. You can never tell if it's going to be any good until you drink it, and price doesn't seem to be any sort of indicator. Some $5 bottles are nicer than some $50 bottles. Not that I drink the latter too often.

"Cool, I'll be there. What's the dress code?"

"Are you serious?"

I am serious.

"I am yes, why?"

"It's a fucking *dinner party,* Oliver, there is no dress code. Just wear what a normal person wears to dinner."

Fuck.

"And what does a normal person wear to dinner?"

Now it's Elijah's time to audibly sigh. Instead of answering my question he simply says, "see you on Friday," and hangs up, leaving me standing in the little kitchen at work holding my phone to my ear, no sound coming from it.

So this is it, then. This Friday, three days from now, I'm attending a dinner party at Elijah and Jennifer's house. Apartment. Whatever. At this dinner party will be a collected assortment of their friends and colleagues and neighbours, and amongst this number: Nicola.

I don't know why Elijah felt the need to organise a whole dinner party just so Nicola and I could spend some time together. And that shit he said about a controlled setting and other people around? He's acting like I'm a baby, like I'm incapable of talking to another human. Nicola is just a woman. Except she isn't, though, is she? Nicola is more than just a woman: she's everything.

I'm absorbed in thoughts of her when I hear her voice behind me and turning, she's there, in the kitchen with me. It's just the two of us, there's no one else around, why is there no one else around? I'm not prepared for this, I'm not prepared to speak to her. Fuck, what am I going to say? She's looking at me, did she say hello, I didn't hear her, but she's looking at me, I gotta say something. What am I gonna say? Oh fuck, here I go.

"I'm good."

Oh fuck, what was that? She's looking at me like I'm an idiot, why did I say that? Why didn't I say hello?

"That's... good," she replies, unsure. I don't blame her, I'm such a fucking moron. Why did I have to apparently choose a line from *I Love You, Man*? Why am I the awkward woman crushing in Sydney in that film, why am I not myself, just being myself? Why can I never fucking be myself?

"Are you looking forward to Friday?" I ask, and she visibly relaxes as I say something normal. Crisis (potentially) averted.

"I am, yeah," she says, looking a lot happier now the conversation is normal. "The invite was a bit short notice and I had to shuffle a few things around to make it, but it should be good."

Shuffle things around? Oh god, has she really? That's so much pressure. But whatever, I can handle it. Nicola is The One, it's all going to work out. That's just a straight up fact.

"Oh, no," I say, trying to sound sympathetic. "Nothing too major had to be moved, I hope?"

"No, nothing too crazy. I was supposed to be seeing

my parents on Friday, so I've pushed that to Saturday and…"

She keeps talking but I zone out; is this what being with someone is like, listening to them talk about boring things? Sure, it's great that Nicola has rearranged her entire weekend in order to spend Friday night with Elijah and Jennifer (and me?), but, like, do I have to hear about it? They never show that in the movies, the mundane daily ins and outs of a relationship, you never see a couple who're falling in love being like, "oh, darling, let's run away together; not this week because I have a couple of dinners and a squash game, and next week I have a couple of big meetings, but the week after that, let's run away together and never look back." It'd be realistic, I suppose, but it'd also be really, incredibly boring. And in that sense I guess also it wouldn't be realistic, because relationships aren't boring. How can they be? How can spending time with the person who was put on this earth to love you be boring? How could Nicola ever be boring? This must be a slip, a glitch in the Matrix or something, and soon I'm sure she'll be back to her usual exciting self. Shit, better zone back in, better be present in the conversation.

"Oh, wow, that's crazy."

"Right?!" she exclaims back at me. "But, you know, whatever, it's just one of those things."

"Yeah, for sure."

"You know, you're a really good listener, Oliver."

She smiles at me coyly, looking a little pleased, a little embarrassed, her cheeks becoming a little red. I have no idea what to say to her. Do I thank her? I suppose I probably should. Thank her and say something nice, that's what they do in movies, right?

"Thank you. It's, like, easy to listen to you to be fair, you're, erm, like, a very interesting person."

What the fuck? Bit weird, bit overdone, but basically okay, I think. She's still smiling at me, she hasn't backed up or run away or anything, so I can only take that as I good sign.

"Thank you," she says to me, and now she's definitely embarrassed, her cheeks are completely red and she's looking at the floor, her feet, anywhere but me. A couple of people walk into the kitchen and the spell of our conversation is broken, Nicola looks at me again before she says, "see you later," and turns and walks away. I watch her go, I can't help it; I'm trying to figure out what just happened but I can't. Did we just have a conversation? Like, did we two people stand here and exchange words, in a normal way, and did the conversation end normally, and she walked away having enjoyed it? I can't know for sure, obviously, but I think so. I think I had a normal human conversation with the woman I love. Because I do love her; if I wasn't sure of it before, I am now. I know we spent the entire day together at the wedding, we danced and held hands and were basically together the whole time, but that doesn't count. That was a wedding, and weddings don't count as normal; you're a bunch of people essentially held hostage for a day: if things were awkward between Nicola and I it would have been tough luck, because there was nowhere for us to go. Sure, one of use could have left early, but that's not really okay, is it? I mean, I did leave early, although not real early, and that still wasn't totally cool. I mean Elijah hasn't said anything about it, but I can kinda tell he's pissed, the wedding can't have been cheap; nothing held in the same building that has seven of the original 500 copies of Frankenstein could be cheap. So yeah we spoke all day, had dinner together and whatever, but it was because we were conscripted, like troops in the trenches. You form a sort of camaraderie there, a

110

wartime friendship. What was it they said about Commissioner Gordon in *The Dark Knight*? He's a war hero, but this is peace time? Nicola and I have a war relationship, but this is peace time. This dinner party is our first proper sit-down affair, our first peace conference. Oh fuck, how's it going to go? I mean, I know it's going to go brilliantly, obviously, she's The One, it's written in the stars, it's fate. But, like, actually how's it going to go? Afterwards we'll be in a great position, but I have to get us there first. Even though it's predetermined, I still have to fulfil the determination. Prophecies are only fulfilled when people fulfil them. They don't happen of their own accord.

The kitchen is getting more crowded now, it must be lunchtime. I manoeuvre my way through the growing crowd and wend my way back to my desk.

"Alright man, where have you been?" Tom says as I sit down. "What happened to your drink?"

"What? Oh, I didn't make a drink, I was on the phone."

"Oh, okay. Everything good?"

Tom's looking at me with hope etched all over his face, like he's hanging his hopes on whatever the answer to that question is going to be. Luckily for him, it's good news.

"Yeah man," I say to him. "Everything is great."

Love and hate are often so similar as to be indistinguishable. Look at *10 Things I Hate About You*, I mean for starters it's right there in the title, the things the person *hates*. The person presumably being Kat, played by Julia Styles, who at the end reads to her class her poem, which happens to be ten things she hates about Patrick, played by Heath Ledger, our heartthrob. RIP to Heath Ledger, obviously. Not thoughts and/or prayers, because they don't mean anything; I'm not a Republican and this isn't the aftermath of a school shooting.

When Kat reads the poem to Patrick, last name Verona — bit on the nose re: *Romeo and Juliet* don't you think? — she hates him. She also loves him, too, and the final line of the poem is about how, despite all the things he does to her, she can never truly hate him. To be honest, watching the film again he doesn't do a great deal. Firstly she hates him because she's aloof, she hates everyone, that's her thing, the school bitch. Secondly she hates him because he won't kiss her when she's drunk, which is an odd thing to hate someone for, because he's doing the right thing. Really, really drunk people can't consent, no matter how much it seems like they can, and so Patrick is correct to say no to her and suggest they do it another time. Weird that she hates him for this; I guess maybe embarrassment, she feels embarrassed by her actions and is taking that feeling out on him? Who knows, ask a psychiatrist, not an idiot. Finally, Kat hates Patrick because she finds out that he was paid to take her out. Now this I can get behind her hatred.

But also, can I, really? Is that sufficient reason to hate someone? Yes, it must be confusing, and frustrating, finding out someone only asked you out for money, or for a bet like Pygmalion. But really, once you get over the initial shock, surely everything would be peaches and gravy, as Scott Pilgrim would say. Yes, the origins of their relationship are wrong, but Patrick genuinely falls for Kat, and it's very obvious. Not just to us as the viewer, but it's obvious to anyone who sees him, who sees how he acts. I mean look at the paintball scene; if that's not love then I have no idea what it is, or what love is. In the words of Kurt Vonnegut, if this isn't nice, what is?

So yeah, understandable that Kat is angry at him, but surely that'd be a flash in the pan anger, it'd dissipate as quickly as it appeared? Like a bolt of lightning illuminating the world for a second before it disappears, and life continues. It's like, hello Kat, he's clearly The One, why are you pushing him away? We all know that underneath your stony exterior, underneath your cold, hard façade you're just a sucker for love like the rest of us. You know as well as we all do that love is all we need.

As if it wasn't clear enough, Kat is a great lover of Sylvia Plath, who is the goddess of romantic people. Her poetry, her only novel *The Bell Jar* — which Kat is reading in the movie — are marvels of romance. Plath understood the human condition in a way few ever will, she understood people and the relationships between them in ways most of us will spend our lives trying to fathom, and still fail. Plath may have committed suicide aged just 32, and whilst she may have done so because she was cripplingly depressed, depression is like hate, in that it's the other side of the coin. You can't have shadow without light, you can't have good without bad, you can't have love without hate, you can't have depression without love.

Kat says that she hates Patrick with the fire of a thousand suns, but how can she? Especially after he does his song, the great romantic gesture. She flashes a fucking teacher to allow him to sneak out of detention; I don't care what Kat says, these are not the actions of someone who hates someone. And to go back to the paintball; wow, wow, wow. This scene, this is the one. They chase each other, throwing water balloons filled with paint at each other, before Patrick tackles Kat into some hay and they lay down together. He takes off his protective goggles, throws them away, and then finally, finally kisses her. The whole film has been building to this moment; Cameron and Bianca, Michael and Mandella, Joey and himself, these subplots are just that, subplots. They're

113

interesting, they give the story depth, they flesh out the fictional version of Seattle that has been created for our viewing pleasure, but they are simply vehicles upon which the plot is delivered. Patrick and Kat, and their first kiss in the hay: it's everything.

I'm in a clothes shop in Brooklyn called Something Else. It's on Smith Street, and whilst I don't normally come into Brooklyn — because the subway is not something that usually falls within my budget and it's a bit far to be walkable — today is a special occasion. I'm shirt shopping for Elijah's dinner party. For the dinner party with Nicola.

It's not my idea to be here: Elijah has been on my case ever since he invited me to this. Hell, ever since his wedding, really. Married life can't be that dull, surely, that I'm now his number one interest? Married life can't be so boring that he's already had to find a new hobby, and that hobby is me? No, must be something else. Maybe it's not that married life is dull, but the opposite: married life is so good that he wants everyone else to experience it, he's so happy and so thrilled to have married Jennifer that he wants me to marry Nicola so I'll get to feel the way he feels. If that's the case, fine by me: I mean, I know Nicola and I will get married one day, we will experience marital bliss for the rest of our lives, but if someone wants to help, wants to try and speed that boat along, who am I to say no?

I'm slowly browsing the aisles in the store, occasionally picking something up, looking at it, holding it against me, before putting it back down. As I say, this trip was Elijah's idea, although apparently not as important for him as it is for me as he isn't with me. It's easy for him to arrange a shopping trip he doesn't have to go on. Easy for him to spend someone else's time, as

114

well as money, getting prepared. I don't think I need to be here, I have plenty of clothes. Actually, whilst that may be technically true, I suppose Elijah is right to an extent. My wardrobe consists of black jeans, which you can wear for any occasion, mostly the reason I own them, a few white t-shirts for evenings and weekends, and a few cheap shirts for work. When I told Elijah I was planning to come in a pair of black jeans and a white t-shirt he gasped — literally gasped — and told me I couldn't. Yeah, he keeps ringing me, it's weird. I hate talking on the phone, but Elijah is so persistent that it's easier just to acquiesce, to let him get it out of his system. I'm hoping it's just the nervous excitement of someone who's shortly to host a party, and maybe from Saturday onwards he'll chill the fuck out.

The store has a few nice shirts, but the prices are staggering. The cheapest I've seen so far, of the few I liked anyway, is $50. $50 for one shirt, what is going on? That's another reason for my Spartan wardrobe: why spend $50 on one shirt when you can spend $20 on multiple t-shirts? It's just good, sound financial sense. But I suppose Elijah is right: being myself hasn't worked much recently in my life, especially my love life, so trying something else can't hurt. Isn't dating just tricking someone into thinking you're a normal person until they like you so much that when you reveal your true self they're in too deep, and have no choice but to stick around? Who knows, I've never had a relationship long enough to be able to figure the secret out. Maybe this is when it all changes for me. Maybe this dinner party will be my *Sliding Doors* moment?

It's quiet in here: it isn't just the melodic trip hop that's very softly playing over the speakers throughout the place, but the clientèle too. There are a few other people browsing, a pair who look like they're probably a

115

couple, and a person of indeterminate gender, some other guy. When I came in someone said hello and asked if I needed any help and I said no by default; really I do need some help but now it's too late. I can't go and ask for it, not after I've previously declined it. I can't walk that back. And so I continue to wander, incredibly slowly, trying to force myself to look at items, to hold them against my body in pretence of seeing how they might look. I'm not that fussed: the longer I spend in here the more nervous I get, the more anxious I'm becoming. I want to leave, to get out, to go home to my familiar apartment. I can feel the tears aren't far away, I have maybe ten minutes before I'm at the point of no return: if I stay in here I'll end up weeping in the store, or in an alley somewhere trying to hide from the world. If I leave now I may be able to salvage the situation, may be able to put enough room between it and myself in order to hold back the flood, in order to keep my calm and composure. I'm going to cry at some point tonight, that's a fact, but if I time it right I'll be okay for the evening and will just cry myself to sleep like every other night.

The store is only small, so when I say I'm walking up and down the aisles, aisles is pluralised in the most minimal sense, being that there are two. I'm not even sure if they count as aisles; there's a rack in the middle holding various pieces of clothing, shirts and t-shirts and jumpers and jackets and stuff. Along the wall to my left are racks of jeans and chinos and other trousers, and on the wall to the right are the fitting rooms and the checkout desk. It's a really tiny place, between the five customers and two people who work here, the place is practically overflowing. I can see one of the members of staff looking at me; she looks to be about 22, very dark skin, curly hair piled up loosely in a ball on top of her head. She's bending over the counter reading a magazine but I don't think she's actually seeing any of its contents as she turns the pages, I think her hand and arm are moving separately from her brain. I'm watching her from the corner of my eye and, oh god, she's standing up straight, she's stretching, she's moving from behind the counter and she's walking over to me. Okay, Oliver breathe, breathe, stay calm, it's going to be okay. She's just going to offer to help you, and that's what you want, that's good, so say yes, accept her help, let her help you choose a shirt and then get out. This small bit of human interaction will speed things along, so it's a worthy sacrifice. Medium risk, high reward. Do it.

"Yes, please."

Oh, fuck, I've been so focused on what I thought she was going to say I answered her before she even said it. Oh, shit, not a good start.

"I'm sorry, dude, what?"

She looks confused and I don't blame her. Fuck it, I'm going full honesty. I'll never see this woman again — I've already decided I can't ever return to this shop, perhaps never to this part of Brooklyn — so who cares if she thinks I'm a total freak. She's not Nicola, so who cares what her opinion is of me?

"I'm sorry," I say, trying to laugh as I do, trying to play it off as if I'm a normal person. "I thought you were going to ask if I needed help, and I was so busy rehearsing my answer I forgot to wait for you to ask and just answered you."

She's looking at me like I'm crazy. I don't blame her.

"O…kay then, sure, okay, right, okay."

She smiles at me, a look of intense pity on her face. It's one I'm well used to. She's wearing a lanyard with her picture on it and the word 'Belle', which I can only assume to be her name. I focus on this mini-face when I speak to her, it's much easier, much less distracting.

"Can I help you find something?"

"Yes, please."

She visibly relaxes as the conversation becomes normal, becomes rote, to her at least. She must have done this a million times before. I bet she's seen people much weirder than I am. I do not find the thought reassuring.

"What is it you're after, dude?"

"I need a shirt."

"Swell. Any particular kind?"

"I don't know."

"O…kay." I'm not being very helpful, I'm not being very normal. I need to be both.

"I'm going to a dinner party tomorrow night and I need a new shirt for it."

She relaxes again — when did she even tense up?

"No worries, no worries. What's the vibe?"

"The what?" Why did I say that?

"The… vibe?" She looks at me as if she's speaking to an alien, and I'm not entirely sure she isn't. It's clear from her face she regrets approaching me, wishes she was back with her magazine. The longer the interaction goes on for, the more I wish this as well.

"Oh, okay, the vibe," I try to recover the fumble. "Erm, I dunno, adults having dinner?"

"Well, yeah, that's a given. But are we talking formal, informal, are we talking actors and producers, music people, marketing people, a bunch of nobodies. Who are we trying to impress?"

Oh, okay, I understand. That's a question I can answer.

"Nicola."

"I'm sorry? Nicola?"

"Yeah, that's who I'm trying to impress. This girl — woman, sorry — called Nicola."

"I see, I see, okay I can work with that." A sly smile has appeared on her face, like she's suddenly understood some intimate knowledge. Has she? "How about this?"

She's holding a lumberjack shirt that's a sky blue with various other shades of blue highlighting the checked pattern. It's okay.

"It's okay."

"Nope, it won't do."

"No, I said it's—"

"—I know what you said, which is why it won't do. We're looking for a special shirt."

"Are we?"

"We are. Now this Nicola, is she special?" I nod. "Well then, we need a special shirt. If you wanna impress her you can't just turn up in any old piece of shit. What about this one?"

The next shirt is red, with yellow and green checks. It's okay.

"It's okay."

"Sure. This one?" Another shirt, this one green. It's okay.

"It's—"

"—okay, I got it. Let's try this another way: what's her favourite colour?"

I don't know. I have no idea.

"I don't know."

"Okay. What colour are her eyes?"

Shit. What colour *are* her eyes?

"I can't remember."

I can see Belle getting tense now, I think her frustration is bubbling away just below the surface. I need to buy a shirt and get out before I cause her to erupt and destroy us all. I pick a colour at random.

"She wears a lot of yellow." I have literally no idea if this is true, but Belle relaxes, the hardness that had come across her face softens a little as I act in a way that appears to be at least slightly human.

"How about this one, then?" She passes me another blue shirt, this one darker, a navy blue. It's okay, which at this point will work for me. I muster up all my courage.

"Oh, yeah, I like this one," I say, reaching out to feel the sleeve. "It's a great colour, and I love the material." Belle is looking at me funny, am I doing this right? Am I being too keen?

"Great! Wanna try it on?"

I nod and she unbuttons it and hands it to me. I slip it on over my t-shirt and button it up, looking around before being pointed towards a mirror. I look at myself and I feel nothing. Whether the shirt looks good or not I have no idea. Seeing my reflection I don't feel good or bad, I simply feel indifferent. If you told me this wasn't a mirror but was a poster, and I was looking at a different person, I wasn't looking at myself, I'd believe you. I swallow these feelings.

"I really like it," I say to Belle, turning away from the mirror and facing her. "What do you think?"

"I think you look great," she reaches out and smooths the front of my shirt, gently nudges my shoulder and I turn around, give her the full 360-degree view. "Yeah, it looks really good. Shall I ring it up?"

I nod, realising I haven't clocked the price but also realising it's too late. I take it off and hand it to her, and then follow her to the counter. She taps a few buttons on the register then says, "that'll be $85 please."

I take out my credit card slowly, wanting to postpone the moment for as long as possible. $85. 85! I was looking at $50 shirts and they were too much, and now I'm spending $85 on one! But there's nothing I can do, she's inserted my offered card into the machine and I'm putting my pin in, I watch myself complete the transaction, horrified. I can't afford this, I'm really fucking myself. But, I tell myself, I might end up fucking Nicola and if that's the case, well, then it's money well spent.

Belle smiles at me as she puts the shirt and its receipt into a brown paper bag and hands it to me, saying "thanks a lot, hope to see you soon!" Despite knowing I'm never coming here again I tell her she will, and I walk out of the store with a confidence I do not feel. Once out on the street I let myself go, remove the mask I've been wearing and finally breathe. I bend over, hands on thighs, and gulping down huge breaths I try and regulate my heartbeat. It doesn't work.

I start to walk back to the Bergen Street Station before remembering the price of the shirt I've just bought and continue right past it, heading to the Brooklyn Bridge. Not only am I walking home, I'm walking everywhere for the foreseeable future. I'm also not eating. I really hope this shirt works. Maybe I can return it on Saturday? I might be able to leave the tags on in a way no one can see, and if I'm careful and don't get it dirty, don't sweat too much or spill any food or anything, I might be able to get my money back.

This idea doesn't reassure me at all because I know that even if it was possible, I wouldn't have the courage to do it. If I walked into that store and Belle was there it'd kill me, the embarrassment would be mortifying. No, the shirt is mine now, I'm never getting my $85 back. I'll just have to wear it as often as possible to try and get my money's worth. I walk the slow miles back to my apartment, avoiding the tourists taking pictures on the bridge, crying the entire time. People stare at me but I ignore them, I'm used to it. When will things be okay? When I have Nicola, that's when. Tomorrow. The dinner party is tomorrow. Tomorrow. I'll have Nicola tomorrow. Then things will be okay.

Maybe I need to move to Seattle. It's where *Say Anything* takes place, and where *10 Things I Hate About You* takes place. People talk about New York being this big romantic city, and I suppose in many ways it is, but it's a bit cliché. It's easy to imagine kissing someone at the top of the Empire State Building, or in Times Square on New Year's Eve, or in the park in the sun or the rain or the snow or, really, any weather. But it's been done a million times, even films that aren't romcoms often have big romantic moments in New York. But Seattle, Seattle hasn't been done much. There's the two films I've mentioned, as well as *Sleepless in Seattle*, but that's about it. Maybe that's where I'll get my romcom moment.

What am I saying? My romcom moment is going to be in New York; I'm going to join the list of clichés. It's going to be here because Nicola is here, and I live here, so this is where our relationship will flourish. We might move to Seattle, or somewhere else in the future, but our relationship has already started to grow in New York, and this is where we'll continue to nurture it, continue to water it and give it plenty of sunlight and see it bloom. I nearly said hopefully, but there's no hopefully needed, because it will bloom here. That's just a fact.

We're building up to the kiss, I just know it. We've had the wedding, the work project will be starting soon, and now the dinner party. All the pieces are falling into place. Maybe it'll be tomorrow, after the dinner party. Maybe I'll walk her home — does she live within walking distance? Where does she even live? — and we'll reach her building, and she'll turn to me, and we'll look at each other, and that'll be it. Maybe this will happen but we won't kiss, maybe we'll just hug like Lloyd and Diane do after their first date in *Say Anything*. Maybe our kiss will come later. Whatever, it doesn't matter when it comes. I want it as soon as possible, obviously, I'm dying to kiss her, but it's okay. We'll kiss when we kiss, and when we kiss will be when we're meant to kiss. This is my romcom, and I know I'm the hero. Maybe after we've kissed I'll be able to sleep without crying. Maybe.

Heath Ledger is sadly deceased now, he died at the ripe old age of 28 in 2008. 15 years ago now, which is absolutely crazy to think of. He died after filming Christopher Nolan's *The Dark Knight*, very much not a romcom. Perhaps he should have stuck to romcoms? I mean it's understandable that he died, he got Julia Styles, and where do you go from there? Unless you're Joseph Gordon-Levitt, who went from getting Larisa Oleynik in *10 Things I Hate About You* to Zooey Deschanel in *(500) Days of Summer*. Talk about an upgrade. He found his one, and then found another one. A two? Lucky, lucky man; most people struggle to find their one and settle for a one. Luckily I've found Nicola. I just now need to make her mine. Tonight is the night.

I'm outside Elijah and Jennifer's building on West 81st. It's a cool evening, the late-September Indian summer sun is nearly back in its bed, the tops of the buildings around me shine with its light but at street level it's nearly night. The building I'm outside, trying and not quite managing to go in, is a white stone apartment block, towering hundreds of feet above me. The entrance is set back from the sidewalk, two brown doors that are watching me pace, that I can feel judging me: they're not open, inviting, like some buildings are, but they're closed, suspicious, they know they haunt the Upper West Side and know as part of this they have a role to play as gatekeeper. They won't let just anyone in, only those who earn it, whether by virtue of being able to afford to live there, like Elijah, or by knowing someone who lives there and managing to wrangle an invite, like me.

It's warm, even though the top couple of buttons on my new shirt are open I'm still pulling at my collar; I feel like a caricature, like a cartoon character, I feel like in my nervousness all my actions are exaggerated, that I look like Wile E Coyote or Popeye or something, only sans the muscles, obviously. And pipe: cigarettes will do just fine for me for now.

I light a fresh one off the end of the one I'm just finishing, throwing the butt into the gutter, then feeling bad I pick it up and throw it into an overflowing trash can. There are bags of garbage lining the curb here, like there seems to be in almost all of New York. In England, London especially, you'd only see rubbish piled up like this when the garbage collectors were on strike; in New York it just seems to be part of the landscape, another ugly part of the city which everyone just collectively ignores. I can't judge anyone, because mostly I do, too; I'm only aware of the garbage right now because I'm outside my window of tolerance, my breaths are quick and shallow and I'm hyper-focusing on everything around me.

There's a couple of white and grey pigeons in the street pecking at what looks like an old, mouldy piece of bread; they fly away when a cab goes rushing past, but once the coast is clear they land and continue eating. There's a woman walking her dog across the street; she's what Sidney in *I Love You, Man* would call a Bowser: she looks just like her dog. It's a poodle, all white with fluffy, curly fur; the woman is old, hunched over, roughly the same height as her dog, and she has a mass of curly white hair perched on top of her head. The pair amble slowly down the street, the dog occasionally stopping to sniff something, the woman letting it. I watch them for a few moments and I feel something akin to jealousy. Maybe not everyone's one is a human; maybe some people find their one with a dog, like this woman seems to have, or a cat or bird or turtle or whatever. You see those documentaries about weird people who have pet monkeys or tigers or whatever: they always seem to have, or at least feel they have, some sort of weird connection with them. Maybe they think that monkey is their one? At least a monkey is kinda human, not like a tiger; does that make it better or worse?

I feel my phone vibrate in my pocket and taking it out see it's a message from Elijah asking where I am. I'm outside, I want to tell him, I'm trying to come in but it's not working. The time tells me it's 7:37, which means I'm seven minutes late. And this being a dinner party, I think I am actually *late* late; this isn't like a regular party where turning up on time is frowned upon, this is an adult party where it's expected. I have been here since 7.14, in my defence, I just haven't made it inside. I guess now's the time.

I drop my cigarette and stand on it, picking the butt up and throwing it into the same overflowing trash can. With a sigh I turn to the building, ignoring the doors still watching me, and with all the courage I have I walk up the short walk and press the button for the intercom; Elijah and Jennifer are *wealthy*, but not *doorman wealthy* clearly. It's Jennifer who answers, a high pitched and inviting 'hello?' I tell her it's me and she buzzes the doors open and I step inside, taking a moment to compose myself before moving across the lobby and to the lift. A man behind a desk, presumably a concierge or whatever, smiles and bids me a good evening, and I just about manage to nod back at him without falling over. I press the button to call the elevator and the one to my left opens its doors immediately, alarmingly quickly, but I step inside nonetheless, pressing the button for 47. The doors close silently and suddenly I'm rushing towards the sky, the elevator fairly flies up. And then it stops and the doors open, and I'm in a corridor, not quite like something from *The Shining* but not far off. It's dark, there are a couple of doors lining each wall and nothing more. It's incredibly unsettling. I see a sign with an arrow pointing right to apartments 47A and 47B, and left to 47C and 47D. I turn left and make my way to 47C, pausing in front of the door for a moment to collect myself. Bracing myself against what's to come, I knock.

A second passes before the door swings open and is replaced by Elijah, who's wearing not only some very expensive looking jeans and a shirt, but also a massive, shit-eating grin. He says hello and pulls me in for a hug, splashing some champagne down both of our sleeves; is he a bit drunk already? When did he start? The hug goes on for longer than I find comfortable but Elijah has me firmly in his grip, I try to extricate myself but am unable, I'm completely at his mercy. He's not much bigger than me but much stronger, and though there's a hint of safety in his arms now isn't the time. He smells like aftershave and champagne, and though the smell is nice due to his proximity it's right in my nostrils and I nearly gag on it. Eventually he lets me go and bids me enter, shutting the door behind me. I'm in another dark corridor, although this one shorter, with just a single door on each side. "Straight to the end," Elijah says, and following his instructions I proceed towards a dark brown door, pushing it open to be assaulted by both light and conversation.

The room in front of me is vast. It's a living room slash kitchen slash dining room; the ceiling towers over it, it must be 20 feet high, I hadn't anticipated it being so high in what looks, from the outside, like a regular apartment building. Obviously we're on the Upper West Side — or at least the Middle West Side, I'm never entirely sure where the boundaries lie — but still. The wall directly across from where I'm standing is floor to ceiling windows looking south over Manhattan; we're high enough that they're still letting in copious light, supported by some large spotlights on the ceiling and, looking around, what feels like a billion candles. It's roasting from all the tiny fires dotted about the place.

Seeing me, Jenn comes and gives me a hug, welcoming me; hers is thankfully both soft and short, her odour also a mixture of perfume and champagne, and pulling away she grabs a glass of champagne from god knows where and hands it to me. I thank her and take a sip, my mouth by this point being so dry I worry I may start literally gasping. The champagne is cool, refreshing, expensive, and I take a second then a third sip in quick succession, and though Jenn looks at Elijah then back at me she doesn't say anything.

There are seven people in the room, including myself. Elijah and Jenn make up a pair; I can see Luna over in the corner, inspecting a tall bookcase overflowing not just with books but ornaments, little trinkets, collections of a life, as well as the requisite candles. It can't be safe, I think to myself, to have open flames on a bookshelf. But looking around the apartment, it's clear that at least one of Elijah and Jennifer knows what they're doing, understands how the world works, so I let the thought go. There's a figure hovering by Luna, I have no idea of their gender or if they're with Luna. But when Luna turns around and spots me, and comes over to say hello, the figure follows her, and she introduces them as, "Gaston, like from *Beauty and the Beast* but he's actually French," and I say hello and hold out my hand but Gaston ignores it and I'm grateful. In the kitchen is another guy, someone I don't recognise. And by the windows, her back to the room, though somehow managing to not come off as rude, is her. Nicola.

She's wearing a black dress, loose and flowing, hanging off her shoulders and trailing all the way to the floor. Her hair is up in a tight bun on top of her head and she's wearing a pair of gigantic hoop earrings, they sway gently from side to side as the hot air circulates in the room. She's holding a glass of champagne in one hand and a small black clutch in the other; she looks peaceful, content, I want to go over and say hello but I don't want to disturb her. Also, now I'm here and I've seen her, I'm terrified. I finish my champagne and even as I look around for a place to put the glass Elijah takes it from me and hands me a fresh one, fumbling it into my hand. "Bottoms up," he says, slurring slightly, clinking his also full glass against mine, before drinking off half of it. I can see Jenn looking at us, mainly at Elijah, and she doesn't look impressed, so as much as I want to down mine I force myself to sip it, to drink it like a normal person.

I'm about to say something to Elijah when he abruptly moves away from me and into the kitchen, returning a few seconds later announcing that, "dinner is ready, please take your seats." There's a rush of movement as we all make our way to the table; there are place cards and I walk slowly around the vast mahogany table looking for mine. Finding it I sit down, my back to the door, facing the windows. Across from me is Luna, to her right Gaston. The unknown man sit down next to me, on my left, and the chair to my right remains empty for just a few moments before Nicola slowly lowers herself into it, smoothing her dress gracefully as she does so. Oh shit, I knew this was going to happen but I'm not prepared. I've spent every waking moment since Elijah invited me preparing but I'm still not prepared. What do

I do? What do I say? I need to speak to her. Oh fuck, here we go.

"Hi," I say, trying to put as much warmth into my voice as possible. "How are you?"

"Hi, Oliver," she replies, smiling at me, a genuine smile, and it melts my heart. I love her so much. "Did you find the place okay? It's an incredible apartment, isn't it? Truly spectacular."

I'm confused, wondering how she knows it so well, before remembering that she's Jenn's friend, she's probably been here a bunch of times. I try to ignore this fact, try to ignore that it feels like we're on her territory. This is neutral ground, I assure myself, we're both guests in this home. She doesn't have anything I don't.

"It's really beautiful," I manage to answer. "I wish I lived in a place like this."

"Well, get yourself a rich ex-husband and you'll be able to."

I'm about to ask her what she means when we're interrupted by a plate being placed down in front of us. Jenn and Elijah are moving about the table like ants, scurrying around placing food in front of everyone, filling champagne glasses, getting a coke for the man sitting next to me who apparently doesn't drink and, based on his performance so far, doesn't speak either. But this latter is fine by me, I want to focus all my energy on Nicola. Just as I turn back to her to ask her a question Elijah speaks.

"Friends, countrymen, Gaston." Everyone laughs, the tension eases somewhat, we're all okay, I think. "Thank you for coming, especially on such short notice. I can't believe you were all free, losers." More laughs, Elijah is a consummate host, despite the fact he's clearly the wrong side of sober. "Jenn has laid on a fabulous spread for the evening, which I hope you all enjoy. Her bosses at

Itterom have graciously given her the night off, but I have not! Sorry babe, I know you were looking forward to not cooking tonight, oops." She smiles at him, her expression exasperated but not seriously, there's absolute adoration in her look as well, his speech momentarily distracting her from his drunkenness. "So enjoy the food, enjoy the drink, enjoy the company. Buon appetito!"

Elijah sits down, and as he does Jenn raises her glass. We all follow suit, six champagne classes and one glass coke bottle raised in toast to Elijah. He raises his own and then putting it down picks up his knife and fork, and following his lead we all do the same. The food is incredible.

"I had no idea Jenn works at Itterom," I say to Nicola once I've finished. She's only halfway through her starter and I momentarily panic, wondering how quickly I ate, whether it was too fast, whether she thinks I'm a pig.

She looks at me, holding a hand over her mouth and nodding. I've caught her mid-chew, fuck.

"I'm not surprised, though," I continue, speaking so she has chance to swallow. "This food is incredible, they're lucky to have her."

"Oh, yeah, she's an amazing chef," Nicola replies, her mouth finally empty. "I remember at college she used to cook all the time, I'd get up in the morning hungover AF and find her apron on, doing all sort of culinary experiments. I never thought I'd enjoy scrambled eggs and hot sauce at 8am whilst trying not to vomit, but Jenn made it so. I am in no way surprised she ended up being a chef, it's definitely her calling."

This is the longest conversation we've had since the wedding and it's going really well. I'm killing it.

"I'm surprised you're not fatter, being her friend." Oh, shit. "Not that you're fat, not at all. You're skinny, like really skinny." Shit, not great. "Not too skinny or anything, you're just right. Like the third bowl of porridge." What am I saying? "Not that you're a bowl of porridge or any sort of inanimate object. Fuck, Oliver," I playfully hit myself on the forehead with my palm, "what are you saying?"

I try to smile, to play off my idiocy as deliberately jokey, and I think I get away with it. Nicola is looking at me out of the corner of her eye while she finishes her starter, and I take a sip of my champagne, the glass emptying as I do. Once again, before I've even set it down Elijah is over and replacing it with another flute, this one filled to the brim. He spills a bit of his also full glass on my shirt as he does, though I don't think he notices. Nicola does.

"I like your shirt," she smiles, "even with the champagne stain."

"Thanks," I reply. Shit, it worked, buying a new shirt worked. Who knew. "I bought it especially for tonight. I was going to come in a t-shirt but Elijah wouldn't let me, apparently I have to dress like a grown up for a grown up's dinner party." I say this in a jokey way and Nicola smiles, finally placing her knife and fork down. She's the last to finish and once she does Elijah and Jenn are up again, whisking away our empty plates and replacing them with mains. The main course is similarly delicious, as is desert, and soon we're all full and satisfied. I feel like a fat piece of shit but by now I've had eight or nine glasses of champagne so I don't really mind.

Elijah opens doors I hadn't noticed before which lead onto a balcony and we all follow him out, Luna and Gaston and I lighting cigarettes as we do. I see Nicola frown and move away from me, so I smoke it quickly before moving over to her.

"Are you having a nice evening?" I ask her.

"Isn't it beautiful?" she asks by way of reply.

"Isn't what beautiful?"

"This," she gestures with one arm, taking in the breadth of the city.

"I suppose so," I say, "If you like steel and light and that."

She looks at me with an odd look on her face, like she's trying to figure me out but she can't. I understand Nicola, I've been having the same problem for nearly 30 years.

"I think it's romantic."

Oh fuck, she said the R-word. Shit, what do I do? Gotta change tactic, go with what she's saying.

"It is kind of beautiful, I suppose, when you think about it. All those people out there living their lives, at the same time we're living ours. Makes you think doesn't it?"

"What are you thinking about?"

"Death," I hear myself saying before I can stop myself. Fuck. "And life," I quickly add. "And everything in between." Shit, think I saved it.

"Yeah," Nicola says, and it's impossible to read her tone. "Would you excuse me for a minute?"

She moves away, heads back inside, I assume to the bathroom or something. Elijah wanders over once she's gone.

"How's it going?" He asks what I think he thinks is quietly, though he basically shouts it. I hope Nicola can't hear. From the look on her face Jenn definitely does.

"Yeah man," I say, "well, I think."

"I think so, too," he says. "I've been watching you two and you seem to be getting along."

"We are, I think," I say, being as honest as I can with him. "It's kinda awkward, but I think I'm doing okay. She's still here and still talking to me so I can't be doing that badly." I smile ruefully as I say this; even though I'm only joking it's a little too close to the truth.

"Keep it up, man," Elijah says quietly, moving away from me as Nicola returns.

"All okay?" I say, before I realise what I've said. Why the fuck did I say that?

Nicola doesn't respond, simply looks at me. I don't blame her.

"Do you want to go inside? I'm a little cold."

"Sure," I say, my heart starting to pound. Fuck, is this it?

She moves inside and I follow her. She heads for the living part of the room and sits on a huge leather couch, it must be two miles long, if I sit at the other end we'll be in different zip codes. I sit next to her, not right up against her but close enough. She doesn't move when I do and I take this as a good sign.

"Are you looking forward to our project starting?" she asks.

"Yeah, it should be really good. I haven't written copy for ages, it'll be good to dust of those muscles."

"I'm looking forward to seeing what you come up with. I never had you pegged as a writer."

No shit, Sherlock, neither did I.

"Oh, yeah," I say, "writing is where my heart is. I may do data by day, but by night I like to put pen to paper."

"Like some sort of literary Batman," she laughs, and I laugh, too. Her laugh is musical, like a symphony. I love her so much.

"It'll be nice to work with you, as well," I say, moving a little closer to her on the couch. From the way she looks at me I can tell she notices, but she doesn't move, either towards me or further away. That's good, I suppose?

"It'll be nice to work together, yes," is all she says, very neutrally. Shit, I think I'm losing her, I need to do something, need to make a move or gesture or something.

She's not looking at me, she's looking at her hands, twisting and knotting them in her lap. Panicking, the weight of the moment, the weight of being alone with her, get the better of me, and before I know what I'm doing I reach out to take one of her hands. But then tragedy strikes.

Because of where her hands are, and because I'm a fairly clumsy individual, instead of taking her hand, my hand reaches too far into her lap, and I brush her crotch. And when I do I panic, freeze, and leave my hand there. And then we're both looking at my hand sitting in her lap, placed far too proximately to her vagina. So close I think I can feel the heat coming from it, though I know really that's only my own sense of embarrassment and shame. Oh fuck, what have I done?

Realising my hand is still there I whip it away but it's too late, it was there too long, we both saw and felt and acknowledged it. Oh shit.

"I'm so sor—"

"—I have to go."

She jumps up and, grabbing her clutch, nearly runs across the room and out of the door. Jenn sees Nicola go and follows her, and Elijah comes over to me just as the door closes and asks me if everything's okay. I don't answer; how can I? What do I say? 'Yeah mate all good, I just accidentally sexually assaulted the woman I love and so she ran away. How're you?'

Elijah sits down next to me and asks me again if everything is okay, and that's all it takes. I burst into tears.

Chapter Six:

Clueless

I can't sleep. And I'm not talking your garden variety 'I've been tossing and turning for a few hours' can't sleep. I'm talking your full on 'I haven't slept for more than a couple of hours for days' kinda can't sleep, the serious kind of can't sleep.

It started Friday night, unsurprisingly, when I eventually went to bed after I eventually got home after Elijah and Jennifer eventually allowed me to leave. I'm saying that like they kidnapped me or something, when all they actually did was take care of me when I was having a minor crisis. After Jenn followed Nicola, Elijah brought me a glass of water and sat with me, not saying anything, not doing anything, just being with me until my weeping became deep sobs, eventually slowing down to very small cries allowing me to get myself back under control. I didn't even notice Elijah had his arm around me, I didn't even try to remove it. *Who is this man?* I thought. I knew him so well so long ago, and now he's back and it's like no time has passed. I adore him for this, even if I don't know him.

Jenn came back not long after I'd regained some of my composure. She asked me what happened and I told her, and she said that pretty much tallied with Nicola's version of events. I was briefly relieved; at least Nicola hadn't taken it to be more than it was, hadn't thought I was trying to grope her or something, at least she knew it was a mistake, just me being a clumsy idiot. But even as I thought this, the whole event replayed itself in my head — not that it had stopped exactly, but I'd at least managed to ignore it — and fresh tears began to stream from my eyes. Jenn passed me a box of tissues and sat on the other side of me from Elijah; she also didn't say anything, simply sat until I got myself back under control.

When I did, and was able to look up, to look at them both, I could tell they wanted me to talk, wanted me to elaborate, but all I said was, "I have to go," and jumped to my feet. I practically flew out of their apartment, back down in the elevator, bursting out onto the street like a man who has actually been held captive, who hasn't tasted fresh air or freedom for many years.

I checked my phone to see it was nearly midnight; you wouldn't have known it from looking around, the streets still teemed with enough people that it might have been midday instead. I walked back down West 81st, passing along the side of the American Museum of Natural History; even though it was closed it was still brightly lit, like a beacon of hope in this cold, dark city. That it's doors were closed was the only sign around to indicate it was night. I crossed Central Park West and entered the park, knowingly doing so, so late on a Friday was stupid but also not caring. By that point I didn't care if I got attacked or mugged or anything; *hell*, I thought, *if someone murdered me at least the pain would be over quickly*. As it stood at that moment, the pain I was feeling had no end date, no expiry; I'd been given a whole life sentence, with the only hope of parole being if I received a reprieve from Nicola. Which didn't feel very likely.

I wasn't paying attention to where I was going, I simply allowed my feet to take me where they would. The paths were dark, the park has never had adequate lighting; you'd think it would after all that's happened there — not least involving a poor, poor woman, some innocent teens, and a certain former President — but no, no such thing. I knew I was using all my male privilege, walking around such a dangerous place, but I didn't care about that, either. Damn the patriarchy, I thought but didn't feel. I had no room in my heart for justice of any kind, except maybe the love kind. And despite the fact that wasn't a thing, that love justice didn't exist, doesn't exist, I still hoped for it. I still prayed for it. Because praying was all I had left at that point; and I could only pray to Nicola, I could only pray that she'd be okay, that our little encounter wouldn't leave a mark on her, that the fact it was an accident, and that she knew it was an accident, would work in my favour.

I walked for perhaps an hour before I realised I was cold; I was still just wearing jeans and my new shirt, my cursed shirt as I'd begun to think of it, and as the night turned towards morning and the temperature dipped to its lowest I began to shiver. What had started as a fine late-summer evening had become a cool autumn night, and stopping to get my bearings, I turned south and began to walk towards West 59th Street. I found it at Columbus Circle but, checking my banking app on my phone, getting the subway was out of the question, so with a sigh I began the slow trek down to Soho and the safety of my apartment.

Once again I let my feet carry me, giving all my brain power to focusing on Nicola, trying and failing to manifest; I knew that would be more helpful than prayer, but, what with prayer being the last refuge of the damned and all, I was still firmly in its territory. I supposed I needed things to improve at least slightly before I could move away from prayer and back to manifesting. Before

I could move away from complete desperation and into slight desperation. That's my sweet spot anyway, being a little, but not entirely, desperate. Just mostly.

My feet carried me down Broadway and to Times Square. Like the rest of the city, this place was bright as the middle of the day, and just as crowded. Despite the fact it was past 1am, approaching 2, no one seemed to be in a rush to go home. There were people in costumes trying to get people to take pictures with them, offering the photos without discussing payment then demanding it when it was too late for the poor exploited soul to say no; crowds of tourists fell for this, but not all, other crowds avoided the street performers, raised their phones to eye level and captured images of the buildings, of the square, of the ball sitting quietly waiting for New Year's Eve to resurrect it. Capturing images of the lights and sounds of a life that finally, for the first time, isn't happening somewhere else, but is happening right here, right now.

There were people who looked like they'd just finished work and were finally heading home passing people who had just gotten up, dragged themselves from their homes and were heading to work. Scores of people had set up card tables and were selling homemade CDs, homemade t-shirts, homemade blunts. I wanted one of these blunts, getting incredibly high would have been the quickest way to dull my pain, even if it only temporarily displaced it until it came back with a vengeance, and I was about to approach one of the card tables when I remembered that the only reason I was in Times Square was because I was walking home because I was broke. No money for subway fare, definitely no money for a blunt.

So instead of completing my approach of the card table I turned and moved towards the steps that function as seats and, moving past the statue of Father Duffy, climbed all the way up and sat down in the back row. It gave the best view, but this was of no concern to me: what it did mean not only was there no one too close to me, but no one could sneak up on me from behind. Not that I expected anyone to, but it was good to have my back against something solid, good to have that reassuring firmness behind me, good to have some structure.

As I sat there watching people the tears started to fall again; all the people I could see seemed so happy, so carefree. Music was playing from who knew where and people were dancing to it, there was a group of perhaps seven or eight people — with their bodies constantly bending to the rhythm it was impossible to say for sure, at times they all blended into one amorphous dancing being — moving to the music, their hips moving from side to side, their feet stomping, their heads by turns swaying and bobbing and banging, depending on the turn the music took, what moves the beat called for. A few feet away from them was a group of boys, probably only 15 or 16, young enough that, for a brief moment, I wondered why they were up and out so late before I remembered where I was and it all made sense. I couldn't be certain but it looked like they were filming Tiktoks; one person would hold the camera up while the others danced in front of it, then after a brief huddle where they'd all crowd around the phone, presumably to watch the video back, the honor of filming would be passed to someone else, and the group would dance once again. They all looked so happy, so carefree, their only worry the number of views and likes their videos would get, their only concern fitting in. I envied them their simplicity, before realising that, essentially, all my worries revolved around the same issue: all I needed was to fit in with Nicola. All I worried about was whether or not she liked me enough, whether I'd be viewed by her enough. *It's all the same really*, I thought, as the tears fell; it's all the same no matter where you are, how old you are, where you've ended up in life. We all just want to be seen and liked by the person, or people, that we love.

The buildings were more visible than ever, their lights silhouetted against the darkness of the sky. Blues, reds, greens, whites, the whole spectrum of colours flashed in front of my eyes like a technicolour rainbow, and each colour felt like a taunt. Sitting there, in the centre of the world, with life happening all around me, I felt beige. I felt like an unperson, a grey shadow floating around the world, watching life happen all around me but taking no part. I was a blob, a misshapen object, perennially in the wrong place at the wrong time.

The colours began to blur as I blinked more and more tears into my eyes, as my ducts continued to overflow and spill into me. Soon everything became a haze, the colours were no longer distinguishable from each other, every group of people became one, a mass of heads and arms. The road and the sidewalk and the sky mixed together and I felt like I was falling, falling, and that I'd never stop. My breathing became quick and shallow and I stood up, stumbled down the steps, moved away from Times Square as fast as my shaking legs would allow me. I only stopped once more on my way home, taking a seat in Washington Square Park to try and recover some composure. Eventually I made it home, not even bothering to take my shoes off as I collapsed into bed. I might as well have done: I stayed awake staring at the clock until around 8am, when I gave up the ghost on sleeping and got up to face yet another fucking day.

Love and hate aren't different sides of the same coin,

they're basically the same thing. I love Nicola, but I also think I hate her too; I hate that she hasn't responded to any of my texts since the dinner party, I hate that she's been avoiding me in the office, leaving her desk whenever she sees me walking towards her and delaying our project together; I hate that she thinks I'm some sort of sex pest or whatever, that I'm the kind of guy who would just grab a woman; I hate that I know she doesn't think that at all and yet can't help but think she thinks it, because otherwise why else would she be avoiding me? Most of all I hate the way she makes me hate myself: I have enough reasons to hate myself as it is, I don't need any more. I'm more than capable of hating myself to a sufficient level without using her hate. I have enough hate, thank you, I don't need surplus hate.

I don't want to hate myself, I want to love myself. I want to trust myself, I want to walk around feeling satisfied, which is how Diane makes Lloyd feel. He says this to his friends, and then asks if they can imagine. I can't imagine; but I can dream. And that's what I dream of feeling. Not hate, pride.

Hate isn't always a bad thing between two people who care about each other, though. Like, fairytale romances, Princes and Princesses and valiant rescues and defeats of monsters and stuff, that shit isn't real. Fairytales are just that, and pretending otherwise is stupid. Look at all good romcoms: there's always some tension between the two star-crossed lovers, there's always at least one moment of misunderstanding, a period of doubt where it seems like they actually won't end up together. Like when Diane dumps Lloyd. But they always do end up together because hate can always be overcome. And besides, hate is necessary, because although love is everything, always and eternally, sometimes love isn't the one. Sometimes, no matter how much you love someone, you get tired of them, you need a break from them.

I mean, I doubt I'll ever need a break from Nicola, once we finally get together, but still, you know, I'm not going to sit here and pretend I know more about life and love than the people who write those movies. They're writing movies, yes, but they're also writing truth up there on the screen. Writers are supposed to write what they know, so I've read — frantically reading anything I can on the art of writing so Nicola and Neil and Brielle and whoever else at work don't find out that I'm a fraud and take me off the project — and so they're writing what has happened to them, and to people they know, to millions of people around the world every day. They're writing true love, real love, the kind of love we all experience. I'm just waiting, hating, I'll be there soon.

Look at Cher and Josh in *Clueless*: for the longest time, hell most of the movie, they hate each other. They're ex-stepbrother and sister, and so have this kind of sibling rivalry thing going on, but also not really, Cher repeatedly tells Josh he's not her brother. They also have this opposites attract thing going on as well: Cher comes across — to Josh at least, we know better — as a shallow, vacuous, fashion-obsessed two-dimensional character, where Josh is this three-dimensional, well-rounded, empathetic cares about the world and all things good college student. They couldn't be further apart in terms of their likes and dislikes — except counting each other amongst their dislikes — but none of this matters, none of this is important. By the end of the movie they get to where we've known they're going to get to the whole time we're watching, and where both we and they know they should be. They end up in each other's arms.

Much like Kat and Patrick in *10 Things I Hate About You*, Cher and Josh learn the most important lesson in

142

the world: you can't fight love. You can try, you can hope to escape it, try and move past it, hell even try and find your own love, like Cher does with Christian, and Kat does with anger, but the fact is: love will find you, love will get you, and love will take you to be with the one who loves you back.

Nicola and I are in the miscommunication and misunderstanding part of our relationship, act two of our movie where things don't seem like they're going to have a happy ending, where the conflict threatens to tear us apart. I know we'll get through it, we'll move into act three soon where we're reunited and have our happy ending. I know we'll have our first kiss soon, and like the first kiss between Lloyd and Diane, between Helen and James, between Tom and Summer, between AJ and Corey, between Kat and Patrick, between Cher and Josh: it'll be everything.

Monday morning and the fresh torrent of pain it brings every week. Some weeks it's bearable, some weeks it isn't but I bear it anyway, but today it's nothing short of torture. In the last week, since Elijah and Jennifer's dinner party, a period consisting of ten nights, from the previous Friday up to last night, the following Sunday, I've slept for a total of 27 hours. 27 hours in ten nights. According to doctors I should have slept at least 60 hours in those ten nights, preferably even more. I've slept for 27. I'm operating on less than half the absolute minimum recommended amount of sleep. And it's not going well for me.

A typical night, at least in my current state, goes like this: I go to bed around 11pm, that is to say I drag my arse from where I'm laying on the couch, brush my teeth, strip down to my underwear, and then lay my arse in bed. Because my apartment is so small I can see the TV from both my couch and my bed, I don't turn it off whilst I complete this process. You'd think it wouldn't take too long, but about half an hour is usually enough time. That's how long it takes me to convince myself that I should at least try and sleep in bed, how long it takes me to convince myself that I must floss and brush my teeth, if only because I can't afford to go to the dentist, which means I definitely can't afford to get false teeth or have any major dental work or whatever. I know you have to pay for everything healthcare-related here, but, like, why are teeth extra? Even in the UK you have to pay for your teeth, where everything else is free. What's going on there? Are teeth special bonus luxuries? Do I not need them, do they not come as part of the standard package? Why are they an optional extra?

Anyway, once I'm in bed, clothes in a pile on the floor, perhaps their own pile, perhaps as part of one of the other ever-present piles, phone and glass of water on the bedside table next to me, I finally manage to convince myself to turn off the TV, shrouding my apartment in total darkness. Well, as dark as it's possible to be in New York, the city which, like me, does not sleep. I roll onto my side, close my eyes, and lay there. And I lay and I lay and I lay, I keep my eyes closed for as long as I can, I feign sleep in order that sleep may happen for real, fake it 'til you make it, baby, but sleep doesn't come. I can usually manage to keep my eyes closed until around midnight, before boredom gets the better of me and I open them and play on my phone for a bit. I do this until my eyes start to hurt, I know it's from the brightness of the screen being pressed basically right up against my retinas but I convince myself it's from tiredness so I close my phone, close my eyes, and try again. And I lay, and I lay, and my frustration grows as sleep doesn't come, and I lay some more, and it's usually around 2am that I give up, sit up, put the TV back on. I don't watch anything in particular, stick on *The Office* — UK or US, doesn't matter — or *Friends* or some other light hearted sitcom and let that play out, not even watching it, not even appreciating the background noise, just having it on and playing because, otherwise, I'm laying in the dark getting wound up at my inability to sleep, one of the very few things the body absolutely needs, and therefore should be fucking able to do without this much fucking drama; it's like, what the fuck is wrong with you brain, literally all you have to do is switch off, why can't you? Surely it's more effort to be awake than it is to be asleep? What the actual fuck?

I always do get some sleep eventually, anywhere between half an hour and two and a half, which is my record longest sleep in this current period. It's never proper sleep, though, not the kind of sleep I awake from feeling well rested. It's the kind of sleep where you only know that you've been asleep because you wake up, and when I do wake up I'm confused, disorientated, not even a little rested, if anything more tired than before I slept. Upon waking I turn the TV off, hoping I can ride the wave back into sleep, inevitably failing. I lay in frustration until around 7am when I finally give up and get up, drink a few glasses of water and then go and stand in the shower and let the hot water cascade over my body, hide the flow of my tears. People say they cry in the shower because then they don't know if they're crying or it's the shower water, but believe me, you know when you're crying. I mean, maybe I know because it's every day, and so I know I am because I certainly am, but really, crying doesn't just happen. A few tears might slip out unbeknownst to you, but that's not crying, that's just a few tears. When I'm actually crying my shoulders heave up and down, my chest tightens, my nose runs, I pound on the walls of the shower until my hands throb. There's no mistaking it.

I shower anywhere from five to 30 minutes, depending on how bad the night has been, how bad I'm feeling. This morning I said fuck it and showered for an hour, knowing today is the day, Nicola and mine's project is finally kicking off. Neil came over to my desk last Monday, when the project should have been starting, and told me about the delay. He was hazy on the details, another project blowing up, something about budgets and deadlines, to be honest I didn't really listen to anything he said after he told me about the delay. I was both devastated and relieved. Devastated because it meant I wouldn't be working closely with Nicola, I wouldn't get to be near the woman I love. Relieved because this had been only two days after the dinner party, after the crotch fiasco, and I wasn't ready to see her, to speak to her, especially as she'd not responded to any of my texts. Part of me wanted to sit down next to her and ask her what was up, let her know that she had read receipts turned on, just in case she didn't know. But really, I was glad to not be near her, glad my hatred of her could be contained to just within myself.

But the project is kicking off today for sure. Neil text me last night; he wouldn't normally do so, he has my personal number but is pretty good about not using it unless he has to, but he violated that self-imposed rule last night. But that was fine by me, because it was a nice text, a good text, he was being not only a good boss but a good person.

"Hi, Oli, apologies to message on a weekend but just wanted to see if you're ready for tomorrow and Nicola? I know last week wasn't great — we don't have to talk about it, don't worry — so I just want to make sure you're in the right headspace. Let me know if not and I'll pull you off it for another week, we'll figure something out. Take care, Neil."

A really nice message, Neil is a really good boss. I replied, feigning enthusiasm I didn't feel, that I was not only aware of the project kick-off but excited, raring to go. It was true in a way: I am very much looking forward to seeing Nicola, to working with her. Even if it's awkward and we only talk about work, talking to her is better than not talking to her, that's just a fact. Even if we sit side by side and the day feels like it lasts 100 years and all we talk about is copy, branding, and slogans and tone of voice and all that super-exciting-shit! then at least we'll have spoken and unlike most days getting out of bed won't have been a mistake.

The weather feels very reflective of my mood today: it's cold, grey, windy, and absolutely pouring down. I brought an umbrella with me but the wind made it basically pointless so after it turned inside out for about the 50th time, I threw it into a trash can I passed and have accepted my fate in getting wet. If life were a novel and not a movie I'd say I was in *Wuthering Heights* or one of the other Brontë books: even though I'm in New York, I could easily be on the moors of Yorkshire. The weather is just right, the atmosphere is on the money; everyone is unhappy, people are walking with their heads down, bracing themselves against the elements. We're all just trying to get to where we need to go with as little damage as possible, staying as warm and dry as we can. If they're anything like me, they're freezing and soaking, but still trying, not giving up. All we can do is try on a day like today, giving up and giving in will not help, all it'll do is make everything worse. It's also like being in a Brontë book, however, because we all have something better waiting for us. For me, the better is at my office, and I'll be there in about ten minutes. Others may not find their better in the office or wherever they work, wherever they're going now, but they'll find it for sure. It may be that the office is simply the next hurdle, and the better is waiting at the finish line. They may see their better at lunchtime, or this afternoon. They may not see their better for 50 years, may not find their better until then. But they will. Everyone I pass, who has their head down, who's wrapped up against the rain, who looks like they want to give up, they're going to find their better. And their better will be The One, because that's why we're all here, that's what we're all doing here. People talk about the meaning of life as if it's some big mystery but it really isn't: the meaning of life is to meet The One and live happily ever after. It's really that simple.

I'd normally take the subway on a day like today, not just because the weather is so foul but because I want to look my best for Nicola, but pay day isn't for another three days and so the $14 I have in my bank account I need to leave in there just in case. I have enough food in my apartment to last me, so as long as any major disasters don't occur I should be okay. If Nicola invites me for a drink I'm totally, completely fucked. After her radio silence for the last week, however, I'm not hopeful she will. I might invite her for one, but later in the week, and only if the project goes okay. I cannot, will not, fuck this up.

By the time I reach my office I'm drenched, my shoes are squelching, carrying their own little puddles within themselves, and my jeans are stuck to my legs. The building is warm, not warm enough to dry anyone, however, just warm enough to make us all feel uncomfortable, and for the building to smell like damp. I cram in the elevator with about five other very wet, very unhappy people. No one says anything as the doors close, the unhappiness is palpable, like a sixth person, and we all just peel out silently at our respective floors.

The office is buzzing as usual when I arrive, despite the fact it's 7.48 and the world is even more of a nightmare than usual. There must be something in the air to be making people feel like this, maybe something has happened in the world that I'm not aware of, a Kardashian has died or gotten married or had a kid or something, a member of the Royal Family has died or got married or had a kid or something. Whatever it is, it must be big, because even Tom is here, not just on time but early, he's here even before I am. Neil isn't in yet which is good, because even though I'm on time, even a bit early myself, it's not a good look to arrive after Tom. Even though we all officially start at nine, but in actuality start at eight, really the official barometer for when the day starts is Tom; arrive before him, even if you're a little late, all is good. Arrive after him, even if you're a little early, all is bad. With this in mind I quickly sit down, take out and turn on my laptop and throw my wet bag under my desk. I'm just checking through my unread emails when I register the presence of someone looming near me. Assuming it's going to be Tom, or Neil finally made it in, or someone else otherwise uninteresting but I have to speak to in order to continue my favourite hobby of being paid, I look up and am startled to see it's Nicola. She's looking incredibly beautiful, impossibly well put together on a morning such as this. Her smile is bright, and I feel like I need sunglasses just to survive her being. I love her so much.

"Morning, Oliver," she says, unimaginable levels of pep in her voice. "You ready to get to it?"

*

149

Alicia Silverstone in *Clueless*, much like Renee Zellweger in *Empire Records*, is impossibly young and beautiful. She's just so incredibly beautiful it's heartbreaking in a certain way; in the way that you know, no matter what happens in your life, you're never going to be able to be with a young Alicia Silverstone. It's literally impossible, short of someone inventing time travel, that I'll be able to spend time with a 19-year-old Alicia Silverstone. Because that's all I want to do, spend time with her. Obviously I want to kiss her and touch her body and see her naked and make love to her, but that's not all; I want to know her, to get to know her, to find out everything about her. I want to watch her, just observe her as she goes about her day being so beautiful, being so perfect; so ethereal. I want to watch her touch things, look at them, study them. I want to watch her watch TV, or read a book, or go for a walk. I want to watch her eat dinner, go to a movie, see friends, have a few drinks. I want to drop her off at a bar to meet her friends, and then pick her up afterwards. I want to listen to her tell me all about it, I want to know what she had to drink, if she liked it, how it made her feel. I want to know it all, now and always, forever. I want to be with Alicia Silverstone.

Even if Sean Bateman says we can never know someone, so what? We can try. If we can never achieve perfection, we can practice and practice and steadily get closer. And that will be enough.

Besides, I have perfection in the form of Nicola. Alicia Silverstone isn't quite the girl of my dreams, but what Paul says in *(500) Days of Summer* still applies here: Nicola is better than the girls of my dreams; she's real.

Nicola *is* the girl of my dreams. And she *is* real. And she *is* sitting next to me, or rather I'm sitting next to her, and we're working together, and talking as if it's all good.

Which it is all good now, after she's explained her absence from my life for the past week.

I joined her at her desk, leaving all my wet shit at mine, taking just a pad and a pencil, accepting the empty chair she offered me and seating myself. After some small talk, the usual shit that happens a million times in a million offices all around the world every day, doubly so on a Monday, I was quite happy just to go with the flow, but she launched into a state of the union, which at the time I didn't want but now it's happened I'm glad it did; but also glad it's over.

"I'm sorry," she said, apropos of nothing.

"Sorry?" I answered, completely caught off guard.

"For last week, I'm sorry, for not replying to you and avoiding you here and stuff."

"That's okay," I said, though it very much wasn't. At least it wasn't at the time, again, but now it's done it's fine, again. It's all part of our journey, I thought. It doesn't matter how we get there, what matters is that we do. We will.

"It wasn't a great week to be honest. I drank too much at Jenn's, and after," please don't say it, "what happened between us I was really embarrassed and I just wanted to hide for a little while, let it all blow over."

"Listen, I'm—"

"—Please, you don't have to apologise. You did nothing wrong, it was an accident, one which I massively overreacted to. I'm really sorry I ran away, that must have made you feel awful."

Obviously it did.

"Not at all," I said to her, looking away to hide the lie in my eyes. "I was just worried about you, what I did was so stupid and I was really scared about what it would do to you. I know they say not all men, but it's definitely all women, and I didn't want to be that guy, you know?"

She touched my hand then, for a second, and it was everything.

"Thank you," she said, looking so deeply into my eyes I had to cough and look away. As much as I wanted to look back into hers it made me intensely uncomfortable and I couldn't hold her gaze.

"You're welcome. Are you okay?" I chanced asking, now I knew the answer was probably going to be yes.

"I am now that we're okay." My heart fluttered at hearing this. "I had a bad one last week, my sister isn't very well at the moment and that's been getting me down, she was supposed to come and stay with me for a few days but she wasn't up to it, and even though I know it's only something minor it set me off, you know, and then…"

She carried on talking but I zoned out. We were okay. We are okay. That's all that matters, we're okay. My little accidental crotch brush has been forgotten about, judged as the accident it truly was and put aside. I'm so glad, because if Nicola had decided that because of that I wasn't The One I would have been absolutely devastated. And worst of all, I wouldn't have blamed her. Sitting there on Elijah's couch after she'd fled I knew it was over, so to be sitting here, once again next to her, knowing it isn't, I cannot comprehend how it makes me feel. Joy beyond joy, relief beyond relief, hope for the future beyond, well, everything.

We've been working away all morning, the campaign is for some new tracking tool that lets companies know in real time where their trucks are. I'm pretty sure a bunch of software like this already exists, but the company we're doing the copy for is really excited about it, and as they're the ones paying us we're finding ourselves really excited about it, too. And hell, I'm finding that I actually am able to write, somewhat. I couldn't write a book or anything I don't think, I couldn't write a billion words or however many they usually are, but I can write slogans, I can write short paragraphs that hopefully sell shitty software to other shitty companies.

"How about: 'know where your trucks are before they do with our new app.'?"

"I like it," Nicola says, and she genuinely seems to. This shit is easy.

"Or something like: 'our app tracks your trucks so you don't have to.'"

"Yeah, that's really good too! Are you sure you haven't written copy before?"

"Nope, this is my first time." If only she knew it was my first time writing anything, at least since my master's thesis.

"Well you're a natural, we should have got you doing this a long time ago."

She's looking at me and smiling and all I can do is look at her and smile back. We must look like a pair of idiots to the rest of the office, two young people falling in love with each other. Which is what we are, but still, from the outside that kind of thing usually looks so funny. People aren't themselves when they're in love, they do things they wouldn't normally do, act and speak in ways that aren't natural to them.

No, that's wrong, completely wrong, I have it the wrong way round. When people are in love, they finally become themselves. All that giggling, the silly way people act, that's how they're supposed to be. Before people fall in love they're not themselves, they're just a poor facsimile of the person they're one day going to be, a lousy imitation. Love for humans is sort of like chrysalis for butterflies: you're born this small, weird, ugly little grub, and you grub along, doing grubby little things, and then you finally meet The One, and you emerge this

153

wonderful butterfly, you become the glorious creature you were always supposed to be. Love is transformative, yes, but it only transforms people into who they should be. Love changes people, but only because they weren't themselves previously.

Nicola excuses herself to go to the bathroom so I take the opportunity to stretch my legs, get a break from all the writing, go and get some water. I'm in the kitchen filling a glass when I hear Tom and Neil laughing behind me, and turning I see them enter the kitchen.

"Well?" Neil says to me.

"Well, what?" I say, feigning ignorance.

"Don't be a dick," Tom says.

"*Tom*," Neil says to him. "Remember where we are. But he's right," Neil says, turning to me. "Well how's it going with Nicola, obviously."

"Oh, yeah, really well thanks, we're getting some great copy down, I think this campaign is going to be a really good one."

"And?"

"And what?"

"For fuck's…" Tom mutters under his breath as Neil puts his hand to his face in exasperation.

"I know I shouldn't say this," Neil says, "but I don't give a fuck about the campaign. How's it going with Nicola, you know, *with* Nicola?"

"Oh, right, yeah," I say, finally giving in and getting to what they want to hear. "It's going really well, I think."

"I heard her apology this morning," Tom says. "Do you believe her?"

I pause for a moment. Of course I believe her, why wouldn't I?

"Of course I believe her, why wouldn't I?"

"I dunno," Tom says. "Women lie don't they?"

Neil and I both look at him, neither of us saying

anything. There are several things I want to say, but none of them possible here in the office if I want to keep my job. Which at this moment I do more than anything in the world. Glancing at his face, I think Neil is thinking the same thing. Luckily we're saved by the arrival of the woman herself.

"Oh, there you are," she says, smiling at me. I die with happiness. "I've been looking for you." Tom and Neil exchange a look which Nicola can't see. I want to frown at them, their immaturity, but I force myself to ignore them and focus on Nicola.

"What can I do for you? Shall we get back to it?"

"We're actually just going out to grab some food, a few of the team. You coming?"

Of course I am, fuck me I am, I've only just heard of this occasion and I immediately can't wait.

"Yeah, sounds good."

Nicola smiles, and it fills my heart with wonder. Her face is a painting when she does, she's beautiful under normal circumstances, but when she smiles it's like her beauty finds another level, she's a car with a 6th gear, we move to plains not even I thought possible. God she's amazing.

"Great, I'll meet you by the elevators in 2?"

She turns and walks away, presumably to her desk to get her jacket and bag and stuff. Tom and Neil exchange another look before turning to grin at me, but I'm already moving, heading to my desk to grab my coat. It's still soaking wet, but a glance out the window tells me the weather has improved, the rain has stopped even if only slightly, so I figure I'll be okay without it. I move into the lobby and when Nicola sees me she smiles and presses the button for the elevators. One arrives and she gets on, I follow behind her, and she presses the button for the ground floor and then we stand side by side, silent but not awkward, not saying anything but not needing to. I feel something on my hand and when I look down I see it's Nicola, she's reaching out her hand to hold mine. I take hers hungrily and we remain in silence, holding each other, and I can feel her, feel her power emanating through her entire body and concentrated in this one hand. Her palm is soft, her fingers small and slender, I feel like an old man holding a tiny child's hand, but it feels right, it feels normal, it feels correct. My hand feels like it's finally, once again, where it's supposed to be. I turn to tell her this just as she turns to face me, and my words get caught in my throat. We look at each other for a moment, and then she closes her eyes and leans towards me, and I close mine and lean towards her, and I can sense her lips close to mine, I can feel that this is it, this is our moment. And then with a ding the elevator doors open and she jumps back from me, I open my eyes to see her composing herself before leaving the elevator and greeting the rest of the team. I'm upset, but only a little. If we didn't kiss then it's because we weren't meant to kiss then. I'm dying to kiss her, of course I am, to move our relationship to the next level, but I can wait. We'll kiss when we kiss, not a moment before. And it'll be perfect.

Chapter Seven:

Fast Times at Ridgemont High

I'm still not sleeping, but it's improving. In the ten days following the first ten I was up to 35 hours sleep, and in the following ten I hit 42. Still far from where I should be, but definitely trending in the right direction. I stopped counting after those two periods, I was worried it might become an obsession of mine, meticulously recording when I fell asleep, when I woke up, creating spreadsheets and all that jazz; apparently tracking data for work — who actually pay me to do so — is too much of a ball ache, but doing it for myself is just fine. Go figure.

The project with Nicola is going well. The work project that is, not the dating one. The dating one has kinda stalled, but that's okay, we'll get there. Since our near-kiss in the elevator there hasn't been any sign that we might be moving things to the next level, but that's okay because there hasn't been the opportunity. When we got our first batch of potential copy done, Nicola took them to her boss who was heavily involved for a little while. Once we had the approved copy Nicola then took it to the design team, who were heavily involved for a little while. And then, once the designs were created and signed off, Nicola took those to the advertising team and the digital team, in order to get the designs both online and plastered on billboards and ads around the city. Billboards for a logistics tracking app, what an exciting world we've built around ourselves.

With all those people being so heavily involved Nicola and I have barely had two minutes alone together. I've considered asking her for a drink but we've been pulling long days, working into the evenings regularly, the client is pumping money into this project like nobody's business so we're being leaned on to make sure the money is well spent, and therefore keeps coming. I can handle it: whilst writing ad copy for a logistics app isn't exactly like writing *War and Peace* or something, or creating a Shakespeare play that will last for hundreds of years in the cultural zeitgeist, at least it's creating something. I can go out into the city now and see my words, blown up hundreds of times in size, proudly shouting from the side of a building, or much smaller on the side of a cab or the front of a newspaper. God forbid newspapers show news, eh? I can walk through Times Square and see my words, see myself become part of the myriad ads shining down on people. I am now both sides of the coin, the dream and the nightmare.

Even though what I'm creating is still disposable, is still fleeting, it's better than just running endless reports, producing a billion different Excel sheets with endless rows of numbers and columns. Sure, they also mean something, but they don't matter. Not that my ad slogans matter, but at least they're there. Other people can see them, so I know they exist. Even if only for a short while.

Cleavage, cleavage, cleavage: according to Regina Spektor that's what summer in the city means. That's definitely true, but sadly the opposite is also true: winter in the city means literally no cleavage, no cleavage, no cleavage. Winter in the city means layers, layers, layers. I'm taking the subway to work more often, I always do at this time of year: New York in December is not the time to be walking around, strolling uptown for an hour in the elements. No, it's the time to be rushing from one covering to the next, rushing from my apartment building to the subway — doing my best not to fall and kill myself on the wet cobbles on my street — and then from the subway to my office building. It's about spending as little time in the open air as possible because the air is sinister, it's out to get everyone. No, that's not fair. Weather can't be sinister, it can't be good or bad, weather has no morality. Only humans have morality, only humans have managed to make it so there are good and bad things. The weather does what the weather does, the climate and all that other stuff guides it down a path. And that path means that in mid-December it's minus five degrees and I hate my life. I mean, even more than usual.

You'd think being from London I'd be used to shitty winters, would find them a piece of cake, but New York winters are something else. The thing about England is, it's not a land of extremes, it's a land of mediocrity. England is grey nearly all year round, but that's all, it's just grey. It rains a lot, but not even that much in comparison to other countries. Look at how much it rains in tropical countries, for example; their precipitation levels put England to shame. It gets hot in England in the summer, but not that hot nor for that long. Maybe 30 degrees for a couple of weeks if we're lucky: again, nothing compared to other countries, take Thailand for example where it regularly hits 40 degrees, and will be above 30 for months on end. Puts England to shame. Even the cold: England is famously cold, but it isn't actually that cold. During the worst parts of winter it might reach minus five, maybe push minus 10, but again only for a week, maybe two. Usually the temperature just hovers slightly above zero, the world not quite frozen but not far from it. We can't even do snow right: we might get a day or two of good, layered snow; mostly, however, the snow comes after rain, which means that rather than being a beautiful white winterland, England is usually just a grey, slushy mess. I can relate to that, though, to be fair, I often feel like a grey, slushy mess. It's not comforting, not by a long shot, but it certainly is familiar.

No amount of winters in London — and I survived over 20 of them — prepared me for winter in New York. The first year I was here, after about three days I wanted to go home. It gets cold here, like real fucking cold. And not just cold, but the city freezes, too; New York doesn't have anywhere near as much rain as London, so when the snow and ice hit, they stay. There's nothing quite like skating down the street, completely against your own will, just praying you won't hit anyone or go flying off the curb and be mown down by a truck or something. As a kid my family had taken me to both Orlando and LA; what this meant was that my idea of America was warped, and in my head it was this land of eternal sunshine, warm all year round, no one even owns jeans, you just wear shorts every day, even Christmas Day. So when I was packing to come to New York, aside from the fact I was only bringing one suitcase so had to be quite strict with what I could pack, I gleefully cast asunder my winter gear. "I'm going to America," I told myself. "Fuck this winter noise, this can all stay in England where it belongs. I'm going where the sunshine is."

And I did, for a time at least. Arriving in the September, it was still sunny, it was still warm, for a few weeks my clothing choice was vindicated. Until it very much wasn't. I now own, once again, all the requisite winter gear, countless pairs of gloves, scarves, hats, all that jazz. But on the third day arriving at lectures with literal ice in my beard, with snot frozen on my upper lip, with my hands shaking and it taking genuinely nearly 'til midday for them to thaw, I regretted a lot of things. And not the usual regret where it's my actions I regret, but the regret of being exposed to circumstances outside your control and not being prepared for them. So I suppose yeah, regret at my own actions, but really regret at my own inaction. I hadn't done anything stupid, but I hadn't done anything, and that was stupid.

One good thing about New York in winter is that the city has this city-wide, like, reverse aircon system. Every building, and even the streets, have these vents that constantly pump out hot air. You'll have seen them on TV, when people are walking the streets there's always steam coming up from somewhere. It comes from these vents, built into the road, the sidewalk, into people's homes; I don't know what the deal is, but I assume they're outlets from the subway. Like the underground in London it's always warm down there, and being a contained system I suppose the warmth has to go somewhere, otherwise it'll just heat up until people are cooking. And it can't go down, because down is just solid rock, the centre of the earth where I guess it's even hotter. And so the hot air comes up, and we all get to feel it. In the summer it sucks, it's warm enough in the city without artificial warmth being pumped in. In winter it's a lifesaver, genuinely I reckon it'll have saved the lives of lots of old people. If there are any in New York: now that I think about it, I don't think I've seen a single one since I arrived. But they must be here, somewhere. Perhaps they're all on the Upper West Side, or up in Harlem, or even upstate. Wherever they are, it's not between Soho and Times Square that's for sure.

The thing about summer is, Nicola is a fan of cleavage, cleavage, cleavage. The thing about winter is, Nicola is a fan of layers, layers, layers. The only skin she shows is from the neck up, and whilst that's not a total bummer, it is a shame. I'll see it all at some point I suppose, but I want to see it now. It'll be great to see her naked, it'll be the culmination of a lifetime's existence, but seeing bits of skin, being teased, is always fun, too. Lets the imagination run wild. Fuck me, I need to ask her out. It's all well and good relying on fate, but fate can't, doesn't, do the heavy lifting. I need to stop relying on it. I'm going to stop relying on it. Oh fuck, I'm going to ask her out. Oh fuck.

Elijah has invited me out for drinks, just the two of us. I know he just wants to find out what's going on with Nicola, but still, it's always nice to be invited somewhere, nice to be included. Especially as he said he'll pay, which is a huge weight off my mind. Sometimes it's good being so poor, because when I don't want to do something, don't want to go somewhere, I have a ready-made excuse that's almost always not a lie. Then again, other times it can be incredibly frustrating when there are things I want to do, like go out for drinks with an old friend, or take a woman out on a date, or eat nice food and put my heating on.

That's my current worry with Nicola, what's stopping me asking her out: can I actually afford to take her out? This city is fucking expensive, and life in general is expensive too, so much of each pay check I get just immediately disappears, whether to my landlord, the electricity company, Netflix, whoever. I don't even get to see it, as this all happens whilst I'm asleep, or at least trying to sleep; the money is transferred from my company to me about 2am, and then at like 2.03am it's sent to all the various companies to whom I give money for the simple pleasure of existing. I see it in the rearview mirror when I check my banking app in the morning but it's not the same. Even knowing I have a roof over my head for another month gives me no pleasure, when I think of all that I gave in exchange for it. My labour is not being sold at a fair price if you ask me; but then again, that price could always be lower, so I guess I should be thankful for what I've got. Even if I don't really have anything.

Elijah and I meet in Ernie's, which is really a student bar full of people impossibly young and impossibly full of joie de vivre, but I don't mind it. Even once I get past beggars being choosers and all that, it's nice to be in a place surrounded by people surrounded by life. The not sleeping has begun to make my apartment seem even smaller and more cramped than it actually is, every night the walls advance on me a little bit more. The quiet becomes overwhelming, and no amount of watching TV will help. It's nice to be surrounded by three-dimensional people, and real people too, not actors like you see on TV, or the ones in reality shows. Because it's all acting, all the way from the top to the bottom. Hell, everyone in here is acting, too, even if only just a little bit, but that's okay because I'm also acting. We're all acting like this is okay! We're having a good time! I'm happy to be alive at this period in time! I definitely don't fear climate change making the planet uninhabitable in my lifetime! New York will be under water in a few years and so will I! Yay!

Entering the bar I'm greeted by a welcome rush of hot air, both from the heater above the door and also coming generally from the many bodies packed into the place. I stand on the doormat and take a moment to compose myself, taking off my hat, scarf, and gloves and shaking the snow off them. I stomp my feet, both to get the snow off my shoes and to try and bring some life back into my toes, and looking down at the mat I feel bad because I've fairly covered it in fine white powder.

But looking at the rest of the floor, the lack of dry space available reassures me. It'd be weird if I was the only one who arrived here wet considering the weather. Once I'm feeling okay, holding what feels like my entire winter wardrobe in my hands, I scan the crowd; I may only be 28, but in here I feel incredibly old. The average age must be 21, maybe 22 at a push; college students home for the holidays, meeting up with old school friends, people they haven't seen since September. The noise is raucous, toasts being called almost continually from the various tables, the clinking of glasses and bottles a continuous backdrop to the hum of energy the place has. There's talking, shouting, singing, laughing, crying, you name it: every emotion that exists in the human range of feeling is in this bar tonight, and being around it, being a part of it, makes me feel good. Well, not good, but okay: I feel a part of life, a part of the world. I don't get this feeling often, mostly I feel like an alien on the outside looking in, so I'm going to try and savour it. How, I have no idea. But I'll try.

I spot Elijah across the bar; he doesn't see me so I take a moment to regard him. He's on his phone, obviously it's impossible for me to hear what he's saying, I'd probably struggle even if I were standing next to him, but I can see his face and he doesn't look happy, his cheeks and forehead are red, his eyes are narrowed and he looks, frankly, absolutely furious. He's gesticulating wildly with the hand not holding the phone, to the point where he almost knocks a tray out of the hands of a passing waitress, who dodges him with a practised ease. She scowls at him before continuing but he doesn't even look at her, doesn't seem to notice. I realise that he's probably not going to hang up the phone until I get over there, if I wait for him to end his conversation I'll be waiting all night, so I move across the room, doing my best to dodge other patrons, flying beer, waitresses. I'm not nearly as practised as the staff and I bump into several people, a couple spilling their drinks on me; by the time I make it to Elijah's table I feel like I've been in a war, although obviously the mildest war in history. The Great Room Traversal of 2023. Doesn't have much of a ring to it.

I catch glimpses of Elijah's conversation over the noise as I arrive at his table, something about an appointment, he'll pay of course, let him know, but when he sees me he quickly tells the person he has to go and hangs up without saying goodbye. Still looking angry, although now looking a bit shaken, too, he stands and embraces me, and I let him. He's damp, whether from snow or sweat or what I don't want to know, thankfully he doesn't prolong the hug and I'm soon released and able to perch on the stool opposite his.

"Oliver, my man, how's it going?"

By the sounds of it he's already had a couple of drinks, and now I look at the table there are two empty glasses and his third is well on its way to joining them.

"I'm good thanks, mate, how're you?"

"*Mate.* God, you don't hear that much over here," he laughs, before polishing off his drink and very rudely waving to a nearby waitress to order another, at the last-minute remembering to order one for me. He doesn't ask what I want, simply gets a pint like he has, but that's fine. Pints are hard to come by in America, beer mostly comes in bottles, and it isn't enough. Sometimes you just need a good pint.

"Nah, people around here look at you like they're insane if you call them mate. Like it's a promise or something, you're trying to get them to sign a social contract. People over here take the word far too seriously."

"You got that right, mate," Elijah says with a laugh and what I think is a tipsy attempt at a wink. It does not go well, but I ignore it and so does he.

"How's Jenn?" I ask, the atmosphere lifting my spirits by the second; the place is packed enough that I can't see any windows, so sitting here in the warmth I can almost imagine winter doesn't exist. The waitress soon returns with our beers and we clink glasses, neither of us saying anything to mark the toast.

Elijah hesitates before he answers, it's only a short hesitation but it definitely is one.

"She's good thanks, away for a few days in Boston seeing some college buddies."

"Oh, cool," I say. "I didn't know she went to college there?"

"Yeah, she went to Harvard, the little genius."

"Wow," I say, genuinely impressed. "That's so cool, what did she study?"

Elijah doesn't answer my question, however; instead he's staring at his phone, which I can just see over the edge of the table, I think he's trying to hide it from me but he's too drunk and isn't doing a good enough job. The screen is lit up white which I think means an incoming call, and I can see a name, Mia maybe, I'm not sure. Normally this kind of thing wouldn't bother me but Elijah is being very weird about it, which means something must be up.

"Who's Mia?" I ask, trying to put a laugh in my voice, make it seem like a casual question. Elijah takes it as an accusation apparently.

"Mia?" he snaps at me. "What Mia? Who's Mia? I don't know, man, who is Mia? What are you saying?"

It's clearly a touchy subject, one I think I should probably explore but I don't, it's not my place, I'm just here for a few drinks with a new old friend, I don't need any drama. I have enough of my own shit going on without getting involved in anyone else's. I don't say anything, just take a sip of my beer, feeling its coolness refresh me, the alcohol warm me, the entire thing settle me.

"You okay, man?" I eventually do say after a few minutes of silence during which Elijah continues to stare at his phone, no longer lit up. He jumps at my words.

"What? Yeah, sorry, distracted. Holidays, you know?"

I don't, but I nod my head regardless.

"It's really busy at work, projects all going off at the same time, the mad rush to get stuff done before the office closes next week."

"They working you hard, then?" I say, trying to keep it vague. I still don't even know what Elijah does, I'm still not entirely sure why this sudden resurgence in our friendship. I'm not unhappy about it, not by a long shot, but some clarity wouldn't go amiss.

"Oh, yeah," he laughs, nervously, "always. Listen, can I ask you something?" He leans across the table conspiratorially as he says this and I can't help but lean in too, the moment seems to call for it.

"Go ahead."

"Thanks, man. A friend of mine, this guy from work called Simon, he's been having an affair behind his wife's back and now the other woman is pregnant."

"Shit man, that's heavy."

"Tell me about it. So now he doesn't know what to do, whether or not to keep the kid or get an abortion, and whether or not to tell his wife."

"Fuck man, that's a pickle and a half."

"Right?"

"Honestly man, not very helpful I know but I have no idea."

"Really?" Elijah says, not impressed. I try and bullshit

a little to make myself seem less useless. Wait a minute, that'd be a good line for my tombstone. Story of my life, as Alison Poole would say.

"I dunno, mate, I think I need more details. Do he and his wife have any kids? How long has the affair been going on? How long have they been married, he and his wife?"

"No kids, a couple of months he said, and they've been married for nearly four years, actually shit no it is four now, it'll be five next year."

"Wow, heavy. So deffo more than a one-night stand if it's been going on for months then?"

"Yeah, I mean he said he really likes her, and he never wanted kids, neither did his wife, but now M—this other woman is pregnant he's realised he does actually want kids, and is really excited."

Did he just...? Surely not, I must have imagined it.

"And what about the two women, who does he love more?"

"His wife, obviously," Elijah says full of confidence. He seems to know an awful lot of intimate details about his friend Simon that he can reel off at the drop of a hat. "He really, really likes the other woman, but he loves and adores his wife."

"Does she want to have kids?"

"No, absolutely no interest."

"Shit man, that's intense. What a shitshow."

"Tell me about it," Elijah mutters into his beer as he drains it off, once again immediately flagging a waitress for another. He looks at me but I shake my head, I'm barely a third of the way through mine. "So what do you think?"

"I dunno, man. On the one hand he loves his wife and wants to be with her, but if he wants kids and she doesn't, then it's complicated. If he's been with this woman for a few months then he clearly likes her, too, and with the kid and all."

"So?"

"So what, mate?"

"So what should he do?" Elijah's beer comes and he signals to the waitress to wait a minute; he downs it in one go and orders another, and I make a mental note to leave the waitress a large tip as not only does she deserve it, but I don't think Elijah will. "Should he stay or should he go?"

It's my turn to laugh now.

"Maybe he should ask The Clash?"

Elijah does not look amused.

"I honestly don't know, mate," I say to him. And I honestly don't; my entire life I've struggled to get one woman to give me attention, so getting two is unfathomable. And anyway, why would you bother cheating on your wife? If you've married the woman clearly she's the one? So why have you gone elsewhere? That's not how it works.

I realise as I say this that I do know, and I tell Elijah.

"He should stay with his wife," I announce, drinking the last of my beer. I'm happy to wait for the waitress but Elijah isn't, waving her over once more.

"Do you think?"

"Yeah, I think, no I know, he definitely should."

"Why?"

"What do you mean why?"

"I dunno, I mean why should I—he stay with his wife, not go off with his mistress?"

Another slip; is Elijah talking about himself? I don't think so, but just in case I'm glad I said 'Simon' should stay with his wife, who definitely isn't Jenn.

"Yeah, he absolutely should. He married her because he loves her, and you said he still does, more so than his mistress. So he should stay with his wife, she's clearly the one."

"Okay, that makes sense." Elijah visibly relaxes, his shoulders slump as if a great weight has been lifted from them. "Next question: should he tell his wife?"

"Fuck no!" I say without even thinking. I didn't realise that this is how I feel, but apparently my subconscious does and is happy to speak for me.

"Why?"

"I have no idea," I say once again. "I just think maybe in this case, ignorance is bliss?"

Elijah relaxes even more, draining his beer and ordering another. I'm a little worried by how much and how quickly he's drinking but I don't say anything, it isn't my place. I guess he's just having fun with Jenn being away, being the college boy he once was again, if only for a few days.

"Enough about m—Simon," he says. "How's Nicola?"

Nicola is The One. Much like how for Stacy in *Fast Times*, Mark is The One, and for Mark, Stacy is The One. Mark knows it right away, the moment he first lays eyes on her in biology class. For Stacy, it takes a little time for the penny to drop; she dates Ron Johnson, and then after her first failed date with Mark, she dates Mike Damone, Mark's best friend, in a classic dick move. She's only a kid though, nearly everyone in the film is, so they can all be forgiven their sins. If a person can't make mistakes in childhood then when can they?

Fast Times is based on a book written by Cameron Crowe, so you know it's all real. Lots of stuff happens, most of it fairly typical high school bullshit, but the most important storyline is that of Mark and Stacy. We see a lot of Linda, Stacy's best friend, who's already found her

170

one, he just happens to be in Chicago for the time being. But really, the most important thing that happens is Mark and Stacy find each other. Hell, she loses her virginity, at 15, to a 26-year-old under a graffiti-covered bridge. She's a long way from The One, until she's right there with him. And then everything's okay: they don't have sex, because they don't need to have sex, They have each other, that's all they need.

That the film is based on a book, a non-fiction book at that, just goes to show how real it is. And the two main people involved, they understand. Cameron Crowe wrote the book, as well as the screen play; he also directed *Say Anything* several years later. Amy Heckerling, who directed *Fast Times*, also directed *Clueless*. These people understand, they know; they know, like The Beatles told us all those years ago, that love is all you need. You just have to find The One.

At risk of sounding like a broken record, *Fast Times* stars Jennifer Jason Leigh and Phoebe Cates, both of whom are, you guessed it, impossibly young and impossibly beautiful. When Mark first approaches Stacy and asks for her number, after she gives it to him and he walks away she bites her lip in a way that honestly could probably end wars, if not also start them. And what can be said about Phoebe Cates, other than two words: red bikini.

Fast Times was released in 1982, 13 years before I even existed on this planet. Stacy regularly describes things as 'classic', and the film, whilst ostensibly about a high school year, is really about meeting The One and falling in love. Some things never change. Some things never go out of style.

*

171

I asked her out. I did it, I asked her out. And face to face and everything, I didn't text her, despite the fact I was dying to. It went down like this:

Friday, the Friday just gone, the last Friday in the office before Christmas. The office closes from the 22ⁿᵈ and reopens on 3ʳᵈ January, giving us all a couple of weeks off, which is sorely needed. A few people have to be on call, check their emails every couple of days, but I'm not one of those, and neither is Nicola. Our project has finished, the final designs have come to life and can still be seen around New York. I'm not sure what's going to happen next year with regards me and copy writing, but I suppose I'll find out. 2024 will have in store for me whatever it does, that is a bridge that will be crossed as and when.

I didn't plan to ask her out, not when I did anyway. Of course I planned in general to ask her out, but I didn't plan to do it on that Friday, it just kinda happened. It was the end of the day, well the end of that day anyway, which was 2pm. Really, work finished the day before and the Friday was just about the end of the year; it was like being back at school, the last day of term. Everyone was giddy, people were packing things away, taking what they'd need from the office for the following two weeks. I wasn't especially involved; since the project with Nicola had ended I was back at my desk, and had nothing to do. All my reports were run, the year closed off with the exception of a couple I'll have to do at the beginning of January. Being away from Nicola, the little enthusiasm I'd garnered for my work was gone, had gone away from me, and I was back in my corner, ignored by the masses, tolerated by Tom and Neil. Normally this was my special place, a spot reserved just for me that if I didn't bask in, I at least was content in. Content-ish. As content as anyone can be when they're actually really, deeply unhappy.

However, spending time with Nicola, I wanted more. I do want more. Now I know there is more, that it *is* possible.

By mid-morning people had gotten into the alcohol we keep on hand for entertaining clients, and bottles of beer and glasses of prosecco were being handed out. I took a beer, not because I wanted it but because not taking it would have led to conversations, and I wasn't in the mood for them. Working with Nicola had lifted me out of my funk for a little while, but I was slowly sliding back into it. The darkness was rising back up around me, was enveloping once more. I was glad it was the last day in the office, was looking forward to a little break, some time to myself. I knew I was going to be lonely, but loneliness is easy, I know loneliness, I *understand* loneliness. It's being around people that doesn't make any sense to me.

So I was reluctantly sipping my beer, trying to draw it out until it was time to go, when Nicola came over to my desk. She was wearing her standard winter work outfit, black jeans and a dark coloured turtle neck sweater; she had them in all colours, from dark red to dark blue, from dark grey to black. Despite being covered from her toes to literally her chin she still looked amazing, she had this easy grace with which she could pull it off. I felt like shit sitting there in my ill-fitting shirt and dirty jeans. I was also overdue a haircut and hadn't shaved for a few weeks: I dread to think how I looked sitting next to her, an unkempt troll person and a Madonna.

Tom wasn't at his desk so Nicola sat in his chair, and for a while neither of us said anything. She had a glass of prosecco at which she sipped, and I sipped my beer, and for a while they were the only noises emanating from us. I wanted to say something, start the conversation, but I didn't know what. While we were working together it had

173

been so easy, we had work to discuss, we had to talk, but it being over meant that our status as colleagues was back to being tenuous, we worked for the same company in the same department but that was all. I was relieved when, after emptying her glass and placing it on Tom's desk, she finally spoke to me.

"Are you looking forward to Christmas, Oli?" I'd grown to like it when she shortened my name; I couldn't stand it when anyone else did, but from her mouth it just sounded different.

"Not even a little bit," I said, completely honestly. "The break from work, yes, Christmas itself, fuck no." She looked incredibly disheartened by my response and I wondered if I should have lied. Never mind, too late.

"I've never been a fan. I mean, I'm away from my family, my friends are all busy, it's a lonely time of year."

"Why don't you see your family?"

"Well they're back in England, and they refuse to fly out here, and I can't afford to fly home, so…" I trailed off with a shrug.

"That's so sad, I'm so sorry." She laid a hand on my arm as she said this, and I could feel the pressure from it, the warmth of her palm. My heart started beating faster, my mouth suddenly became very dry.

"What do you have planned?"

"Oh nothing fancy, I'm going to stay in Boston with my parents, and my brother is coming from LA with his new wife. It's going to be a total hassle to be honest," she said, sighing. "My parents much prefer him to me, and they're not shy about mentioning it. Perfect Ben with his perfect education and perfect wife and perfect job and soon I'm sure he'll have some perfect little children so my parents will have perfect grandchildren. It's just like, urgh, can you not?"

I nodded as she spoke as if I understood what she

was saying, but once she finished speaking I had nothing to say, didn't know how to respond.

"That sucks," was my incredibly lame reply. But she seemed to appreciate it.

"It does suck, Oli, thank you for saying so."

"So when do you leave the city?"

"Tomorrow morning, my train leaves Grand Central at 11.30."

"Do you want to go for a drink tonight?"

The words were out of my mouth before I even realised what was happening; I think it took her a moment too because something flashed over her face, it looked like a shadow, and she was quiet for a moment or two before she answered.

"Yeah, that sounds great."

"Awesome," I said, my heart now pounding in my chest, my stomach tying itself in knots, my every dream coming true. Although my bank balance flashing across my mind quickly dampened my excitement. That is until Nicola spoke again, and my excitement reached fever pitch.

"Instead of going out, though, shall I just come over to yours?"

Oh fuck. Fuck yes.

"Yeah, if you'd like."

"I mean, if you don't want me to…"

"No, no, no, I'd love for you to, I mean I'd like you to, I mean, erm…" I was panicking, I couldn't get my thoughts aligned nor get my words out of my mouth with any kind of sense. "I'd be delighted if you came over to mine. Not just because it's 3 days before Christmas and I have no money!"

I tried to say this jokingly, despite the words being true, but if Nicola got it she didn't find it amusing. She gave me a wan little smile, before slowly rising from

Tom's chair, not a moment too soon as he returned to take her place.

"I'll text you my address," I said to her as she walked away. I wasn't aware the conversation was over, but her departure made it harder to continue.

"Text her your address, will you?" Tom said, a sly look on his face. I didn't say anything, just looked at him, trying to keep my own face as neutral as possible. "And just why exactly will you be texting Nicola your address?"

I could see Neil looking at me now too from the corner of my eye, the pair of them had turned to face me and were apparently hanging on my every word, despite the fact I hadn't actually said anything to either of them.

"Wait," Tom said, a look of seriousness falling on him. "Is Nicola actually going to your apartment tonight?"

"She is," I confirmed, continuing to maintain my façade of neutrality.

"And you're going to be there?"

"I am."

"Oh shit, this is big," Tom said, a huge shit-eating grin now on his face. Neil had one, too, and it was all I could do to keep my calm, not flee from these grinning freaks, or even start grinning like them.

Thankfully I was saved from any further interrogation from the sound of a spoon being tapped against a glass. Silence descended on the room as we all turned to the source of the noise and saw Brielle standing on a small box, apparently about to give a speech.

"Thank you, everyone," she began, to rapturous cheers and applause. Evidently some people had imbibed more of the holiday spirit than others. "Thank you for an excellent year. We're on course to not only surpass our targets but smash them. All metrics are up across the board, with brand awareness hitting an all-time high amongst consumers."

Another cheer greeted this piece of information, and from the way some people hugged each other you'd have thought it was fucking VJ day or something, that we'd all been saved from a terrifying, bloody death.

"Soon it will all begin again," light-hearted boos greeted this, "but for now, go and enjoy your Christmases." No one moved. "I'm serious, go home. Or go to the bar, or go wherever; you don't have to go home, but you can't stay here."

She stepped down from her box and people started streaming away. I quickly shoved everything into my bag and, grabbing it and my coat, practically ran to the elevators, and after they took several million years to arrive and grant me entrance, I practically ran to the subway. Nicola, *the* Nicola, was coming over. I had to fucking clean.

It's 6pm. My apartment is as clean as it's ever going to be, at least without the intervention of a small army of underpaid, overworked labourers. I haven't done much cleaning because the place didn't require cleaning per se, but tidying; most of what I've done is shove piles of clothes into my wardrobe, shove piles of books haphazardly onto shelves, shove my lazy personality back into its box.

I stand in the living room area of the apartment and look around. It isn't the most inviting place, being tiny and filled with man things, but considering by the time I got home I had just three hours to sort it out, I don't think I've done too bad a job. Short of a team of carpenters guided by the *Queer Eye* gang, I'm not sure who could have done much better.

I just wish I had some Christmas decorations, even just a string of fairy lights or something. I have nothing: I don't decorate for Christmas, I never have, but it's never been an issue until now. Hopefully Nicola won't mention it, won't focus on it; I'd say I hope she wouldn't notice, but if she didn't I'd be worried for her powers of sight. It's pretty fucking obvious, this must be the only apartment in the entire city not lit up for Santa's arrival. I guess except for the Jewish and Muslim ones? And whoever else doesn't celebrate?

I stopped at a liquor store on my way home and spent the last of my cash on a couple of bottles of prosecco; nothing too fancy, because I can't afford them, but not the really cheap stuff, as much as my budget wanted me to, because I like this woman, hell I fucking love this woman, and I want to treat her as well as I'm able. Which I don't think is very well, but I'm trying my best, I'm doing everything I can.

She's due any second; when I messaged her my address earlier she asked if six was okay, said she didn't want to be out too late, still had to pack and even though her train wasn't until nearly midday she said she'd like to be up early, make sure she was ready. To me this definitely means she won't be staying over, which means sex is definitely off the table, but I'm getting too far ahead of myself, anyway. I definitely am not thinking about sex, not at all. I'm just thinking about seeing her.

I'm startled from a reverie I didn't even know I'd entered by a knock at the door. That must be her. Fuck, this is it. This is when it all starts. This is the beginning of the rest of my life.

"Hi, Nicola."

"Hi, Oli, thanks for inviting me."

"Not at all, thank you for coming. Can I take your coat?"

"Here you go, thanks."

178

"No problem. After you."

"Thanks. Where shall I put these bottles?"

"What are they?"

"Prosecco."

"Oh wow, thanks. The fridge will be fine. It's just there in the corner."

"You already have a couple in here."

"Great minds and all that."

"..."

"You made it here okay, then?"

"Yeah it was fine, subway was a bit carnage, drunk people going out and going home and going god knows where, but basically it was a piece of cake."

"Good stuff. I'm so glad you could make it, I've been wanting to do this for ages."

"Me too."

"Here you go."

"Thank you. Cheers."

"Cheers to you. Happy Christmas."

"Happy Christmas to you, too. Oof, this stuff is a bit..."

"It is, isn't it? I don't normally drink prosecco, but even I know this stuff isn't great. I'm sorry."

"That's okay, I'm sure we'll live. As long as it gets me drunk I don't mind."

"Is that your plan, get drunk?"

"Absolutely. I'm going to be drunk for the next few days, it's the only way to survive my family, so I might as well get a head start."

"Are they really that bad?"

"My family? Don't even get me started."

"I'm sorry, let's talk about something else."

"It's not that they're bad, per se, it's just, I dunno..."

"I'm sorry."

"I guess it's just different, since my mom had her

affair."

"Oh wow, shit, I'm sorry to hear that, that sucks. Refill?"

"Please."

"Here you go."

"Thanks."

"So your mum had an affair?"

"..."

"You don't have to talk about—"

"—I don't even know if affair is the right word, to be honest I'm not really sure what happened. I know my mom definitely slept with someone else, on at least two occasions, but that's all I can get out of my brother."

"Your brother?"

"Oh yeah, Mom and Dad will discuss things with him, but god forbid I find anything out."

"Shit. How come?"

"I dunno, I think they're just old fashioned, conservative with a small-c. I'm a woman, my fragile heart doesn't need to be burdened with things like this."

"But what about your brother?"

"Oh, he's just like dad, that's why he and my mum both like him so much."

"Shit, I'm sorry."

"Thanks. It's just like, I'm 26 you know? I'm an adult, I can handle it. I've been cheated on myself, I know how it goes."

"I'm sorry you've been cheated on, that must be awful."

"It is, yeah, literally the worst thing I can imagine."

"I bet, it must be awful. Refill?"

"Thanks."

"Do you mind if I ask what happened?"

"Oh, the usual, he went on a friend's bachelor weekend and fucked a stripper, classic tale.

"Shit."

"Yeah, very shit."

"I didn't realise that actually happened in real life, I thought it was just the movies."

"Tell me about it, I was surprised too. I think that made it worse."

"What did?"

"How, I dunno, how *typical* it was ."

"Yeah."

"It's just, fucking men you know? No offence, present company excluded, but men are just fucking awful, you know? Like, if he'd met someone and fallen in love with her, that would have sucked but I would have understood, but the fact it was a stripper? I mean, come on, cliché much?"

"Yeah, at least if he met The One it wouldn't be so bad to stand aside and let them be happy."

"What do you mean?"

"Well, like, The One, if the piece of shit who cheated on you found the person he was supposed to be with, was destined for, then there's nothing you could do, and besides, it'd be a good thing, because that would mean they weren't *your* one, they were out of the way, and your quest for The One would be easier, you'd know it wasn't him so could move on."

"Wait, wait…"

"Yeah?"

"Are you saying that it's a good thing he cheated on me?"

"Well no, obviously, but…"

"But what?"

"But, like, hold on, I don't think I'm explaining myself very well."

"Whatever, take your time."

"It's like, we're all looking for The One right? And

we meet people, and think we've found them, but then they do something, cheat on you or fall out of love with you or whatever, and you realise you haven't found The One?"

"O...kay..."

"And so it's like, yes that sucks, being cheated on is brutal, but now you know for sure they're not The One, and you can start the search again."

"O...kay..."

"It's like, if someone was going to cheat on you, they were always going to cheat on you, and it's better to find out now than in 40 years when you're married and have kids and stuff, when you and that person have made a life together, and then you have to unpick that life."

"I mean, I guess, but I think it's a very simplistic way of looking at things."

"How do you mean?"

"Well, I mean what you're saying makes sense, and probably looks good in a book or in a movie, but life isn't like that, is it?

"Isn't it?"

"Well, no. Do you think it is?"

"I mean, why isn't it?"

"Well it just isn't, is it? The One? Do you think we're all searching for The One, and we'll all find them?"

"Well, I mean, yeah? Don't you?"

"I used to, until he cheated on me. That set me back a bit."

"I can imagine. But still, you must be looking again?"

"For The One?"

"For The One."

"I mean, I'm looking for *a* one, I don't know if I'm looking for *the* one. Does that make sense?"

"No."

"Okay, let me rephrase. I'm looking for someone I

like, to spend time with. I'm not looking to fall in love, get married or whatever. I'm not *not* looking for that, and if it happens great, but that's not why I'm here."

"Oh."

"Oh?"

"Nothing."

"No, go on."

"No, it's okay."

"No, please tell me, I want to know."

"I am."

"You are what?"

"I'm looking for The One."

"Oh."

"Yeah."

"Shit."

"Right?"

"Right."

"Well just because you are, and I'm not, doesn't mean we can't, you know."

"We can't what?"

"Hang out."

"Really?"

"Yeah, absolutely. I like spending time with you."

"I like spending time with you."

"Can I get you a refill?"

"Are you trying to get me drunk?"

"I thought *you* were trying to get you drunk?"

"I am, but you're helping."

"What can I say? It's easier."

"Huh?"

"What?"

"What did you say?"

"Nothing."

"No, tell me, what did you say?"

"Oh, I just made a shit joke."

"Oh okay. What joke?"

"Nothing, it's okay."

"No, go on, tell me."

"I was just joking that I am trying to get you drunk, because then it'll be easier to seduce you."

"What the fuck?"

"I know, I'm sorry, not cool."

"No, not cool at all."

"I'm sorry."

"Whatever. Listen, I think I better go."

"What?"

"Yeah, I still need to pack, and my train is early tomorrow."

"I thought it was 11, or 11.30 or something?"

"No, I switched earlier, I'm going at 9am now."

"Oh, okay."

"Can I get my jacket?"

"What? Oh yeah, sorry, here you go."

"Thanks."

"Will I see you—"

"—I really should be going. Merry Christmas."

"Happy Christmas to you, too."

I know exactly how Damone feels when he said that he woke up in a great mood and didn't know what the hell happened. Me too, Damone, me too.

Chapter Eight:

Sixteen Candles

Ladies and gentlemen, boys and girls. And non-binary people and everyone else in between, may I present to you, back for another year due to overwhelming demand: Depressed as Fuck Christmas!

Returning with Depressed as Fuck Christmas are all your favourites: blacking out drunk on Christmas Eve at 7pm; receiving precisely one text, and that being from your parents, on Christmas Day; having a bagel from the Jewish Deli down the block for Christmas Dinner; receiving a notification that your parents have transferred you some money on December 27th, two days late because they clearly forgot, but you don't care because it means money for fresh booze and your supplies had been running out; texting a certain woman twice a day every day and receiving no replies; spending more time crying than not crying; suicidal thoughts!

Depressed as Fuck Christmas is back, bigger and better than ever. You thought last year was brutal? This year is on a whole other level. You thought you'd done enough during the year, been social enough and worked up enough karma, to avoid it, well think again. Because that's the beauty of Depressed as Fuck Christmas; it'll find you! You can't outrun it, can't escape it, can't hide from it: Depressed as Fuck Christmas is coming for you!

*

I haven't slept for more than an hour a night since December 22nd. I slept okay then, my last night of okay sleep, because I didn't think it was too bad; sure I'd made a bad joke, one that definitely didn't hit the mark, and Nicola left, probably earlier than she'd planned to. But then her plans had changed, she had to leave Grand Central like three hours earlier; plus she said she hadn't done her packing, so it made sense, at least I thought at the time, that she left at a decent time. That it happened to be right after my bad joke was just bad timing, or maybe even good timing on her part, she saw a window and she took it. So going to bed on the 22nd, I wasn't feeling on top of the world, and yet I wasn't feeling on the bottom of it either. I had some feelings of optimism; Nicola had spent the evening in my apartment, we'd hung out just the two of us, had a few drinks, had some conversation. It had gone really well I thought, that joke aside, and I was feeling, not upbeat, but not especially downbeat. I messaged her an hour or so after she left, telling her I'd had a lovely time, that I hoped her packing was going okay, and that Christmas wouldn't be as bad as she feared, I was sure of it. She didn't reply, but I figured she was still packing or was having an early night or something.

Waking on the morning of the 23rd, Saturday, I was disappointed not to have any messages from her. But then again, I told myself, it was two days before Christmas, she was lugging a suitcase home to spend a few interminable days with her family, I probably wasn't at the forefront of her mind. I shot her a text saying I was thinking of her, and then I began my day. Well, began a day of staring at my phone, willing it to buzz with an incoming message or call, anything from her. When I hadn't heard from her by mid-afternoon I messaged again saying I hoped her train ride hadn't been too bad, she'd gotten to her parents okay, that no one had killed anyone yet!

After sending that I put my phone down, tried my hardest to ignore it, put on a film, *Jaws*, an all-time classic. Though I didn't exactly watch it, I was too pre-occupied with staring at my phone. I tried pacing the room, but it was so small that walking the perimeter took me no more than about 12 seconds, walking as slowly as I could without standing still, and I soon gave up on this. I stood at my apartment window, looked at the building opposite. So many lights were on, and not just the usual yellow-ish white lights of regular lighting but greens and reds and golds, the colours of Christmas. I could see silhouettes of people living their lives, and god how I wished to be amongst them. I was so lonely, so alone, I just wanted to die. I just wanted to hear from Nicola. I poured myself a glass of prosecco. Nicola and I had only gotten through one bottle, and she'd forgotten to take hers back with her, which meant I was sitting on three unopened bottles, a veritable Christmas treasure trove. I only had a couple of glasses that night, finishing the film by about midnight and turning in. Sleep didn't come easily, in fact barely came at all, but I didn't mind too much, I still had the hope of hearing from Nicola.

24th, Christmas eve: waking to nothing. Complete radio silence still operating, the Iron Curtain had apparently fallen between us with immediate effect. I tried not to let it bother me and sent her a good morning text, wishing her a happy Christmas Eve. I didn't put anything else, I didn't want to say anything that might pressure her to reply to me. I figured that she hadn't messaged was because she was having a pretty crappy

Christmas, and I didn't want to add to that. Once I messaged her I put my phone down, for a few seconds anyway; I put it face down on the bed next to me, and as I did I felt it vibrate. I jumped and picked it up, flipping it over with a nuclear bomb of excitement having gone off in my chest. Nothing. I was disappointed; I was sure, I was positive, it had vibrated, but there was nothing on the screen, just the time, the date, a picture of Nicola staring back at me. I put it down again, and even though it was only 11 in the morning, I poured myself a glass of prosecco. "It's Christmas Eve," I told myself. "Besides, the bottle has been open since yesterday, if I don't drink it, it'll only go flat. Waste not and all that."

My apartment felt smaller to me on Christmas Eve, like it had shrunk the previous night. Not whilst I slept, because I basically didn't, but it had shrunk anyway, the walls had closed in on me, the ceiling had lowered itself. I felt trapped, like an animal in a cage, though one that had been forgotten about, I wasn't in a zoo but left behind in some warehouse, in an empty space, no one knowing where I was, no one caring.

I finished the first bottle of prosecco and, feeling a decent buzz, despite the fact it was still only early afternoon I opened a second. It was going down easily, and my growing drunkenness was a good distraction from checking my phone every 15 seconds. I mean, I tried to pretend it was. I was having another classic fight to the death, ego vs id. My id was telling me to check it, to pick it up and look. Phones can misfire, I told myself, not all notifications always cause vibration and noise, sometimes wires get crossed and you'll just get a silent alert on the screen. Of course each time I checked there'd be nothing, but it didn't stop me. Even as my id repeatedly told me, correctly, that nothing had happened, that I'd definitely get a notification when she messaged, it didn't help to check my phone that often, all I was doing was making myself feel worse.

My ego obviously won every time. To the point where, when I'd look at my phone screen and see it blank, I'd tell myself that maybe the app wasn't working properly, and I'd have to go on it, sometimes the crossed wires meant the messages only came through once you opened the app, they sometimes couldn't come through when the app was closed. My id knew this for the idiocy it was, but its complaints were just noise in the wind. I opened the messaging app perhaps every 30 seconds, hoping to spur it into action, but to no avail. It stayed dark, stayed quiet, the conversation stayed one-sided.

By mid-afternoon I was wasted and it was everything I had in me not to call her. The sun was sinking, the day slowly ending, and my hopes were going with it. Darkness was starting to spread across the apartment, and a certain darkness was spreading across my chest, across my heart. I sent Nicola a message saying I hoped she was okay, I was there for her, she could ring me if she wanted. When she hadn't replied a couple of hours later I messaged her again saying I hoped her Christmas Eve was going okay, that I was going to bed soon, I'd speak to her in the morning. I passed out fully clothed, some shit horror movie or another playing on the TV still, the bright colours and loud noises washing over my limp body, finding no receptacle in me.

I woke up — came to? — at 5am on Christmas Day confused, disorientated. I wasn't sure where I was, how I'd got there. I was in bed, but fully dressed, a stain on the sheet next to me I prayed wasn't urine. My mouth was dry, my phone was still in my hand. With a start I unlocked it, and was devastated to see I had nothing from Nicola; no messages, no missed calls, not even anything on any socials. Her radio silence was still happening, I was still receiving the silent treatment.

Details of the previous day slowly came back to me as I dragged myself into the bathroom, and checking my sent messages I was a little embarrassed, but only a little. My messages, though perhaps more frequent than they should have been, were nice, were decent messages, I came across as a kind, thoughtful, caring person I thought. I had a piss then turned on the shower, waiting for the water to warm, and once it did I climbed inside and broke down, wept and wept, sobbed out loud, my neighbours must have been able to hear such was the volume of my despair, but I didn't care, I couldn't. Nicola, the one person I loved the most in the world, the one person I needed, was ignoring me. I tried to tell myself it was her shitty family, maybe they had shitty reception wherever it was they lived, but this didn't help. I sank down to the floor of the tiny shower cubicle, wrapping my arms around my knees and resting my forehead on them. I cried until I ran out of tears, and then I cried some more, the crying equivalent of dry heaving, whatever that may be called. The water fell on me, around me, the hot water ran out after a time but it took me an age to notice, and even when I did I didn't care, the iciness of the water felt appropriate, it felt apt for how I was feeling. Being splashed by cold water felt like what I deserved for being such a fucking loser, for being such a waste of space, a waste of time for both the world and everyone in it.

I don't know how long I was in the shower for but when I was able to drag myself to my feet and turn it off I didn't even bother drying myself, I just dragged my wet, naked self to bed and collapsed. I felt the wetness of the sheet under me and once again prayed it wasn't urine, though without any conviction. There was an overturned bottle of prosecco on the floor that I could see from where I was laying. Not knowing whether I had any left I got off my bed, and with nothing less than a gargantuan effort moved to the fridge; I was relieved to see a bottle still inside, and was about to open it when my stomach gave a huge growl. When had I last eaten? I had no idea, I wracked my memory but nothing came to mind. Dressing in the first clothes I could find, that's when I went and got my heavenly Christmas Dinner, my proper traditional Christmas Dinner, of a plain white bagel with cream cheese on it. The Jewish Deli was the only shop open in Soho on Christmas Day which was a lifesaver; I had no food in my apartment, no food in my system, nothing. Stumbling back home, the few people I passed looking down as I approached, avoiding meeting my gaze, the streets icy and dangerous, a chill in the air which I was aware of but barely felt, I took my clothes off, all except my underwear, and opened the final bottle of prosecco. With a glass of it in one hand, I held my bagel between my teeth and messaged Nicola. All I said was 'happy Christmas!' with a couple of emojis, a couple of celebratory ones, and that was it. She obviously didn't reply, but by that point I didn't expect her to. I put the TV on but ignored it, I lay on my front on my bed and stared at the floor, at the walls, stared at nothing. How long I lay there for I have no idea, but soon the bottle of prosecco was empty and I was drunk once again. I got up and took a piss, then, finding a bottle of rum in one of the kitchen cupboards, I took that back to bed with me, not even bothering with a glass. Rather than collapsing back into bed I sat up, leaning on the headboard, and I went onto Nicola's Insta. No posts for the last few days, which reassured me slightly; perhaps she wasn't ignoring me, but was ignoring her phone, wasn't replying to anyone, it wasn't just me being neglected — maybe she was having a phone cleanse, a social detox, whatever they're called. Or perhaps she was having such a shit time she didn't have the energy to reply; a feeling I could well relate to. I didn't want that to be the case, but if it was it worked in my favour somewhat. I looked through her old pictures, taking frequent and massive sips from the bottle I cradled in the crook of my arm, the firmness of it somewhat reassuring, an anchor holding me in the real world, and even before the clock had passed into later afternoon I was wasted again, on the verge of passing out again. I didn't think it was a great way to spend Christmas, but I also didn't care. If Nicola wasn't replying, what was the point in anything?

I sent her one final message, something about hoping her Christmas had been okay, when was she coming back to the city, before I passed out. When I came to the next morning my head was pounding, my mouth dry, the light shining across my apartment floor was so bright I wanted to die, and I had nothing from Nicola, still nothing; no words, no pictures, no thoughts at all. But for a little while I didn't mind, for one main reason: it was December 26th, and I was still alive, which meant I'd survived another Christmas.

There is, however, still the spectre of New Year's Eve to get through. What a fucking pointless evening. The American Founding Fathers or whoever talked about truths that were self-evident: well it's a truth self-evident that New Year's Eve is pointless and everyone knows it but for some reason we all go along with it anyway. Everyone knows it's impossible to have fun, the pressure is too high, and besides it's cold, dark, usually wet, probably windy. The temperature now, 8pm on New Year's Eve, the sun already long gone, the snow also gone to be replaced by dull, driving rain, is minus six degrees. Minus six, and yet no doubt people have been in

Time's Square since midday, maybe earlier. To a certain extent I don't blame them; the first year I lived here I did New Year's in Times Square. You kind of have to, in a way; New Year's Eve in Times Square is like this mythical beast, this creature you've heard about but need to experience with your own eyes and ears, your own senses, to understand completely. It's a rite of passage.

My first year I went down with a couple of other people on the master's course. I can't even remember their names; as I sit here now and dig through the murky depths of my memory, what passes for it anyway, their names are long gone. It was a couple of other guys anyway, clearly no one interesting or I would at the very least be able to name them, short of having stayed in touch or whatever. Clearly our friendships weren't meant to be, they weren't the friendship one.

We got there about two in the afternoon, and from the moment we arrived it was clear that we were late. The crowds were already huge, nearly all of the standing space taken up. We had to squeeze in the back of one of the specially made areas, fit in where we could. Luckily it wasn't like a gig or anything, there was no stage to try and see, just the ball, which is hundreds of feet up in the air so unmissable from any vantage point. And so we stood there for ten hours, counted down for ten seconds, then went home. Total damp squib. I never did it again, would never want to. It's one of those things that's super romantic on paper, in theory, the kind of thing that, when it's explained you can't imagine anything more romantic, can't imagine anywhere better to take Nicola. But really it's large, loud, jostling crowds, it's queueing for half an hour just to piss in some disgusting porta-potty. It's numb toes, numb fingers, being too sober, being too tired. The reality is fucking far away from the theory, believe me.

I never went again, I never will. Unless Nicola asks me to. I have no idea what she's doing tonight, where she is, if she's even in the city. She still hasn't replied to me and her Insta feed is still dark. I haven't heard a peep from her in nine days, since she was in my apartment. How can we go from that to this? It just doesn't make sense.

I have no plans this evening. Actually no, that's not true. I have no plans to go out, no plans to see other people. I do have plans of a sort. They are to stare in the mirror and try and figure it all out.

And that's just what I'm doing. There's a floor to ceiling mirror on the front of one of the wardrobe doors in my apartment and I'm sitting in front of it, cross legged, looking at myself, trying to figure it out. Trying to figure myself out. And I'm failing.

Sitting here, looking into the mirror, looking back at what, for all intents and purposes, is a human. The person looking back at me has all the features of a human: a human-shaped head, hair and a forehead, two eyes, a nose, two lips, which when parted show a tongue, teeth, gums. The person staring back at me has a chin, though barely visible through its beard. It has a neck, shoulders, a chest, arms and hands and legs and feet. When I turn my head, the person in the mirror turns theirs; when I lift my arm the person in the mirror lifts theirs. Sitting here, regarding the mirror, everything seems perfectly normal, everything seems fine. But there's something off about the scene.

Firstly, the person looking back at me is crying, and I wasn't aware that I am. Seeing the reflection of tears I touch my cheek and sure enough my finger comes back wet, and when I lick the moisture off my finger it's salty, so it must be a tear. Secondly, the person looking back at me has no expression; they don't look happy, sad, angry, hungry, horny, anything. They're just sitting there, their face a blank, staring at me. I want to break eye contact but I'm unable, they're holding me enraptured in their gaze, I want to look down, look to the side, but I'm incapable.

Because, and this is thirdly and perhaps most importantly, the person looking back at me has nothing behind their eyes. They're grey, like mine, attached to a face I know to be a facsimile of mine from pictures I've seen, but that's where the likeness ends. I have a rich inner life, I have thoughts, feelings, opinions, memories, hopes and dreams. The person looking back at me does not. They have nothing below the surface, nothing inside; their hopes and dreams are long gone, their aspirations lay rotting, going to waste. They look like they might have had optimism, once upon a time, but that optimism is long dead, buried with every other good thing they ever felt.

I'm struck by this complete lack of depth; the person looking back at me looks just like me, but that's where our comparisons end. They're simply a picture, but I'm a real person. They're a moving image on a piece of incredibly highly polished glass, but I'm here, in the flesh. Cut me and I'll bleed, pinch me and it'll hurt. I am a real human. I think.

My phone buzzes and I jump to my feet, dash the few feet to where it lays on the coffee table and grab it. Nicola Nicola Nicola please mother of god let it be from Nicola. It isn't. It's Tom from work asking if I want to come to a party. It's very kind of him, but I can't think of anything worse. I've had messages from Elijah and Luna as well, both of which made me feel a little better; Christmas may have been a time of isolation, but now it's New Year's people have remembered I exist, which is nice. Except the one person I want to, she apparently has forgotten any trace of me was ever present not just on the planet, but in her life. I want to die.

Chucking my phone on the couch I sit back down in front of the mirror and have a very sudden, very stark realisation; the person in the mirror looking back at me is, in fact, me. That nose is my nose, those lips are my lips. And those grey eyes, those two circular blanks showing nothing? Those are my eyes. I have no hopes, no dreams, no optimism. I used to, but then I met Nicola, and all my plans for the future became her. She's The One, she is my future. The problem is, I'm beginning to doubt whether she is The One, and whether or not The One exists at all. Because surely if she's The One, she'd be talking to me? I'm no relationship expert, but I believe that acknowledging each other's existence goes a long way to building a foundation? Can The One be The One if they don't want to talk to you?

The grey eyes devoid of all hope are mine. The frown, the tears, the slumped shoulders; the person in the mirror who has nearly lost all hope, who is 1% away from giving up, is me. And then Nicola texts me and it's all okay.

Because sometimes that's all it takes, that one moment where everything changes. That *Sliding Doors* moment. It happens for Sam in *Sixteen Candles* when the love test she fills out in class finds its way to Jake, and he reads his own name upon it. That's the moment it all changes for Sam, even if she doesn't become aware of it until later.

Jake is The One for Sam, she knows that, she's always known that. Because Sam knows. She knows that even though Jake is dating Caroline this is only a small bump in the road, a minor obstacle to be overcome. Initially, in the early stages of the film when Sam's family forget her birthday, her faith falters, she doubts.

Everything's just getting shittier, she says, and it's impossible not to have the utmost sympathy with her when she does. Because Sam's life *is* shitty, until Jake properly enters it. Then it becomes everything it should always have been, it becomes worth living. Jake makes Sam's life worth living.

Because that love, the love you feel for The One, is the only love that matters. The love I feel for Nicola is the only love that matters. The whole premise behind *Sixteen Candles* is that Sam's family forget her 16th birthday, and that sums up The One really; family are meant to be there for you, always and forever, they're meant to be your safe spot, your home. But family let you down. Family will always let you down. They'll arrange their wedding for the day after your 16th birthday, already overshadowing it. And then because of this they'll forget your 16th birthday, totally ruining it. Not to mention that as part of your stupid sister's stupid wedding you'll be kicked out of your room and be forced to sleep on the couch. Your older siblings won't care, neither will your younger. Family will abandon you, will hurt you. Only The One will ever truly love you and treat you the way you deserve to be treated.

It isn't just Sam; Jake has a really shitty relationship with Caroline because she's not the one for him. They have fun together, lots of fun, but neither of them are happy, because they know in their hearts that they're with the wrong person. For Caroline, it's not clear who The One is. It might end up being Anthony Michael Hall, who knows? It doesn't matter, because that's not what's important. What's important is Jake becoming aware of Sam, and slowly learning she's The One for him. The party Caroline throws at Jake's house is a disaster, because she's wrong for him! If Sam had thrown a party it would have been spectacular, there wouldn't have been any destruction of property or fighting, nothing untoward like that. If Sam had thrown the party it would have been perfect, because she gets Jake, she's made for Jake.

The film takes a little while for Sam and Jake to get there, but when they do it's everything. When Jake turns up outside the church, and Sam asks him what he's doing there, and he replies that he heard she was there. Oh my god. And then when they're at Jake's place, with a cake, and Sam has finally gotten her sixteen candles. She blows them out and Jake tells her to make a wish, and Sam says it already came true. Oh my god. And then they kiss. They finally, after nearly 90 minutes of not being together, are together. And it's everything.

I'm beginning to worry that Nicola and I are not going to end up together. No, that's not true. I know we are, I'm just beginning to doubt the timeline. In movies, people always get together sharpish. Not just because movies, by their definition, are usually only an hour and a half, two hours, maybe three hours max, and so the entire story has to be told in that timeframe. But even within the movies, people get together fast. *Empire Records* takes place in 24 or so hours. *Sixteen Candles* is probably 36, max. Yes, *(500) Days of Summer* takes place over 500 days, but that's slightly different, and it's not really relevant here. *Fast Times* takes place over the course of a year, but when you're 15 or 16, a year flies by, so it probably only feels like a day or so to Stacy and Mark. The point is, love happens fast. Which is why I'm getting frustrated that Nicola and mine's love is taking it's time.

Because obviously we are going to end up together, but when? I need it to be soon, because the thought of it is the only thing keeping me sane. Well, as sane as I am. It's the only thing keeping me going; if I don't have Nicola I'll fucking kill myself, what's the point otherwise?

But the thing is, I need her soon. Knowing we'll end up together is one thing, but if it doesn't happen for 50 years? What the fuck am I supposed to do? Am I supposed to be like Sam, just sit back and watch Nicola with her Caroline, watch her with someone else, kiss them, hug them, not know that they aren't The One and so act as if they are? Because that would fucking kill me.

And it's like, what more do you want from me? I don't know what doubts Nicola could still be harbouring, what could be holding her back from investing fully in me. She knows me now, knows all about me. The wedding, the dinner party, her coming over here for a few drinks; between all of those things — not to mention the project at work, all that copy we spent hours writing together — she knows me. I haven't held anything back from her — well, not much anyway — I've given her my full self, my truest self. I've given her my all — nearly — and laid myself bare. So what's stopping her? I'm here waiting, she's there choosing. Choose love Nicola, choose me.

Her message was a very simple one. Sent at 8.14 on New Year's Eve, it said: *Happy New Year's Oli x.* Nice and simple, four words and one letter. Simple, stark, straight to the point. I was hoping for more, I hadn't heard from her in nine days, but this one sentence is better than nothing. Besides, she ended it with a kiss, so that's promising. Maybe things aren't so bad after all, maybe New Year's Eve is a good evening. Maybe I should go out, message Elijah back and see where he is, insert myself into it. I need to see Elijah, anyway, find out how his friend Simon is getting on with his pregnant other woman. See if Elijah is ready to admit it's actually him he's talking about, because I'm fairly certain it is.

Looking around at my apartment, the walls and ceiling are back where they belong, even though it's night and I have on no lights the place is lit up, there's hope again. I've been very stupid: this place isn't a cage or a prison, it's a jail cell. A prison is a place of permanence, a place where you spend 10, 20, god knows how many years; a jail is a place of transience, it's a holding cell until you go somewhere permanent. I'm not in this apartment permanently, it's just a holding cell until Nicola is ready for me. Wherever she is, that's my permanence. I know this now, because that kiss holds within it so much promise, so much hope for 2024. That kiss is all I need to carry me into the new year, I shall ride it like a surfer riding a 50-foot wave, I'll catch the break and let it carry me to shore, carry me to victory. And besides the content of the message, that's perhaps less important than the fact she messaged me at all, because even though her words are nice, the entire existence of the message says one thing: I'm thinking about you. I don't know where Nicola is, what she's doing, but wherever and whatever, she's thinking of me. She might still be with her parents, be back in the city at a party, be at home alone, whatever. The only thing that matters is that wherever she is, whatever she's doing, I'm on her mind. I, Oliver, am on the mind of her, Nicola. That's basically all I want. Well, I want her to realise this is all that matters and commit to being with me, but that'll happen. But when?

I messaged her back right away, because obviously, why wouldn't I? I kept it simple, too, I just sent *Happy New Year's Nicola xxx*. Three kisses felt like a risk, especially as she'd only sent me one, but you have to take risks in life, and in love too, especially in love. Love doesn't just happen; well no that's not true, it does, but relationships don't just happen. Nicola and I are in love, that's just natural, but we're not in a relationship, because we haven't made it happen. You gotta risk it to win it.

I sent that message two hours ago, it's just after 10pm

now, and she hasn't replied, but that's okay. It's New Year's Eve, she's doing what she's doing, she'll message when she can. I'm on her mind, that's enough for now. And by replying to her, she knows she's on my mind, and that's most likely enough for her. We've only being playing this game, doing this dance, verbing this noun for a few months. Most likely Nicola made her New Year's plans many more months ago, before we even started talking, and so she's committed to them. No one wants to be the person that goes to a party and just sits on their phone, so really I'm not expecting to hear from her. I'll message again at midnight if I haven't heard, wishing her a Happy New Year when it does actually come. Until then, we're all good.

Actually, I'll just message her now, so she definitely knows I'm thinking of her. Nice and easy, all I'm going to send is *Hope you're having fun, thinking of you, speak soon xxx*. Three kisses again, solidify that risk. If it was anyone else I wouldn't have put that I was thinking about them, but it's Nicola so I do. Anyone else and I might not be so keen, might try and pretend I was blasé, that I didn't mind how it worked out. But not Nicola. You can't fuck around when it comes to The One. You can't fuck with fate.

I've decided to go for a walk. I haven't heard from Nicola, the only contact I've had was Elijah who sent me a garbled voice note of which I could understand about 4%, and none of which made me want to go and be where he was, is, whatever. So I put on my shoes, got my big coat and hat and gloves, put my headphones in, and here I am.

I used to walk a lot, both when I first moved to New York and for a while afterwards. Very different kinds of walking, though; when I first arrived I was walking in awe, walking around this wonderful city, trying to take it all in. Something I had seen constantly as I was growing up, this cultural monolith, was now in front of me, and I was simply trying to be a part of it, trying to comprehend its existence. It was in front of me but I didn't think it was real, it didn't feel real, so I tried to spend as much time as I could walking around, trying to absorb it. There are still days now, seven years later, when I feel like I don't fit in. I get that seven-year itch — not *that* one — and I have to try and absorb it again, try and replenish what I've lost. Because it does feel like a loss in a way; living in New York feels like a constant task, a challenge. It feels like having a muscle, one you have to constantly train to keep fresh. They say you gotta train your brain like any other muscle to keep it in good shape; living in New York is like that. If you don't stay on top of it, it'll get on top of you.

The second type of walking, the kind I do much more now, the kind I'm on at the moment, is despair walking. When things feel too much, when everything becomes overwhelming — though not so overwhelming that I get stuck in bed — I have to walk it off, to go out and get some fresh air, stretch my legs, look for a new perspective. I find thinking on things, ruminating, outside of my usual haunts, can help a lot. I mean, nothing ever gets solved, but it doesn't anywhere else, does it, so where's the harm? I also sometimes try and walk to find something. What that something is, I don't know, but I'll know it when I find it. It might be life, it might be hope, it might be a big fuck off pile of money. I dunno, I'm looking for something when I walk. Right now I'm looking for Nicola. Not literally, obviously, but yeah, I'm looking for her.

I used to take walks without any headphones in, I used to just absorb the sounds of the city; traffic noises:

engines revving, wheels spinning, horns being honked in anger, despair, frustration, joy. The sounds of a million conversations: people talking to their friends they're walking with, talking into phones, on phone calls and recording voice notes and live streaming for social media. The sounds of a billion different businesses happening: trucks delivering things, metal doors being rolled up with loud crashes and bangs and boxes being hauled off, thrown into warehouses; bike messengers weaving in and out of people, flying along at god knows how fast, risking life and limb to ensure documents get where they're needed; food deliveries and taxis taking people places they need to go and people selling things on stalls, in front of shops, hawking their homemade CDs to unsuspecting tourists who have no idea that it isn't free, that something will be demanded in return. Ain't that the story of life, though; that unsuspecting cost that accompanies everything, things that should be free, things that should be readily available, and which seem so at first, until the bill comes due. Because the bill always comes due. In love as in life.

Right now I need music; it's all well and good trying to gather your thoughts when you have the usual mix of good, bad, happy, sad, exciting, reluctant, whatever. When you have a range of thoughts, when your emotions cover the full scope of human experience, it's okay. Walking and taking in the city is a good way to straighten them out, get a handle on them and get some sort of order going in the chaos of my mind. But when all you have are the bad thoughts, the bad feelings, the last thing you want is to be alone with them; I can't walk without music right now, because once I get inside my own head I get stuck there, and no one can get me out, I can't even get myself out; I just have to hope my brain, with its twisted ideas, gets bored of me and spits me out, and then I can try and live my life. No, I need music, I need sounds, I need distractions. I need distracting from my distractions.

The scene: it's 11.36 on New Year's Eve 2023, and I'm standing in East River Park listening to Maisie Peters sing about Brooklyn as I look at it across the water. There are millions of lights reflected in the vast blackness, the reflection broken only by small ripples caused by the tide of the nearby ocean. It's oddly beautiful, this doubling; from a distance Brooklyn looks so innocent, so peaceful, it looks like it holds the key. That I don't know what it's the key to is irrelevant, just the fact it exists at all is enough. "If you're looking for the girl of your dreams," I am Maisie, I am, "she's in Brooklyn with me." Is she, Maisie? Is the girl of my dreams out there somewhere, in amongst all those lights, all that life. Is Nicola on that island, right now, waiting for me? Is she at a party checking her phone, hoping I'll message again? Is she this very second taking her phone out, seeing my message for the first time, and typing out a reply? Maybe. Maybe she is. According to Maisie Peters she is, and I have no reason to doubt her.

I take my phone out of my pocket for reasons I immediately forget once I see it lit up with an incoming call. And my heart immediately stops: it's Nicola. She's calling me; maybe she is in Brooklyn, and can see me right now looking for her. Maybe she picked up on my thoughts of her, my wishes were transported into her brain somehow, subconscious microwaves or whatever, and she just had to call me. Maybe these last nine days have been her thinking time, and though it's taken until nearly the very end of the year, she's finally figured out what she wants, and that what she wants is me. Whatever, who knows, I'm about to answer it, I'll know soon enough.

"Hello?" I answer, wanting to be much more familiar, say 'hey you' or something along those lines, but figuring after this much silence I should play it safe. So much for taking risks.

There's no response right away, instead all I can hear is a lot of noise. Nicola must be at a party or something, maybe in someone's house or in a bar or club; all I can hear down the phone is music beating away, the bass thumping so much I can nearly feel it in my chest; the sounds of people talking, shouting, screaming to be heard over said music; people laughing, cheering, bottles and glasses clinking. What I can hear down the phone is life, and standing here on the edge of the water, the freezing cold wind buffeting me, I find in it a certain comfort. Not only am I not the only person alive, but life is happening elsewhere, on a much bigger, grander scale than it is in this park, which I occupy alone. Somewhere out there, be it in Brooklyn, Manhattan, Upstate, in fucking Nigeria or whatever, life is taking place. People are appreciating what they have — at least I hope so, anyway — and appreciating those around them. I hope someone is appreciating Nicola the way I am from a distance. I hope she's safe and warm and happy.

When I don't hear Nicola's voice after another 10 seconds or so I say, "hello," again, and still getting no response I repeat myself a third time, adding Nicola's name in the hope of gaining her attention. No dice.

I'm about to hang up when I hear my name in her voice and I stop; my name is coming out of her mouth and it's everything to me. In my head all this time I've been thinking of us reunited, our first kiss, the first time we sleep together, the first time I take off her clothes and truly see her, all layers shed, see her as vulnerable and frail, as real. And yet, I've been skipping over something that I hadn't realised how much I missed, how much I needed, until just now. Hearing my name in her voice, coming from her mouth, is everything. I thought our first kiss would be everything, the way it is in the movies, the way Sam and Jake's first kiss is everything, the way Lloyd and Diane's first kiss is everything. Nicola and my's first kiss will still be everything, of that I'm sure, but I'm also now learning that there can be more than one everything. And this is the first.

"Hey, you," I say with a confidence Nicola has instilled in me. There's still no response, at least not *to* me. Nicola does begin to talk, and it isn't long before I realise that she wasn't saying my name to me, that in fact she's talking *about* me. It soon becomes clear that this must be an accidental dial, and that she has no idea I'm listening, no idea I can hear her. I wish I couldn't. I wish this phone call had never happened. I wish I was dead.

"Oli, Oli, Oliver. That fucking guy."

Mumbled noises I can't hear, it must be whoever Nicola is talking to, because the mumbling ends and then Nicola starts again as if answering a question. I can't move.

"I thought so, too! I mean, I still think he is, you know like inside somewhere. There's definitely a nice guy in there underneath all that, I dunno, crap he hides behind."

More indecipherable muttering.

"Yeah, yeah," she laughs, "but we didn't do anything. I wanted to, don't get me wrong, and the prosecco helped, to be honest I was going to, but then he made this weird joke, really inappropriate, and it killed the mood."

More mumbling, as I contemplate the proof of something I suspected but didn't want or need confirming.

"I dunno. He's text me like five times a day this last

week while I've been away. It was sweet at first but I dunno, you know what it's like."

I still can't hear the other person, so I have no idea what it's like.

"It's just, you know, we work together. What happens if it gets awkward, like what happens if the weirdness isn't a mask, but it's who he really is? What happens then? Because if we get together and it doesn't work out," no chance my love, "then we break up, I'll still have to see him every day? Thank god that project is over with, it was too much."

What the fuck? The project was too much? What does she mean? I thought it was amazing, I thought that not only did the work side of it go really well, but the personal side of it, too. I thought us spending so much time together was unparalleled, I thought we really grew close. What the fuck is going on?

"Yeah another please, prosecco, actually no fuck it get me a vodka lemonade please. Double. Thanks, doll."

Whether she's at a bar or a party I cannot tell. I can picture her in both; at a party, hanging out in the kitchen, red solo cup in hand, standing in a group of three or four people, all of whom are hanging on her every word. Music drifts in from another room, some popular song, and Nicola's head nods slightly, she's taking in the music even as she's entertaining the crowd. She's wearing something simple, a pair of jeans and a crop top, her perfect stomach on show, the tops of her breasts. I want to be there, I want to stand next to her, admire her, grow in her warmth. I can picture her in a bar, the lighting low, she's dancing, drink in hand, being careful not to spill any of it as she's twisting her body to the music, people are watching her body move, watching her vibrate at a frequency they'll never be able to access. She's wearing a little black dress, tight to her perfect, tight little body, the

material covering only the bare minimum of her torso
and crotch, tantalising, teasing, she's enrapturing guys
left, right and centre, poor unsuspecting guys who think
she's on the market, who don't know I exist, who don't
know she's spoken for. Even if she isn't 100% sure of it
yet. She will be. Even in spite of this conversation, she
will be: she's The One, how could she not be?

"Jenn, ohmygod Jenn how are you?"

Wait, is that Elijah's Jenn? And does that mean Elijah
is where Nicola is? Shit, I shouldn't have been so quick to
blow off his indecipherable voice note. If I'd have known
Nicola would be there I'd have tried much harder to
track Elijah down.

"Yes babe, Happy New Year to you too, come here
give me a kiss, mwah mwah. Where's Elijah? What? What
do you mean? What the fuck?"

She shouts this last and I have to move the phone
back from my ear. It's so frustrating only hearing what
Nicola is saying and not whoever she's talking to, right
now presumably Jenn; I have no context, I have no idea
what Nicola's *what the fuck?* was in reference to. It's killing
me to not know.

"She's pregnant? And he's moving in with her and
they're going to start a family? Are you fucking kidding,
babe?"

Oh fuck, I know what this is about. I knew there was
no Simon, I knew Elijah was talking about himself. And
now he's apparently told Jenn, and has decided to leave
her and move in with Mia and have the baby. Shit, heavy.
That's probably why he was so drunk earlier. I wonder if
he's even still awake, has made it this far, will make it to
midnight? At least now I'm less concerned about not
being with him, because by the sounds of it he's not with
Jenn, and therefore not with Nicola. Some slight relief on
what is otherwise turning into a pretty awful evening.

Am I weird? Was Nicola right in her assessment of me? I mean, I know I'm weird, but I didn't think I was that weird? Or at least, I thought I hid it better? Nicola's words have stung, but there's no time to dwell on them now as she's speaking again.

"Oli knew? What do you mean he knew? And they talked about it behind your back?"

Nicola sounds angry, and I don't blame her; but then again so am I. I didn't know! Elijah and I had one conversation, in which he was talking about a friend. And I told him to tell this friend to stay with his wife! Why am I getting dragged into this, I've done nothing wrong. Why am I being stoned for Elijah's crimes?

"That's disgusting, I can't believe it. No offence babe Elijah doesn't surprise me, but Oliver?" Back to my full name, that can't be good. "I thought he was better than that. That's one of the things I like about him, he seems totally drama free." I am! I want to scream, I am drama free, I'm collateral damage in all of this, Elijah is both Bush and Blair and I'm just an innocent Iraqi citizen. Leave me out of this!

"I do like him, I do, I was just saying to Zarah how much I like him, but, and come on Jenn you know this, you've met him, he's a bit odd. He's a bit much. He's texting me, like, loads every day, it's creepy. And now this? I dunno, I don't know what to do."

I do! Leave them and be with me! If I'm being weird it's only because I love you and want to be with you. I'm weird because I care!

"I did message him before, and he replied, it was all perfectly normal, and I thought maybe I'd been overreacting, overthinking things. But then he messaged me again, I know I should probably reply, but it's like, you know, if I do how many messages will he then send me? I'll message him tomorrow I guess, and no doubt get

14 in return. God he needs to fucking chill."

Mumble mumble mumble.

"Yeah I'll deffo see him again," she says, and my heart beats out a rhythm even louder than the one coming from the speakers wherever Nicola is. "But it might be the last time. I'm only giving him one more chance because I think maybe I've been a bit hard on him, I haven't been entirely present."

"One final chance? What the fuck?"

I don't realise I've said this out loud until Nicola says, "Hello? Hello?" in a way that makes me realise she isn't talking to Jenn or this Zarah or anyone else, but she's talking into the phone. There's panic in her voice, and rightfully so. She may be The One, but she can't treat me like this, can't talk about me like this. I've done nothing but worship her, done nothing but lay the groundwork for us to be together, and this is how she repays me? Fuck that. I'm still going to meet up with her, obviously, and it won't be the last time, also obviously, but I'm not happy. Happy fucking New Year, indeed.

"Oliver, Oli, hello?"

When I don't respond she talks to her friends again, I hear her briefly before she hangs up. "I think I called Oli," she says, laughing. Fucking laughing. "I think he heard all that..." and then the line goes dead and I'm left standing in East River Park, phone still held to my ear, no more noise coming from it. The only noises are the sound of the wind blowing across the water and the sound of my heart breaking. But I'll fix it. I have until I meet up with Nicola to put it back together so I can be my best self and finally win her over. Oh fuck, what a fucking day it's been. I'm going home and going to bed; let's try again next year.

Chapter Nine

Pretty in Pink

I lasted until nearly 2pm on New Year's Day before I messaged Nicola. She didn't reply. I was good and restrained and only messaged her a couple more times that day. Now it's over a week later and I still haven't heard from her, but that may be because I haven't messaged her. Well, not much anyway. Just a couple of messages here and there, letting her know I'm still here, I'm still thinking about her, I'm not mad at her.

She hasn't been in the office at all this week. It's Friday, closing time, and I'm going to meet Elijah for drinks. Now there's someone I've been hearing a lot from. To be honest, I can't fucking get rid of him, I'm only going for drinks in the hope it'll allow him to get everything out of his system and then he'll leave me alone for a bit. I'm sick of jumping at the sound of my phone chirping only to see it's a message from him. I like Elijah, but he's not who I want blowing up my phone.

I know that Nicola hasn't been in the office this week because I've been here every second of every day and I haven't seen her. I asked Neil on Thursday where she was but he didn't know, didn't have much to say. It's weird, before Christmas he was always up for talking about her, he seemed, if anything, a bit too interested in how it was going between us. I don't know what's happened since, but he doesn't seem bothered at all now. Which is good, I suppose, one fewer complication in the mix. And less pressure, too; it's one thing to fuck something up when it's just you and another person, but when the relationship has like fucking cheerleaders and stuff? "That's too much, man," as Sarah Lynn would say.

Not seeing Nicola all week has me a bit fucked up, I won't lie; I get her not responding to my messages, she hardly ever does, but then I thought seeing her would be good, we could blow past that awkwardness of the accidental call, of everything I heard her say about me. Which reminds me, another reason I'm seeing Elijah: ask him what the fuck is up with him dropping me in it re: Mia and the baby. I'm assuming he just dragged me down with him, was panicking when talking to Jenn and blurted my name out, but I want to know for sure. And I want a fucking apology. I feel like Gerry's friend in *Sliding Doors*, except this is not funny. This is a potential life ruiner.

Elijah is meeting me downstairs. In fact — my phone has just pinged — that's him saying he's in the lobby. I throw my stuff into my bag and head out, saying bye to Tom and Neil, receiving little by way of return. Weird, but whatever; I guess it's not weird, we're just going back to our pre-Nicola relationship, that of colleagues and boss. We're not friends, I don't need them. As long as Neil keeps paying me, we're all good.

Arriving in the lobby I see Elijah, but I also see something else, a flash of something, of someone. A whisper of brown hair on the edge of my vision, just for a brief moment. I could swear it's Nicola, I could swear that was her I saw dashing into the ladies' bathroom in the corner of reception. I walk over to Elijah and say hello, ask him how he is, we shake hands and all that, but I'm not present, I'm not paying attention. I'm thinking of that flash of auburn hair I saw going into the restroom, disappearing quickly as if it was fleeing something. I need to hang around, need to wait for that brown hair to emerge so I can see upon whose head it rests. Telling Elijah I'll be one second I walk over to the reception desk. A young woman comes over to meet me, her skin a dark shade of ochre, her hair pulled back into a bun. On her face is plastered the hideously distorted smile of someone who works in customer service in a country where you can be fired any time for any reason, and rent is obscenely high.

"Hi there, how can I help you, sir?"

"Hi, yeah, erm…" I'm panicking, I have no idea what to say. What can I say to give me reason to be here, to be hanging around in a way not totally suspicious.

"Is everything okay, sir?"

The woman is looking at me with a small look of concern on her face, and a large look of boredom. I'm keeping my eyes firmly on the ladies' bathroom door, willing it to open and the person, who by now I'm absolutely certain is Nicola, to emerge. Out of the corner of my eye I can see Elijah tapping his foot impatiently. Fuck that guy, he can wait.

"Yeah, no, erm, I work upstairs on the 27th floor and I was just wondering…" I trail off, still no idea what to say. Matthew, the agency's receptionist, walks by and looks at me without smiling.

"Yes, sir?"

She's beginning to look pissed off now and I don't blame her, this woman no doubt has much better things to do than listen to me say, well, frankly, not a great deal.

I try to speak but nothing comes. I have nothing, no words. I have literally nothing I can think of to say to this woman to prolong this conversation.

"Never mind," I mumble, "it's nothing." I begin to walk away. "I'm sorry," I say to her over my shoulder.

She's already left, already gone back to whatever she was doing before I pointlessly interrupted.

"Is everything okay?" Elijah asks when I return to him.

"Yeah it's all good," I say, "some work thing. Shall we?"

I don't want to go but can't hang around. Short of going into the ladies there's nothing I can do, so with a sigh I follow Elijah through the building's revolving door and onto the street.

"Where to?" he says, looking at me as if I'm a man capable of making a decision. I'm beginning to think that Elijah might be really, really stupid.

New York is frozen once again. There was a little respite to the weather over Christmas; funnily enough the days I spent confined to my apartment were actually quite mild, according to the forecast. Mild enough, anyway, that all the snow melted. The only problem is that water didn't go anywhere, and now it's turned cold again it's all freezing, meaning the streets are death-traps, long stretches of ice just begging for people to fall down and not get back up.

Despite the fact I'm only 28 I walk carefully; being young doesn't necessarily save you from a hard fall, and I'll be no good to Nicola with a broken leg or something. I need to present the best version of myself when we finally meet up, not present myself as some broken thing. Even if that's what I am, both inside and out, she doesn't need to know that. I'll let her know how broken I am once she's fixed me, that way we can laugh about it. Much better to laugh at the danger when you're out of it; fires aren't as funny when you're still inside the house.

Despite the ice everywhere Elijah leads us on a merry chase, eventually ducking into Rudy's Bar and Grill on

9th. The place is crowded, I get one of the last remaining empty tables while Elijah heads to the bar, returning quickly with a pitcher of beer and two glasses. He pours us each one then holds his out in a toast. I say nothing, wondering what he's toasting to.

"Happy New Year, Oliver," he says, and we clink glasses. "Here's to 2024 being better than 2023."

I continue to say nothing. Now we're here, sitting down, each with a drink, my anger is rising. If he wants to fuck up his life he's more than welcome to, but I refuse to have mine fucked up with it. He's bored of Jenn? Whatever. I haven't even gotten started with Nicola.

"You okay, man?" he says to me, finally noticing my silence. I stay silent, take a sip of my beer, look at all the happy people around us, people without cares or problems. How I envy them their simplicity, the ease of their lives.

"Whatever, cheer up man, it might never happen." *Not if you have anything to do with it*, I think. "Anyway listen, there's something I need to tell you."

Here we go, is he going to admit it?

"Mia and I are moving. We're going to the west coast, she's from there and that's where her family are and she wants to be near them for the baby and stuff."

Nope, still all about him. Fucking dickhead. I continue to hide behind the Iron Curtain. I can sense him becoming annoyed.

"So yeah," he continues when I don't say anything. "Her family lives up in Portland, so we're moving there next month. Jenn has bought me out of our apartment, and my company has offices up there, so I'm good to go. Mia quit her job, she says she might get another but honestly, the cost of living up there compared to here, she probably won't need to. That's another thing," he says. "I've been promot—"

"—I don't care!" I blurt out, unaware I'm going to vocalise the words and not just think them until I do.

Elijah blanches, he's totally taken aback. I don't blame him, based on the number of people looking at us I think I might have shouted that, and quite loud too.

"I'm sorry, man," I say to him, lying. "I don't mean that," I do, "I'm happy for you," I'm not, "it's just that, well…"

"Well, what?" he says in a monotone, I think he's trying to keep his anger in check. Well fuck him, it's my turn to be angry.

"You threw me under the fucking bus, man!" I say to him, my anger failing, the hurt that's replaced it making itself known through my tone.

"I did what?"

"Don't play innocent with me," I say, though even as I do I realise he probably genuinely has no idea to what I'm referring. I enlighten him all about the overheard conversation, about what Jenn said about me, which can only come from what Elijah said to her. When I finish he's looking suitably abashed, which pleases me. He may be a dickhead, but a dickhead with contrition is better than nothing.

"I'm sorry man," he says, his voice so quiet I can barely hear him over the thrum of noise in the bar. A glass smashes somewhere and I look around, try to locate the source of the noise, before looking back at Elijah.

"Thanks," I say to him, before he continues speaking, his voice shaking, his footing now less than firm.

"I didn't mean to, man, and I am really sorry." He looks so genuine that I can't not believe him. "I thought so much over Christmas — Jenn was with her parents and I was with mine, so we were apart for five days — and realised that, even though I love Jenn more than Mia,

I'm going to love that kid more than both of them combined, and that's what really matters. Mia and I might not work out, in fact it looks like we probably won't, I'm pretty sure she fucking hates me, but I need to be in my kid's life. I couldn't have my kid growing up as the child of the other woman, as the child of someone other than the woman to whom I was married."

He stops, finishes his drink, pours us each a refill, emptying the pitcher in the process. Lines of condensation run down the outside of the glass jug, I watch them pool on the varnished wood of the table, and it takes everything I have to pull my eyes off them and put my focus back on Elijah.

"I didn't mean to throw you under the bus, man, I'm really sorry. When Jenn and I both got back to the apartment I'd made up my mind, and I told her there and then. I mentioned you and I spoke about it without even thinking, I was just relating facts to her at that point. She ran with it, I think she was so angry she was looking for people to hate, and you're an easy target."

"Wait, what do you mean?" Why is he turning this back on me?

"Come on, man."

"No seriously, what do you mean?"

"Don't pretend you don't know," Elijah says, his fear and shame now replaced by incredulity.

"I honestly don't," I say to him, and he takes a sip of his beer before responding.

"Before I say this, let me preface it by saying these are not my words. They may not even be Nicola's words; this is just what Jenn told me before we broke up, that Nicola had told her." I take a sip of my beer, bracing myself. "Have you been messaging Nicola a lot?"

"I mean, a bit, I guess, I wouldn't say a lot."

"How often?"

"Not that often."

"Every day?"

"Yeah," I reluctantly admit.

"Multiple times a day?"

"I guess," I mumble, shame beginning to wash over me in a dreadful wave.

"Do you double text?" I can no longer bear to speak and so simply nod into my rapidly emptying glass. "Has she been replying to you?" I shake my head. "There you go then, man, that's what."

I look up at him, still not fully understanding. My facial expression must convey this because he continues, but now his voice is patronising, pedantic, it's like he's explaining a very simple concept to a very stupid person.

"It's too much, man! You're doing too much to Nicola, being too much. She likes you, she has feelings for you, but you're scaring her, man."

"Scaring her? What the fuck?"

"You can't message her ten times a day, it's not cool, it's just weird. You can't message her multiple times a day, when she's not replying, *at Christmas*. Fucking hell man, I know you're no expert at this kinda thing but this is basic stuff, everyone knows this."

"What do you mean?" I ask, genuinely not understanding what the fuck Elijah is talking about.

"You need to chill," he says, his voice softer now, kinder. "She likes you, okay, but you're being a bit much. Maybe don't message her so much, maybe wait for her to message you."

Yeah, like that'll happen. What's he even saying, how is it possible to not message the person you love? Why would you even want to?

"I guess," I say sullenly, like a child who's just been admonished for getting dirt all over a clean room. I feel five years old. "That makes sense, I suppose, but still.

Why doesn't Jenn like me?"

"Oh, Jenn doesn't not like you," he says, waving his hand dismissively. "She's just being protective of her best friend is all. Listen, I'm telling you man, give Nicola some space and it'll work wonders, trust me."

"I'll try—" I begin, but Elijah slams his glass down on the table so hard I'm surprised it doesn't break. Beer shoots upwards from it and splashes us both, the table, our bags.

"—Don't try, Oliver, just fucking do it."

"I said I'll try."

"Don't try, just fucking do. You don't want to drive her away like you did with me do you?"

This takes me by surprise. Drive her away like I did him? Drive Elijah away? What's he talking about?

"What do you mean?"

"What?"

"You said I don't want to drive her away like I did you. What do you mean?"

"I mean, like, Oliver, it's— Do you not remember what happened between us?"

"Yeah of course I do. We had a fling, we hung out, whatever you want to call it. That ended, for whatever reason, I think it just fizzled, and we lost touch with each other."

"Are you fucking kidding me?" Elijah is looking at me, his mouth open, his beer suspended halfway between it and the table, his arm frozen mid-raise. His face would be a picture if I wasn't so sure he was about to completely devastate me.

"What?" I say, quietly, trying to prompt the onslaught. I know it's coming, so might as well get it over with. But what is it going to be? What's he about to say? I don't remember everything from that period with 100% clarity, but I remember enough. What have I forgotten?

"What's that film you like, the dodgy one from the 80s, the romcom?"

"You're going to need to be more specific," I say in a monotone, trying to stay as neutral as possible.

"You know, they go to England at the end, the dad's in prison for theft or fraud or something, I dunno. The dad from Frasier is in it, he plays the guy in prison."

"*Say Anything?*"

"Yes, *Say Anything*. You fucking Say Anything'ed me."

"I...what? I sent you to prison for fraud?"

"Don't jerk me around, man."

I'm not jerking him around, I genuinely have no idea what he's talking about. I don't say anything, wait for him to continue.

"I was in bed one night, it was just a random Tuesday or something, and I was just nodding off when I heard music. I looked out of my window to see you standing there, holding a fucking boombox above your head."

What? I never did that.

"I know what you're thinking and yes, you did in fact do that. It was 2014, man, I don't even know where you got a fucking boombox from! And that was the least terrifying thing you did."

"What are you talking about?"

"I can't believe you don't remember this. When I broke up with you, Oliver, you went nuts. I promise I'm not making this up. You were sending me hundreds of messages every day, turning up at my place at all hours of the day and night. You even came into some of my classes, once my roommates started threatening to call the police so you had to stop coming round to the apartment."

What the actual fuck? Why is he saying this shit? Why is he making up these lies about me?

"Do you honestly just think we drifted apart, and that's why we lost touch? Oliver, *I fucking dropped out of college because of you*. I left midway through second year and didn't come back. I had to, it was the only way to escape you; I knew you'd never quit, you'd never leave me alone, so I had to bail. My parents came and got me, literally in the middle of the night. They flew over, stayed in a hotel, and then one night they came and picked me and all my shit up in a rented car. I didn't even tell my roommates where I was going in case they slipped and told you. I didn't tell anyone except the admin staff who had to complete the paperwork. Oliver, you drove me away from college, you drove me away from London. You drove me out of the fucking country."

Is this true? It can't be true? Surely I didn't do that? I wouldn't, why would I? Elijah didn't dump me, we just fizzled. He was still at uni, I know he was, I saw him at graduation, we went for a pint before getting our degrees. Didn't we? Now I think of it, I can't say for certain that we did. I assumed I did see him there on that day, and maybe that assumption has crystallised into a fake memory. Oh shit, did I really do all these things that Elijah is saying? Am I really guilty?

"Did I—"

"—you did, Oliver. I'm sorry to be the one to bring it all up, but I didn't realise how bad it was with Nicola. You need to be careful, man. You're the reason we didn't speak for nearly a decade."

These words are harsh, they sting, like a knife through my heart, but if what he's saying is correct, then I only have myself to blame. Nah, fuck that, I don't believe him. I refuse to believe him. Why would I do all of that, for someone who isn't even The One? I might do the boombox thing to win back Nicola, but not Elijah. Elijah was just a bit of fun until I found The One, he was just a speed bump delaying me as I travelled to my destination. Which I have now arrived at; I just need a parking space and then I can attend and begin my future.

"I have to go," I say to Elijah, once again surprising myself.

"Oliver don't—" he starts to say but I'm already up, I've already left the table. "Please, Oliver, don't ruin her life the way you ruined mine…" I hear him shout across the room, then I'm outside and the door is closing behind me with a *thunk*. I need to speak to Nicola. I take my phone out to text her and then decide fuck it, I press the call button. It rings once, twice, three times, I'm just about to hang up when the ringing stops and I hear a soft, tentative, "Hello, Oliver. How're you?"

A voice. Sometimes all you need is to hear a voice. That's all I need right now, in this moment, is to hear Nicola's voice. Her soft tone coming down the line, the way she says certain words, her soft east coast American accent, all of it. When Nicola says my name my heart seems to be unable to decide whether to stop beating altogether, to simply shrivel up and cease to be, or to beat at a million beats per minute, beat so hard and so fast it bursts from my chest for the world to see. It eventually opts for the latter and for a few seconds I can't breathe, my throat constricts and no words are capable of leaving my mouth. Then I realise that I need to say something, this is the start of a conversation, it doesn't work if I contribute no words, so I try and find some. I hadn't expected her to answer, so I hadn't prepared anything to say.

What can I say to her? Tell her she's The One? She is, but if what Elijah said is right I don't want to scare her away. Tell her I've missed her? That might be even worse. Ask how her family is, how Christmas was? Wait, that might be a good one. Christmas isn't too far behind us so she's probably desperate to talk about them, to talk about it, to begin to unload whatever fresh trauma has been imparted on her.

Because that's what families do, what families are, a fresh and ever replenishing source of trauma. Everyone knows it, even the movies; they show it on screen with constant abandon, knowing it's the truth we're all mostly too afraid to acknowledge.

I mean look at Andie in *Pretty in Pink*; her dad does his best, but he's just not capable. All of Andie's trauma comes from her parents, from the fact her mom left her and her dad three years ago, and the fact her dad never got over it. He just lays in bed, moping, unable to work, unable to parent his child, unable to so much as even look after the dog. It's pathetic really. But then again, I don't blame him. He's under the misguided impression that Andie's mom was the one, and so he thinks he's lost her, that he's lost The One, and that he'll never be happy again. I want to grab him and throttle him, scream in his face to get up, get off his arse, get his act together; if Andie's mom left him, that means by very definition she isn't The One. What he needs to be doing is a) looking the fuck after his daughter, and b) sorting himself out and getting back out there. This is the 80s, long before the internet, and so people had to meet in real life. Andie's dad isn't going to be able to do this hiding away, lamenting the loss of his great love. Someone needs to give him a slap across the face and tell him that she wasn't his great love, just *a* love, and that his great love is still out there.

It's amazing Andie turns out so, well, normal in *Pretty in Pink*. Between her failures of parents, and the fact she's in an upper-class school and constantly ridiculed for being below the poverty line, it's a wonder she's so well-adjusted. Even after she meets Blane and he treats her like shit, over and over, she continues to keep her chin up, to do her best at everything. And she wins, ultimately, in the end: she doesn't just win Blane — which she of course does, he's The One, she's obviously going to win — but she wins in general, too. After Blane chickens out under pressure from Steff and reneges on his prom invite, after her dad tries, but fails miserably, buying her the hideous prom dress; even after turning up to prom alone, in a school where she's already an outcast, Andie wins. She transforms the hideous dress into a beautiful masterpiece, in which she looks amazing by the way. She meets Blane at the prom and they sort out their differences, they kiss in the parking lot, they finally end up together. Blane finally realises what he has right in front of him and accepts his fate.

As if it would be a hard choice; it isn't just Andie that's amazing, but Molly Ringwald is just something else altogether. How do you sum up the 80s in two words? Molly. Ringwald. She is, as anyone with a pair of eyes and a brain can see, impossibly young and impossibly beautiful. Even in *Pretty in Pink* in which she's poor, and makes all her outfits herself, she's irresistible. Hell, you know *Pretty in Pink* is going to be an amazing film right from the off when there's a close up of her putting on her tights. Fucking hell, that scene is something else. Molly Ringwald is something else, something else entirely. She's a goddess in a world of mere mortals, she's operating on a level to which the rest of us can only aspire. It's one of the things that makes Blane so insane, that he doesn't see this right away. But then, he can't be blamed, because sometimes one party of the couple doesn't always see what's in front of them right away. Look at Stacy and Mark in *Fast Times*, Jake and Sam in *Sixteen Candles*. It can sometimes take one half of the perfect couple a little time to realise that they're supposed to be one half of the perfect couple. But they always come around; as long as one person knows the other is The One, the other will figure it out before the end. And we'll always get the kiss.

Because the kiss is all that's needed. In *Pretty in Pink* when Blane finally asks Andie to the prom, and she says yes, and they finally have their first kiss: oh my god, it's everything. As Andie's dad says, in one of his pieces of wisdom — he's the ultimate advert for do as I say, not as I do — a good kiss can scramble anyone's brain. A-fucking-men brother. I'm desperate for that first kiss with Nicola, although when it finally happens I think my brain will just shut down, it won't be able to handle it. My life will finally have fulfilled its purpose, so perhaps that'll be it, my brain will pack it up and go home. It'd be fine by me; my brain is nothing but trouble, it does nothing but haunt me. I managed to escape my family, put several thousands of miles between us. So whilst I can avoid trauma from them, I can't avoid trauma from the organ sitting inside my skull at this very moment. It's my worst enemy.

I just know a kiss from Nicola will be shock therapy. It'll get all those misfiring synapses or whatever and reset them, get them on the right track. Nicola's lips on my lips will blow away anything else, any little thing that for so many years has pretended to matter. The kiss will be Andie and Blane outside her house after he asks her to prom, it'll be in the parking lot during the prom; it'll be Sam and Jake kissing above the candles, it'll be Tom and Summer kissing in the copy room, it'll be Stacy jumping over the counter to kiss Mark in the fast-food joint. It'll be everything, everything in the world, in the galaxy, in the observable and knowable universe. And then it'll be so much more on top. It'll be everything else. Because Nicola is everything. Really, she is truly everything.

Everything that has come before, the past that doesn't exist; everything still to come, the future that looks dark and uncertain; these things will finally take their rightful place in the background. All I need is Nicola in the foreground. She isn't a backing character, she isn't part of the scenery; she's the entire script.

"I'm okay thanks, Nicola, how're you? Did you have a nice Christmas? How are your family?"

Silence from the other end, only for a moment, like composure being gathered, like a line being silently rehearsed before being said out loud, like a feeling being confirmed.

"Christmas was okay, thank you," her response is very quiet, very timid. She's probably just nervous, I wonder if she's finally realised I'm The One and now she's a bit scared, a bit apprehensive. Maybe she's finally where I am, which is living in a constant state of fear of losing the other person. Maybe her eyes are finally open. My heart flutters, it swells up and threatens to burst out of my chest like in *Alien*, though much less horrifying and much more beautiful. "My family are fine, thank you. Same old."

"I bet, families can be like that. No one killed anyone, I hope?"

A small laugh, one that sounds like it might be coming through tears, but it's impossible to say.

"No, no one committed murder. Although I think a few people came close on a few occasions. I know I did."

I laugh now, her words amuse me, I can picture the family Christmas perfectly in my head, brothers and sisters and fathers and mothers and sons and daughters all on top of each other, unable to move for crashing into each other, slowly losing the plot, loving the holiday but begging for it to be over. I'm surprised as a tear falls on my hand, and I think: is this what I'm missing?

"Did you have to stay long? When did you get back to the city?"

"Thankfully no, I left on the 27th. My brother and his wife were leaving then, too, so it made sense, my parents dropped me at the station on the way to the airport."

Oh wow, so she's been back in the city for a while? I won't pretend I'm not hurt that she didn't reach out, didn't want to see me, but hey ho; what can you do? She's here now, we're talking now, we'll arrange to meet up no doubt, have our next date.

"Did you have a good New Year's Eve?" I ask, somehow momentarily forgetting about the phone call. The silence from Nicola tells me that she has not. "I mean, like," I scramble, "sorry, I'm not putting you on the spot, I'm not fucking with you or anything, I'm genuinely asking."

"That's okay," she says, still speaking incredibly slowly, as if she's calculating every word, making sure she says the exact right thing. Her voice is incredibly soft, she's sniffing as she speaks, I want to somehow pass her a tissue through the phone, put my hand on her arm, make her see that everything is going to be okay now. Her voice is barely above a whisper, and on the street I struggle to hear it over the sound of passing cars, of human conversation. "New Year's was good thanks, I enjoyed it."

"I'm glad." I really am.

"Listen, Oliver," she says suddenly, quickly, she startles me. "I'm really sorry about New Year's, I'm sorry you had to hear that."

She doesn't need to apologise, I don't need to hear one, but it's nice, nonetheless. It shows she cares, that she considers my feelings. My cheeks become warm, I must be blushing. I try and look in the window of the store front behind me but the glass is too clean to reflect anything, it simply shows me the inside of the shop.

"That's okay," I say, "it happens." And I mean this: it does happen. Things happen, that's just what life is. Didn't someone once say something about the path of true love, or the path to true love, never running smoothly. Or was it a river? Who knows. But yeah, basically love isn't always straight forward. We're in the part of the movie where there's some tension between us, some conflict, and whilst it isn't fun to live through, it's vital to the story. We've come together, and now we're in conflict, we've moved apart, but all it means is that when we finally get together at the end of the movie it'll be all the sweeter. A little bit of bad really makes you appreciate the good.

"I didn't want you to hear any of that, that was only supposed to be for Zarah and Jenn," she continues, and though I don't need to hear this I get the sense she needs to say it, and so I let her. "I was just so drunk, and had no idea I'd called you. I'd had, like, a long Christmas, even though I got back to the city pretty soonish afterwards it still wore me down, I was still a bit of a mess. I, erm, I drank more than I should have on New Year's and that's why I said those things. I didn't," she hesitates, as if unsure of what she's going to say next, or unsure of whether she means the words about to come out of her mouth. "I didn't mean what I said. You're not weird," it stings to hear again, I won't lie, "you're just different, that's all, you're just not like other guys."

Now my heart does stop beating, it no longer wants to burst from my chest, it simply wants to just stay where it is, safely ensconced in my ribcage. Because these are the words I didn't even know I've been waiting to hear, words that I have been desperate for my entire life. I've always suspected I'm not like other guys, always felt apart from them, I've always felt like something else. Not necessarily in a bad way, either, just in a neutral way. It isn't bad or good I'm not like other guys, it's just a fact. However, to hear Nicola say it I now realise that not only is it a good thing, it's the best thing in the world; I'm different from other guys, and she likes that. I'm different from other guys, and that's why she likes me. I'm different from other guys, and that's what's made her love me. Because standing here on the street listening to her talk, I know she loves me. She's finally seen the light, and the light has shown her the path. I've been on the path since day one, and it's been fine to be alone, waiting for her, knowing she's on her way. And now she's finally joined me, and I know everything is going to be okay.

"Thank you," I practically whisper to her. It's all I can manage without my voice breaking, and I don't want her to hear me cry. She won't understand. "You're not like other women, you're completely different. You're something else entirely."

"Thank you," she says with a sniff.

"How come you haven't been at work this week?" I say suddenly, changing the subject abruptly. I'm not sure why I say this, I mean I asked because I want to know, but why now? Why not continue praising each other, complimenting each other? It was much more fun than this probably mundane line of conversation.

"Oh," she says, hesitant. "I haven't been very well."

"Oh no, nothing too bad I hope?"

"No, just a cold, I've been working still, just working from home, keeping my germs to myself."

"And we in the office thank you for it," I say with a smile. Such a normal conversation, just two people in love discussing life, as people in love do. I am just like the other guys, now I am. She's made me like them, and that's more than fine by me.

"So listen——"

"——I was thinking…"

We both start to speak at the same time, talking over each other, cutting each other off. I laugh and apologise, tell her to go on.

"I was thinking, do you want to grab a drink after work on Monday? I'm feeling much better so should be back in the office, and it'll be good for us to sit down and catch up properly. I want to hear all about your Christmas."

And I want to hear all about yours, I think. I'm dying to. I want to learn all about your family, people who will be my family one day, once we're married. I want to know about your home and your traditions, your decorations; do you go to midnight mass? Who puts the star on top of the tree? Do you have mimosa on Christmas morning, or hot chocolate, or do you do whatever each individual wants, no traditions at all? I want to learn everything about you, Nicola, I want to take the information in and memorise it and use it to make your life perfect. Because you deserve a perfect life, Nicola, and I'm going to be the one to give it to you.

I don't say any of this of course, instead I simply say, "that sounds great, I'd really like to."

"Perfect," she says, "it's a date."

A giant grin spreads across my face as she says this. It's a date. Our first official date. We had the wedding and she came round to mine, but those were just hangs, in the words of Corey and D.C., they were just scams, they weren't dates. This is a date.

"It's a date," I echo. "I can't wait."

"I gotta go, but Monday. Have a great weekend."

"You too, Nicola, bye."

We hang up and I put my phone in my pocket but don't move. I stay where I am on the sidewalk, the wind blowing the world all around me. *This is it*, I think. Nicola asked you on a date. This means that your suspicions were correct, she does love you, and she's finally not only accepted this fact, but is acting on it. I start to walk, fantasies of Monday evening filling my head. I'm finally going to get my first kiss with The One; I just can't believe I have to wait three whole days for it.

Not only is it amazing to have a date lined up with Nicola because, well, I have a date lined up with Nicola, but it's also amazing because it means I don't have to spend the weekend checking my phone every two seconds to see if she's messaged. I still do jump up whenever it goes off in case it is her — it isn't, she doesn't message all weekend but that's fine — but when it's quiet, I'm happy for it to be quiet. It can stay quiet; the date is in the bag, nothing can change that.

As well as this, I only message her a few times myself. I message her Friday when I get home, telling her it was great to speak to her and I can't wait for our date. I message her on Saturday saying that I hope she has a great day, and then a little later letting her know I'm thinking of her. On Sunday morning I simply message 'tomorrow', and then on Sunday evening I tell her I hope she sleeps well, and that I'm looking forward to seeing her the next day. Which is perhaps the biggest understatement of the century, of all time; I haven't slept a wink this weekend, not even half an hour, but it's fine, because now I'm not sleeping due to excitement. It's one thing to lie awake at night under a veil of dread and despair, watch the bell jar slowly sink upon you, but it's something else entirely to be cloaked under a veil of excitement and anticipation. They're not two sides of the same coin: dread and despair is a dirty penny pulled from the gutter, where anticipation and excitement is a fresh, crisp $100 bill. They exist in the same world, but they're not even close to being in the same league.

It's nice to not have to spend the weekend like Andie, hoping Blane will call, or like Helen, hoping James will call. It's nice to have it in the bag so I can enjoy my weekend, can let my mind be worry-free for once. Which is a wonderful theory, but obviously doesn't happen. The dread is still there, even if it's much easier to ignore now. It still exists, it still haunts me, it's just quieter; for once optimism reigns in my mind, a positive outlook is the way forward for me, I'm no longer treading water, I'm swimming for the gold.

I spend Saturday clearing out my apartment, getting rid of crap I don't need and crap I can sell. Because in spite of all this excitement, there's still the worry of how I'll be able to pay for the date. And the second date, and third, and so on. Dating is expensive, and I'm about to face a lifetime of it, so I need to be prepared.

The first thing I do is lug my box of vinyl down to Octopus Records in Brooklyn. It's a trek, the box is big and unwieldy, not to mention it weighs a tonne, but I take the subway, cringing as I pay the fare but telling myself it's worth it, you have to spend money to make money, speculate to accumulate and all that. The trip is worth it: the two buck fare nets me just over a hundred bucks in sales. Less than I expected, to be honest I think I got ripped off, I think they saw me coming a mile away, but I don't care. I was desperate for money, and now I have some.

This trip is so tiring — I force myself to walk back, despite the fact it takes over two hours — that I do little else on Saturday except lay on the couch, stare at the TV, will time to pass. I don't know that I've ever wished a weekend away this much, and though it feels counter intuitive, I know it's right. Monday holds so much more promise than every other day combined. On Sunday I clean; I properly clean my apartment, the way I half did when she came over last time. There's no guarantee she'll come back to mine, not at all, but I want to be prepared just in case. I change my sheets, lug all my washing to the laundrette down the street; I find a duster buried underneath the sink and go over every surface meticulously, getting rid of god knows how many spiders and their webs, how many dead flies. I'm actually pretty shocked to see just how bad it is, how dirty my apartment is, but I don't dwell on it. The best time to find dirt is as you're erasing it, so it's all good.

By late Sunday afternoon I'm happy with how the apartment looks, and also absolutely exhausted, so I stop. I make one quick trip to the Jewish Deli down the street and get some supplies, nothing major, just the basic stuff most adults have, that I'd imagine Nicola would expect me to have: tea, coffee, sugar, milk, bread, butter, jam. Again, I don't have any expectation that Nicola will come to my apartment, but it'll be nice to resemble a proper, functioning person if she does. She may be in love with me, of that I have no doubt, but love can only do so much, and I have to do the rest.

I also bought a bottle of prosecco which I put in the fridge. I'm tempted to open it now, have a glass, but I don't have any stoppers, once the bottle is opened it's on a countdown until it's flat, so I stop myself. I don't need to drink anyway, for the first time in god knows how long I feel okay. Scratch that, I'm feeling good. I'll go to work tomorrow, smash out a few reports, maybe write some copy, not for a project or anything, just for fun, just because I can, to keep practising my skills. Nicola said the best way to get better at writing is to write, that practice makes perfect and all that. Maybe I'll do so tomorrow. Whatever; I'll do whatever, patiently counting down until

6pm, when my new life will begin.

With this in mind I turn off all the lights, turn off the TV and, getting into bed, prepare for a night of staring at the ceiling. A few tears tonight, but tears of excitement, I think? Maybe there is hope for the future? Scratch that, because I know for sure there is hope for the future. The future is going to be wonderful. Nicola and I against the world. With her at my side, I can't fail.

Chapter Ten

The Breakfast Club

Monday is interminably long; I imagine this is how people on death row feel, spending their days going through appeal after appeal, and then once their avenues of appeal are exhausted waiting for an execution date, and then once they have a date, waiting for that date. It's the waiting, always waiting. I spend the morning going through the motions — which doesn't actually make it much different from any other morning, to be fair — running weekly reports for last week, answering a few emails, deleting a load more. All the boring stuff that happens every Monday, not just here in this office, not just in this company, not even just in this building or this city, but all over the world; Monday mornings are being had by everyone, whether they want to or not. Not everyone's are the same, but for my fellow white-collar workers, this Monday is also last Monday and the Monday before that, repeat ad infinitum. It's always Monday morning.

Nicola is in the office today, as she said she would be, and she looks resplendent. I don't know if it's because we're going for a drink later or what, but she looks even more beautiful than normal. They say that pregnant women glow; I've never known what they mean until now, because Nicola has a glow about her today. There's a light around her, actually more of an aura; her brown hair is brighter than normal, shinier but, like, not in a greasy way, in a gorgeous way, her hair is glowing. Her skin is light, pale but not delicate, firm, fierce; even her eyes are shining more than usual, it almost looks like she's been crying. I'm sure she hasn't, I'm sure it's just the anticipation running through her body much like it is mine, I'm sure she's just as excited about tonight as I am. She keeps looking at me, sneaking little glances; I look up from my computer, my phone, my feet, the abyss, whatever, and I'll look over to her desk and see her looking at me, and then she'll quickly whip her head around, her hair flying out around her as she looks back at her computer, at her phone, whatever. It's really sweet, actually, how nervous she is; I find it reassuring as well, that she's as nervous, if not more so, than I am. It makes me feel better knowing we're both in the same boat.

Tom and Neil have been oddly distant this morning, but it's all good, I just assume they each had heavy weekends and so want quiet Monday mornings. I'm more than happy to oblige. Neil even cancelled our Monday morning check-in, which is good: I hate meetings at the best of times, but especially Monday mornings. I need those few hours not just to run my reports, but to come to life. I don't wake up when my alarm goes off, oh no, I slowly wake up as the morning minutes are eaten by the clock, and it isn't usually until after lunch when I feel alive. As alive as I ever do anyway, as alive as it's possible for someone as dead as me to feel.

There was an awkward moment this morning; I went into the kitchen to make a drink and, returning to my desk, I saw Nicola going into a room with Sophie, that horrible HR woman from the incident in the pub last year. Awkward mainly because I know Nicola doesn't like her, because of that incident. To have been a fly on the wall in that meeting; I could see the room from my desk, the glass walls only providing an imitation of privacy, and from where I was sitting it looked awkward. I don't know the purpose of the meeting but Sophie looked concerned the entire time. Nicola was sitting with her back to me so I couldn't make out her features, but judging from Sophie's face Nicola was giving her somewhat of a pasting. Good for her. And good for me, too: I have someone fighting my corner, and it's wonderful. If I didn't already know that Nicola is The One, here's yet more proof. God, life is simple, straightforward, when you're in love. They were in the meeting for 47 minutes; when it finally finished the HR woman disappeared, presumably to wherever HR are located, and Nicola went into the bathroom, I assume to calm herself down; I imagine the meeting got pretty heated. Anyway she was in there for 8 minutes, before she emerged looking as beautiful as ever. I smiled at her, though I don't think she saw me, despite looking in my direction, because she didn't smile back. Probably lost in her thoughts, bless her: that can't have been an easy meeting.

It's nearly midday, which means nearly lunchtime. I'm not hungry, I'm too excited and nervous to eat, but I'm going to go for a walk anyway, stretch my legs, get out of the office for a bit. Even though it's a horribly cold day the January sun is flooding the streets and the city looks gorgeous. The sunlight is shining off the melting frost on trees, the sidewalk, on cars; it's truly beautiful, each little twinkle like a drop of Heaven. Even though it hurts my eyes I don't mind it, I can imagine there are worse things than being blinded by beauty. Though if I was to go actually blind I don't think I could go on; I can't imagine never seeing Nicola's face again, never seeing her smile, seeing her laugh. Never seeing her naked; yes, I'd be able to feel her body, learn to read it like braille, but it wouldn't be the same. I need to know what she looks like, not just how she feels. They may be two of the five senses, but they're worlds apart in reality. I need both to make the full picture.

I'm just gathering my things to go, and by things I mean my wallet and phone, when Nicola approaches me. Though still ostensibly pale her face is red, and her eyes are red, too, more so than earlier; I wonder if she had a little cry in the toilets after her HR meeting, if the adrenaline coursing through her system crashed out of her in the form of tears. I know how it is, emotion coming out in the form of tears; it's somewhat my speciality.

"Hey, you," I say to her, unable to keep the grin off my face.

"Hi," she says quietly, and it breaks my heart to see her so hurt. I want to take her in my arms, tell her with both my words and my embrace that everything is going to be okay, that I'm going to make everything okay.

"How's your Monday going?"

"Fine," she says, still very quietly, sniffing as she does, her nose scrunching up, yet another adorable trait of hers.

"Good," I say, "I'm glad." And I am, I really am. For the first time in my life I'm experiencing what it's like to appreciate someone else's emotions, and I quite like it. "I'm really looking forward to tonight."

"About that," she says. "Have you got two minutes?"

"Sure," I say, delighted. "I was just going for a walk, that can wait."

I stand up as she walks away and I follow her; I have no idea where we're going, what she wants to talk about — actually no, she probably wants to talk about her meeting with Sophie. She leads me into the same room, and I want to make a joke about this but I don't, it's still probably a very sore topic to Nicola. Jokes can come later, now is the time for comfort.

We reach the room and Nicola lets me go in first; I sit down in one of the two chairs but she stays standing by the door, closing it but never removing her hand from the handle.

"Are you okay?" I ask, more tenderly now, less as a colleague and more as a future lover, now we have privacy.

"Oliver, I don't think it's a good idea for us to go out tonight. In fact, I don't think us speaking at all is a good idea. I need you to leave me alone."

Time stops. My heart moves up into my throat and I can't breathe. The walls start moving in, the glass is upon me before I know it and I'm trapped. The air in the room is suddenly too hot, the lights too bright. I think I must be in the wrong room with the wrong person because this person, who looks like Nicola, who sounds like Nicola, is saying words Nicola never would. I'm in the wrong place, part of the wrong conversation.

I don't say anything; what can I say? How am I supposed to respond to this? There are a million incoherent thoughts rushing through my mind, a million different fragments of ideas, half sentences, mismatched words. None of them are correct, none of them sculpted enough to come out of my mouth. However Nicola isn't saying anything either, she's waiting for me, for my response. I have to do something. I open my mouth, lick my lips, moistening them with what I feel is the last moisture my mouth will ever create, and I see what happens.

"What?"

Great, nice one, Oliver. Really good, insightful response to her statement. Brilliant work you fucking idiot.

Nicola still doesn't say anything, so it's my turn to go again. I force myself to speak an actual sentence this time, to use actual words properly. It's a titanic struggle. In fact the Titanic itself has got nothing on me. This is a fucking tragedy of epic proportions.

"I'm sorry, I'm not sure if I heard you correctly." There we go, full sentence, proper grammar and syntax and everything. Nice one. "Did you say you never want to see me again?"

She looks down, apparently unable to continue making eye contact as I say these words. She's still standing by the door and now I understand why, it's so she can make a quick escape. I recognise that posture. Even as she stands perfectly still I imagine her running through things in her head, picturing herself opening the door, leaving me in this room, leaving me behind.

"I'm sorry," she says, and she's so sincere that for a moment I believe her. But then I don't, because this can't be real, can it? This must be a joke. That's it, this is a joke. That's what Nicola was discussing in this very room with Sophie, how to pull a joke on me. Sophie did it amazingly, so Nicola wanted some tips. When she did it at the wedding she failed, so she went to the expert. That's how we've ended up here. I sigh with relief. Good one, Nicola.

"Good one," I say, standing up, smiling now. Nicola tries to back away as I rise but she only bumps into the door, she has nowhere to go; I assume this is only part of the joke, however. I move towards her and she stiffens. She's really committing to this bit, fair play to her.

"What do you mean?" she asks, the very picture of innocence.

"You had me for a second there," I say to her, "I won't lie. I thought my life was over for a moment."

Her expression has changed now, from sadness to

confusion. She cocks her head at me like an animal might, regarding me as if *she* now doesn't understand *me*. It's a bit much, I think, but whatever, I guess she's just committed to the bit.

"Oliver—" she starts, but I interrupt.

"—For a second there I thought you were being serious, you were actually cancelling our date." I laugh as I say this; hearing it out loud makes it sound even more absurd than it had been in my head. Once I start laughing I can't stop, and soon I'm bending over gasping for air, tears falling from my eyes. What a joker Nicola is. I can't wait to spend my life with her.

"Oliver, I am being serious." Her voice is flat, all emotion removed from it.

"It's okay, Nicola," I say, forcing the words out between my laughter, standing back up, wiping the tears from my eyes. "I'm nervous too, I get it. It's going to be a wonderful evening, I promise."

"Oliver!" she says, exasperation lacing her words.

"Nicola!" I say back to her, mimicking her tone, her expediency. This game is a little weird, but it's all good. I'd play any game with Nicola. I'd have fun with her even in a Turkish Prison, as Blane says to Andie. I feel that line whenever I watch *Sixteen Candles*, and I feel it standing here, now, talking to Nicola.

"We're not going out tonight, Oliver," she says, all trace of humour long gone. If it was ever there to begin with. "I was being serious, I *am* very serious. This isn't going to work, Oliver, you're a nice guy but it's not meant to be."

These final five words trigger something in me, some kind of understanding, and suddenly it all rushes in on me. She *isn't* joking, she *is* being serious. What the fuck?

"But it is!" I practically shout. Behind Nicola, through the glass, I can see people stopping what they're doing and looking at us. "It is meant to be, this, us, we are meant to be together."

"But Oliver—"

"—You're The One, Nicola!" By the time I say this I am shouting, and everyone in the office has stopped and is watching us. I see Neil and Tom moving towards the meeting room, a few others moving with them. "We're meant to be together, Nicola," I say, pleading entering my voice. "You're The One, you're made for me and I'm made for you."

"I'm sorry, Oliver," she says, opening the door behind her and slowly moving forward as it swings into the room, then slowly backing through it. I follow her, unable to stop myself.

"Nicola, please," I say, everyone can see and hear me but I don't care, I don't fucking care about them, they don't matter. Only Nicola matters. "Nicola, please," I shout, my voice breaking. "You can't leave me, you can't leave it like this. My job is to be a great date for you, how can I not?"

She continues walking away, her back to me, ignoring me. She moves between Tom and Neil and so do I, they turn as we pass but neither of them move. Nicola glances over her shoulder and seeing me she speeds up, so I increase my pace to match hers. The office is eerily quiet, the only sounds Nicola's footsteps walking away and mine chasing them, muted and hushed on the scuffed, grey, carpet tiles that comprise the floor.

"Nicola wait, what about our ideal kissing moment? The boat," I say, scrambling to get my words out coherently, "the moon, all of it. You can't not be there!"

She moves through the office and into the lobby with a practised ease, making for a door in the corner. I chase after her, grab her wrist, try and stop her, but she jerks her arm so suddenly I lose my grip and then she's opening the door, rushing into the room, and I grab the door before it closes and follow her. Behind the first door there's immediately a second and it slams into the wall with a deafening crash as Nicola throws it open. There's another loud banging immediately afterwards and it's only when I see a cubicle door shutting and hear the sound of the lock scraping closed that I realise where I am, what I've done. In my desperation to catch her I've followed her into the ladies' toilets.

I know I need to leave but I can't move my feet, they're welded to the floor.

"Please, Nicola," I say, and even I'm annoyed at the desperation I can hear in my voice, but only momentarily. The annoyance is quickly replaced by sadness and fear and devastation. This can't be it, can it? I think of *Friends*, the early season episode where Rachael dumps Ross after he cheats on her. He tells her that it can't be the end, begs and pleads, literally on his knees, and she simple replies with great finality that it is.

"Nicola, please," I say. "I love your smile. I love your hair. I love your knees. I love how you lick your lips before you talk. I love the heart-shaped birthmark on your neck. I love it when you sleep." I don't know what I'm saying any more, words are just falling out of my mouth. "I love *you*."

And there it is, the three words that are the pinnacle of human existence. Those three words and the feeling they convey are the only reason to live, the only point to this species. That we're able to fall in love with each other is why we're here, the entire raison d'être of humanity. It's what separates us from the animals, from plants and buildings and everything else, our ability to fall in love. It's what makes us, us.

Nicola doesn't respond, all I can hear from the cubicle in which she's ensconced herself is an occasional sniffing sound, a cough; she's crying but trying not to let me hear.

I stand there, in the middle of the floor, the forensically bright lighting making me uncomfortably warm. I'm just thinking of what to say when there's a bang behind me and I jump, letting out a little yelp as I do. I don't turn around, don't take my eyes off Nicola's cubicle, but I don't need to: to my left is a wall made up of sinks and, above them, a huge mirror, and in this mirror I can see Tom, Neil, and what I can only assume from his outfit is the building's security guard. They all stand in the doorway watching me, waiting for me to do something, but I don't do anything. The four of us simply stand, letting the moment play out around us.

I don't know how long we stand for, but when Nicola sniffs again it breaks the ice that had been encasing us all, and Neil steps forward, he squeezes past the security guard and speaks to me.

"Oliver, can you come with me, please?"

I don't move. I can't move.

"Oliver, please," he says, and now it's his turn to plead.

"Neil, please," I say, "this is between Nicola and I."

He sighs, mutters something under his breath, but stays where he is. I still don't move either, except to jump when I feel something on my arm. Finally tearing my eyes away from the door behind which Nicola sits I look down to see a huge white hand on my arm: the security guard, apparently having had enough of my silence, has moved over to me and has grabbed me. And before I know what's going on he's pulling me out of the room, I'm trying my hardest to fight him but to no avail, he's much bigger and stronger than me, not to mention trained for this type of scenario. I have lost all agency, I am no longer able to control my movements, they've become as alien to me as my emotions. I'm just an idiot in love.

Despite my best efforts, my loudest protestations, I'm dragged into the elevator and then held firmly as it descends to the ground floor. The security guard escorts me out onto the street, and with a shove finally lets me go. Stumbling to a halt I rub my arm where he's been holding me, it's sore, his grip was not light. I turn to face the building and see him standing in front of the revolving glass door shaking his head. I move towards him and he raises his hand, palm facing me in a 'stop' gesture. I move towards him regardless, try and push past him to the door, and when I'm unable try and push him out of the way. He doesn't move so much as a millimetre. I try for about 30 seconds before I give up, exhausted, pain and fear and frustration and sadness coursing through my body, causing me to tremble. I take a few steps away, move towards the curb, before turning back to face the building. I see the security guard tense, as if he's expecting me to take another run at him, this time literally, but I don't move. Behind the security guard I can see Neil standing in the lobby. He has my bag and my coat, and after a brief conversation the security guard stands aside to let him pass. I consider making a run for it, trying to squeeze into the building whilst the security guard is momentarily distracted, but my legs have turned to jelly, whatever adrenaline I had in me has passed, I'm weak and pathetic once again. Neil approaches me slowly, the way you might approach the T-Rex in Jurassic Park. When he's close he holds out my bag and coat to me and I take them from him, dropping them at my feet, not caring how wet and dirty they get in the pools of brown water gathered in the gutter. Neil follows their trajectory with his eyes before looking at me.

"Oliver, what the fuck?"

"I love her, Neil," is all I can say, it's all I can think, it's all I am. "I love her."

"I know, Oli, I know," he says tenderly, his voice soft. I begin to think I know how old people feel now being talked down to, being patronised to the nth degree. "I know you do, but you can't," he gestures behind himself to the building, "do whatever the hell that was in there."

"But I love her!" is all I can say. If I say it enough the words will get through to him, surely? How could they not? Once they do everything will be fine, he'll let me back in, Nicola and I will be reunited. For now, however, he stands firm.

"Oliver, why don't you go home? And stay home for a few days, yeah? Officially you're suspended on full pay, but unofficially, between you and I, I think you need a break. Go home, sleep it off, read a few books, watch some Netflix, distract yourself, relax, and then let's go from there. How does that sound?"

Fucking terrible.

"I want to see Nicola," I say, moving towards the building once again, but the security guard moves with a speed that belies his size and then his massive hand is on my chest, holding me back with almost embarrassing ease.

"For fuck's sake, Oliver," Neil says, one hand on his hip, the other on his forehead, all trace of sympathy now gone from his voice. "Don't make this any worse than it is. Just go home and I'll call you in a couple of days, yeah?"

When I don't say anything he nods at me then turns back to the building. He says something I can't hear to the security guard who nods, and then Neil is back in the building, he presses the button for the elevator and gets in without looking back, and then the door closes and he's gone, and I'm left on the street with just the security guard. Reluctantly I pick up my coat and bag and, putting them both on, ignoring how wet I immediately become, how bad both items smell, I start to walk away from the building, start to walk home. I cry, I weep, the entire way.

Love and hate are still, will always remain, two sides of the same coin. Just as Nicola seems to hate me right now, she'll pull through, of that I have no doubt: look at Claire throughout the majority of *The Breakfast Club*. She hates Bender from the start, constantly telling him off, trying to force him back into the box society — and the school — has cast him into. She despises him and makes no pretence of doing otherwise. But it's all just a cover, she knows, deep down, that she doesn't hate him really, that she in fact loves him. We can see it even if she can't; the way she bites her lip after correcting his pronunciation of Molière, the way she happily follows him out of the library, even though she doesn't know where he's going; the way she covers for him even when he's underneath her desk and sneakily looks up her skirt, looks at her underwear. Claire knows, even if only subconsciously at first, that Bender is The One. Because it follows the usual pattern, which is just a reflection of real life: Bender knows right away that Claire is the one, and this is all it takes. As in other romcoms, it sometimes only takes one side of the couple to know, and that's enough. So long as one party knows, the connection has been made, and it'll never be broken.

I just want to see Nicola's panties, I want to hide under her desk and look up her skirt, and I want her to let me. She seems to hate me right now, I mean what else can I surmise from her current actions? But it's okay, because we're still in act two. I've been crying all week, moaning her name, holding my pillow tightly and wishing it was her; but these acts aren't unique to this week, this behaviour is par for the course. And as I say, we're still only in act two; in act one Nicola and I got to know each other, spent a lot of time together, now in act two we're facing conflict and strife, we're in the 'will they or won't they?' phase of our relationship. We're in the phase where Nicola doesn't know I'm The One, but it's okay, because I do, and so the connection has been made. She'll come around, like Claire does, like Stacy does, like Blane does, like they all do. There's no stopping it, no keeping us apart. Neil can send me home all he wants, all it means is the distance between us is only physical. She's in my heart, and soon I'll be in hers. I just have to wait. There's no stopping true love.

I'd be lying if I said the waiting isn't hard, though; I've been at home for three days now, three long, tough days. I've messaged Nicola and haven't heard back from her, but that's fine. Even before we entered into this temporary conflict, she was terrible at replying. No matter; some people are texters, some aren't. I am, she isn't. It's whatever, it'll be fine.

Speaking of texting, Neil text me this morning, he wants to have a call this afternoon. I'm assuming it'll be to apologise, to un-suspend me, invite me back into the office, back to work. Whilst I can't forgive what he did, I can understand it. Workplaces, especially offices like ours, 90% of it is all about show. What you're actually doing matters little compared to what it looks like you're doing, to how you look whilst you're doing it. I'm sure Neil didn't want to call security, didn't want to escort me out of the building and suspend me, but I'm also sure he had to. Admittedly, things did get slightly out of control; finding myself in the ladies' toilets was not my finest hour. So yeah, understandable, after the whole office had seen me do that, that he had to do what he did. And now

I assume enough time has passed, it looks good to Brielle and her bosses, it looks like Neil really cares about the company or whatever, keeping everyone healthy and happy. I assume he's calling to tell me all is good, that I can come back to work on Monday. Not that I particularly want to go back to work, but I'll be able to see Nicola so it'll be okay. Seeing her face, being in her presence, overwrites everything else, makes everything else bearable. Blane's Turkish prison all over again.

Whilst I wait for Neil to call — he's due to in about half an hour — I'm actually trying to put Nicola out of my mind for a change. Despite the fact I know the call will be fine, it's like how I know Nicola and I will be fine: I still have to actually go through the motions. Nicola and I will end up together, but only because I'll make it so; the call with Neil will go fine, but only because I'll make it so. I need to put her out of my mind so as to not mention her on the call, leave her out of it. I need to make it about me, and then it'll all be good.

It's easy, temporarily at least, to get Nicola out of my mind. I've simply replaced her with someone else, someone nearly as incredible: Molly Ringwald. There's a scene in *The Breakfast Club*, towards the end when all the barriers have come down, when they're all finally seeing each other — when Claire has finally begun to realise that Bender is The One — where they're sharing secrets. Some serious, some not. Claire's secret is that she can put lipstick on with her cleavage, and when no one believes her she shows them. And it is just incredible. It's sexy, oh so sexy: to think that the lipstick is resting between her breasts, they're sufficiently close together to be able to hold it there; because they do hold it, it isn't just balanced but nestled, held firmly enough that Claire can rub her lips on it and it stays put. I'm not sure I can adequately put into words how this scene makes me feel, each and every time I watch it. I picture the inside edges of Molly Ringwald's breasts, the pink skin, how soft and smooth they must be. I picture the rest of each breast, equally pink and smooth, and it makes me want to melt, it fills me with a longing that's so far beyond wanting it becomes painful, it's a chore; short of time travel being invented, due to the existence of linear time I'll never be able to feel Molly Ringwald's breasts as they were in 1985. Like *Fast Times*, *The Breakfast Club* pre-dates my existence by over a decade; I can only dream of being there, of being a part of it. I never actually can.

I wonder how Molly Ringwald's breasts compare to Nicola's. At least with Nicola's I'll one day know, I'll see them and touch them and take her nipples into my mouth. I wonder about Nicola's breasts perhaps less than Molly Ringwald's, because with Molly Ringwald it's an abstract fantasy that will never be fulfilled, and with Nicola it's simply a matter of time.

My phone is ringing, Neil's name on the screen. I wonder: is this the end of act two, and the beginning of act three, or will act three begin upon my triumphant return to the office? It doesn't matter, not really, I'm just wondering, daydreaming. Soon all will be revealed. I take a moment to compose myself, put on my work mask, take a couple of deep breaths in through my nose, out through my mouth, and then I answer.

"Hi, Neil, how are you?"

"Hi, Oliver. I'm okay thanks, how're you?" I'm about to answer when he speaks over me. "Just to let you know Oliver, you're on speaker."

"No worries."

"Great. And I have Saanvi from HR here with me, too."

My initial thought is that this is odd, a strange

development, but then I figure it must be a formality, a third party to witness the conversation.

"Okay, cool. Hi, Saanvi," I say.

"Hi, Oliver," comes a high pitched yet very soft female voice across the line. "It's great to meet you."

"You, too," I say, and although I obviously don't mean it I'm sure she doesn't either, so it's all good. There's a moment of silence, now the introductions are over, before Neil resumes speaking.

"So, Oliver, about the other day…"

I'm not sure if he trails off because he doesn't know what to say or just doesn't know how to start, so I jump in and save him the effort.

"Listen, Neil, I'm really sorry about what happened on Monday. My behaviour was incredibly inappropriate, and I'm not only sorry towards Nicola but towards you as well, I'm sorry for the position I put both you and the company in."

Another moment of silence, no doubt the pair of them absorbing my words, taking them in, being impressed by them. I don't say anything, let them have their silence, bask in my victory. It's Saanvi who speaks next.

"Oliver, thank you for that, it's great to hear you acknowledge what happened and admit your mistakes." Her voice is so soft it's making me sleepy, I want to curl up in it and go to sleep, wake up on Monday when it's time to see Nicola again.

"Unfortunately," she continues — unfortunately what? What's unfortunate — "unfortunately your behaviour was completely and utterly unacceptable, it was behaviour we absolutely cannot tolerate. You scared Nicola half to death; she's been off work all week, and I think she will be for a few more weeks. And we're having to pay her, of course, because it happened on company property, during work hours, and was done to her by a fellow employee." Her tone has shifted now, the softness has been replaced by something hard, something firmer. I don't like where this is going, I want Neil to speak again. "So with that in mind, Oliver, we're going to have to terminate your employment with immediate effect."

The silence returns, only this time it's Neil and Saanvi waiting for me to speak. They're going to have to let me go? Am I fired?

"What do you mean?" I ask. "Neil, what does she mean?"

It's a moment before Neil speaks, and when he does his voice is soft, quiet, the voice a person might use when speaking to someone who's unstable, who's liable to take whatever is said badly. Is that how they see me? Am I unstable in their eyes?

"I'm sorry, Oliver, but Saanvi is correct. We have to let you go."

"But Neil, mate, come on," I laugh, suddenly realising what's going on. "Oh, I get it, well done, nice one. You really had me going for a minute there."

"What do you mean?" Neil's voice is all confusion now, like this conversation has taken a turn he didn't anticipate.

"Very funny, guys," I say, a huge weight lifting off me. I don't know what it is about me that makes people do this so often, but whatever. "I actually believed you for a minute there. Fired, me. Ha!"

"Oliver…" Neil begins, but Saanvi speaks across him.

"Oliver," she says, the softness from her voice long gone. She's all business now. "I'm afraid this is not a joke, you are indeed being terminated with immediate effect."

Terminated? Fuck me, that's not a nice word.

"But—" I begin, but Saanvi now cuts across me too.

"You'll be paid up until the end of the month, and we'll provide a reference for your next employer, but otherwise this is the end of your relationship with us."

Relationship? End of it? What does she mean? I'm not in a relationship, I don't have one, I'm waiting for Nicola. Fucking hell, Nicola. Does she know what's happening? Surely she'll stop this? I need to get in touch with her, get her to speak to Neil, to set him straight. She can sort out this whole mess.

"Have you left anything in the office?" Saanvi says this but I don't answer, I can't; her voice suddenly sounds very far away, as if I'm at the top of a mountain. Her words don't mean anything either, they're just empty sounds. Fucking Saanvi. She'll be eating her words when she sees Nicola and I together. Maybe we'll invite her to the wedding just to say a proper 'fuck you'. The idea makes me smile, thinking of Nicola makes me feel better. So I'm being fired, so what, it's just a job. I'll get another. And yes, the other won't have Nicola in it, she won't be in the office, but that doesn't matter. Quite soon we'll be together, spending every day together, so a few hours apart won't kill us. Distance makes the heart grow fonder and all that. If anything this firing will strengthen our relationship.

I can hear Neil talking now but I'm not listening, I'm done with this, I'm over it. The two are talking to each other, and after a while I get bored and hang up. Whatever, I don't work for them, what are they going to do? Instead of speaking to them I open my contacts and scroll to Nicola, call her instead. Speaking to her will make everything okay. The call goes straight to voicemail and I leave her one saying I hope she's okay, I'm looking forward to speaking to her when she's ready. And then I hang up, put my phone down, wonder what to do.

Luckily I'm saved having to figure this out by my phone ringing. I jump to answer it thinking it's Nicola calling me back but it's Neil again, this time from his personal number. I answer it, ready to be vindicated; I assume he's now calling to apologise for the last call, for the shitty circumstances, tell me Saanvi was wrong and everything's okay, I'm not fired. I assume this is Neil my friend calling, not Neil my boss. How fucking wrong can I be.

"What?" I say by way of answering, I don't know what else to say.

"Hi, Oliver," he says, sounding very downbeat. "I'm sorry about what just happened, but it was out of my hands."

"Out of your— what do you mean? What's out of your hands? I'm not actually fired, am I?"

"I'm really sorry," he says, still speaking as if I'm a loaded gun.

"Fuck," I say, the realisation dawning on me that this call will not be my vindication, that I am indeed fired. "Well, whatever, it's all good."

"All good?" Neil says, sounding genuinely confused.

"Yeah, it's all good." I repeat to him my thoughts about not working with Nicola, spending time apart.

"Yeah, about that." Silence envelops us for a second before Neil breathes in deeply and continues. "Listen, Oliver, and I mean *really* listen. I shouldn't be about to tell you what I am, but I like you, and I don't want to see you get in any trouble." Trouble? What does he mean? "You need to leave Nicola alone." Oh fuck. "I mean it, like really leave her alone."

"But—"

"—No buts, Oliver, no buts at all. This is the end, the final straw. You have to leave her alone."

"But I love her!" I shout, unable to stop myself. "I

254

love her, she's The One. She just needs time, she'll see it, I know she will."

"Oliver—" Now it's my turn to interrupt.

"Neil, mate, you listen to me. I know it probably doesn't look like it from where you stand, but Nicola and I are going to end up together. We belong together, and fate will see that we get married and live happily ever after."

"Oliver, for fuck's sake," and now Neil is shouting, to the point I have to hold the phone a little away from my ear so as not to be deafened. "She wanted to call the police, okay? After what happened on Monday she wanted to call the police, but I managed to talk her down. That's what I mean about you getting in trouble: I stopped her calling the police, but I can't do anything else. When she finally agreed to not call them, she told me that one more attempt at contact from you and she would, and I don't blame her if she does. She's changed her number, so don't try and call or text her, she won't get them." He sighs, exasperation flowing from his voice in waves. "You gotta leave her alone, bro," he changes his tone, from angry to pleading. "She doesn't like you, she isn't in love with you. She's scared of you bro, she's actually terrified of you."

What is he saying? Nicola, scared of me? How can she be? Scared of her love for me maybe, the size and strength of her feelings? She just needs time, she'll come around. Okay, so maybe she is actually scared of me right now, but it'll pass. Act two, I keep telling myself, act two. I'll give her some time, like Neil says, I won't try and contact her. She'll come around in act three.

"Like I say," Neil continues, "I shouldn't be telling you this, but I don't want you to get arrested. You gotta move on bro, you gotta let her go. She doesn't like you."

"But—"

"—No, stop it, stop saying *but*, stop trying to rescue the situation, there is no rescuing it. Nicola doesn't like you, she doesn't love you, and the sooner you figure that out the better it'll be for everyone."

"But—" I try again, but Neil isn't interested. Throughout the conversation I've gotten the sense he's holding something back, and I must finally have pushed him to the edge, because he snaps and shouts at me, and the words he shouts change everything. The words Neil shouts at me change my life, and not for the better. No, for the much, much worse. They fucking ruin me. Four words that can break a heart, break a man. Four words that can end a life. Four words that become a *Sliding Doors* moment.

"She has a boyfriend."

Epilogue

Say Anything

March in New York is wild. Each day is different from the last, the climate seems to run with no precedent, it just throws out whatever weather it feels like. It might be 30 degrees and sunny, it might be minus five and a blizzard. It might be mild and rain, or cold and rain, or mild and sunny, or cold and sunny. Every day is a gamble, the weather playing roulette.

It's been two months since I found out Nicola has a boyfriend, two months since everything changed. I told myself I'd wait three months and then message her. It's been hell. But it needs to happen; three months is enough time for her to have fun with her boyfriend, get him in and out of her system; three months is more than enough time for her to forget her apparent fear of me — as if she ever felt any anyway, ha — and realise what she's missing. I'll contact her in a month, and then our love will truly begin.

I haven't been sleeping, but there's nothing new there. I found a new job, same shit different agency. So far the new company is okay; like all digital marketing agencies, it's much of a muchness. Different people, different department names, different clients, but the work is all the same. I run the same reports, on the same days, give them to the same teams, blah blah blah. It pays the bills, so I can't complain. There are a lot of people struggling financially, so I shouldn't count my chickens. Plus, like, I'm struggling so much mentally at the moment that having a steady job is a wonder for me, it's one less thing keeping me up at night.

I've cried every day since Neil called and told me, delivered those four words. Some days it's just a few tears, I'm basically able to carry on as normal, I tell people its allergies and whether or not they believe me they don't question it, which is fine by me. Other days the tears are such that I can't get out of bed, I have to text my boss that I have a migraine or something and then roll over and weep into my pillow. I weep for Nicola, for her boyfriend, I weep for myself. What am I? Why am I? Who am I?

I'm having one of those days today. In fact, it's late afternoon and I've only just made it out of bed, and the only reason I've done so is because I'm out of alcohol. Oh yeah, I'm drinking a lot now, at home, by myself. It isn't good for me I know, but it's necessary. If I stay sober, I think, and right now I can't think, because I only think of her. And I have to — *need* to — wait another month before I speak to her. I can't fuck this up again.

So I'm on the street, wearing just my pyjama bottoms and a dirty t-shirt, a white one covered in stains, but who cares. Unless I bump into Nicola, and I very much doubt I will, it doesn't matter how I look. I'm only going to the Jewish deli for some more vodka, so fuck it.

Thankfully the street is quiet, I think it's about 4pm so I guess most people are at work or whatever. The few people I pass on my walk avert their eyes when they see me, they suddenly become very interested in the sidewalk or their shoes or some imagined thing off in the distance. Whatever, who cares, these people mean nothing to me, their opinion of me is just sand in the wind. I almost want to tell them I don't care, but I don't care enough to. Too much effort.

The bell above the door to the Jewish deli tinkles as I push it open, and a "hello" drifts across to me from somewhere in the back. It's a voice I don't recognise, a female one, it sounds young, maybe 19 or 20. I'm immediately curious.

Grabbing two bottles of Grey Goose — my bingeing is currently very expensive — and moving out of an aisle filled with sugary confectionery, I'm about to walk to the counter when I stop, when I see her.

She must be the owner of the voice; I was right, she looks no older than 20. She's tall, maybe nearly six foot, so still much shorter than me. She has black hair, long, flowing down her back, and dark skin, a cool shade of brown like pine or something, I dunno, I don't know woods. A deep burnt ochre maybe. She must have heard me walking towards her and then stop without reaching her because she turns to me, and she looks at me with the most beautiful eyes I've ever seen; even from here I can see they're green, the colour of spring grass, and within them is contained a promise, a secret, the potential for so much more.

I force myself to move, I pick up my feet one after the other and finally reach the counter. Placing the bottles down I look for a name badge on her chest and find one pinned on top of a small, soft looking breast: 'June'. *Hi June*, I think. I don't know who she is; the owners of the deli, an old Jewish couple, are as white as it's possible for people to be — their skin is like grocery paper, I wonder if you got a little water on them would they become completely transparent? — whereas June is very dark, she looks like she's Indian, or descended from an Indian family, or something like that. I wonder if she's in any way related to the Jewish couple, then realise it doesn't matter. It doesn't matter who she is, where she's from, all that matters is the future. All that matters is that we've met.

As she scans the bottles and tells me the total, as I put my card in the machine and enter my pin, lines from a Maisie Peters song float through my mind, "if you don't want me, then you're not the one." I must be thinking about Nicola: I thought she was The One, but clearly she isn't. If she doesn't want me, she isn't The One, like Maisie says. I'm surprised to realise this, but not massively disappointed. After all, lots of people get it wrong. Look at Duckie in *Pretty in Pink*, pining after Andie when Andie is meant to be with Blane. Or Corey in *Empire Records*, who is so convinced she'll lose her virginity to Rex Manning, when in fact AJ is The One. People make mistakes, it happens, it's easy to misread the signs and go in the wrong direction.

Which is what I've been doing, clearly. Nicola is not The One; June is.

Acknowledgements

Kurt Vonnegut wrote that all writers, no matter how broke or otherwise objectionable, have pretty wives. Thank you to my wife, who continues to make this true even as I stay broke and become more objectionable with age.

Thank you to Stuart at SRL, who continually has faith in me even when I have none in myself.

Thank you to John Hughes, Amy Heckerling, Cameron Crow, and all the other filmmakers who made the films this book is about. You made me the person I am today, so I suppose thank you, but also, what the hell!?

SRL Publishing don't just publish books, we also do our best in keeping this world sustainable. In the UK alone, over 77 million books are destroyed each year, unsold and unread, due to overproduction and bigger profit margins.

Our business model is inherently sustainable by only printing what we sell. While this means our cost price is much higher, it means we have minimum waste and zero returns. We made a public promise in 2020 to never overprint our books for the sake of profit.

We give back to our planet by calculating the number of trees used for our products so we can then replace them. We also calculate our carbon emissions and support projects which reduce CO_2. These same projects also support the United Nations Sustainable Development Goals.

The way we operate means we knowingly waive our profit margins for the sake of the environment. Every book sold via the SRL website plants at least one tree.

To find out more, please visit
www.srlpublishing.co.uk/responsibility